PIECE
by PIECE

Also by Laura Bradford

A Daughter's Truth
Portrait of a Sister

The Tobi Tobias Mysteries

And Death Goes To ...
30 Second Death
Death in Advertising

PIECE *by* PIECE

LAURA BRADFORD

KENSINGTON BOOKS
www.kensingtonbooks.com

KENSINGTON BOOKS are published by

Kensington Publishing Corp.
119 West 40th Street
New York, NY 10018

All Kensington titles, imprints, and distributed lines are available at special quantity discounts for bulk purchases for sales promotion, premiums, fund-raising, educational, or institutional use.

Special book excerpts or customized printings can also be created to fit specific needs. For details, write or phone the office of the Kensington Sales Manager: Kensington Publishing Corp., 119 West 40th Street, New York, NY 10018. Attn. Sales Department. Phone: 1-800-221-2647.

Kensington and the K logo Reg. U.S. Pat. & TM Off.

ISBN-13: 978-1-4967-2596-7 (ebook)
ISBN-10: 1-4967-2596-4 (ebook)

ISBN-13: 978-1-4967-2595-0
ISBN-10: 1-4967-2595-6
First Kensington Trade Paperback Printing: August 2020

10 9 8 7 6 5 4 3 2 1

Printed in the United States of America

For Tasha and Andrew

For giving me a place to visit that invites clarity of mind,
and a friendship that feeds the soul.

Thank you.

Dear Readers,

Grief, as defined by dictionary.com, is a cause or occasion of keen distress or sorrow. From my own book of life, I know grief can be so powerful, so overwhelming, that it can literally bring you to your knees. But to grieve means you've loved—another person, a pet, a career, a passion—and I, for one, wouldn't want to live any other way.

Here, in *Piece by Piece,* we see what grief can do, how Danielle Parker's world is positively shattered by unimaginable loss. Suddenly, the simplest of tasks are akin to climbing the highest mountain . . . Silence becomes deafening . . . An endless mental parade of could-haves and should-haves makes sleep an impossibility . . . And the thought of going on? Of traveling the rest of life alone? It's more than she can fathom.

But if you've loved—really loved—another, you're never truly alone. Love is bigger than all of us. It digs into our very being and stakes a forever claim on our minds and hearts, ready and able to glue our pieces back together. It's getting there, to that knowledge, though, that is a journey in and of itself.

Happy Reading,

Laura

My Day's To-Do List

- Muffins to Roberta's. ✓

- Call and decline book club invitation. ✓

- Finish writing Ava's thank-you notes.

- Check calendar/write tomorrow's list.

- Prepare and freeze meals for Tuesday (Soccer) and Thursday (Scouts).

- Find and make gluten-free snack for Monday's practice.

- Final decision on Jeff's client lunch and make ressie for Friday at noon.

- Maggie: practice piano, 1 hour.

- Spencer: finish 100th day project, read aloud for 30 mins.

- Ava: add drawings to thank-you notes, stamp envelopes.

Chapter 1

Setting the final thank-you note atop the stack at her elbow, Danielle Parker glanced up at the clock above her kitchen desk, its gentle yet ceaseless ticking drowning out her usual sense of accomplishment in the wake of a completed task.

Twenty minutes to the exit...

A minute or so to park the van...

Ten minutes to climb across every rock between the parking lot and the playground...

Twenty minutes of swinging and sliding...

Ten minutes for snack...

Her gaze jumped to the freshly wiped counter on the opposite side of the kitchen while her mind's eye began a mental inventory of the tote bag her mother had all but snatched out of her hands mid-protest.

Pretzel sticks for Ava.

Veggie straws for Maggie.

Spencer's favorite rainbow-colored—

She pulled in a breath. Had she even gotten the cracker box out of the pantry, let alone sealed them in a baggie and added them to the tote? Pushing back her chair, Dani crossed to the notebook she kept beside the toaster and ran her finger down the list she'd made just that morning—a list she knew by heart but still wrote, item by item, every time a trip to the park was on the day's schedule. Or, in today's case: not on the schedule but insisted upon by one's visiting-from-out-of-town and refused-to-take-no-for-an-answer mother.

Bubbles.

Frisbee.

Butterfly net.

Picnic blanket.

Ava's snack.

Maggie's snack.

Spencer's snack.

Sure enough, the day's green checkmark was present beside the five-year-old's name just as it was next to every other item on the list. Sinking against the side of the refrigerator, Dani waited for her heart rate to normalize as her focus traveled across the center island to the hardcover book marking her spot at the kitchen table and, finally, onto the list she'd temporarily abandoned in order to—

Sliding her view back to the oak table and the book she hadn't noticed until that moment, she parted company with the magnetized pictures at her shoulder and made her way around the island, her eyes playing across the unfamiliar cover. Intrigued, she fingered the embossed envelope, followed the long black dashes denoting a breeze, and noted the whimsically inviting harborside village at the base of a hill, the muted glow of light from a single window both calming and alluring all at the same time.

Below the cover art and positioned across the book's title was a blue sticky note with her mother's bold handwriting:

> *There's nothing on your to-do list you can't do tomorrow.*
> *Let this time alone truly be Dani time like you promised.*
> *Now fill your well.*
> *Love you!*
> *Mom*

"A promise made under duress, I might remind you," Dani murmured.

And it was true. She didn't need Dani time; she had Dani time every day. She had it in the mornings when she was making breakfast for Jeff and the kids, she had it in the car while singing along with the kids to whatever song came on their favorite kid-friendly station, she had it when she was sewing on Maggie's latest scout patch, she had it when she was running to the food booth on the other side of the field to cover whichever teammate of Spencer's had failed to bring a snack to practice that week, she had it when she was playing in the rec center pool with Ava while waiting for toddler swim to start, and she had it at night after the kids were in bed and she was helping Jeff brainstorm his latest client pitch.

That was the Dani time she wanted, the Dani time she craved regardless of what her mother believed. She didn't need to go off on girls-only trips like Roberta, or join book clubs or card groups to fill some sort of inner well. She was a wife; she was a mother. She didn't need time away to discover herself. She didn't need to sit in a circle with other women and search for the meaning of life inside the pages of a book when her help was needed in Maggie's or Spencer's classroom. She didn't need to enroll Ava in a kids' day out class so she could go shopping "in peace" as her friends were fond of saying. And she most certainly didn't want her kids to come home to a babysitter the way she, herself, had while growing up.

No. Jeff and the kids were her inner well. They filled her up just fine all on their own . . .

Reaching out, she peeled off the note, crumpled it inside her hand, and then flipped the novel over, the summary's promise of adventure and self-discovery for thirty-four-year-old Amanda Frawlings sliding Dani's gaze back to the clock and then below it to the day's list and the next few items awaiting her attention.

Tomorrow's list needed to be written . . .

Tuesday night's baked ziti and Thursday night's chicken and dumplings needed to be prepped and frozen . . .

She still needed to find the perfect snack recipe for—

A gurgled reminder of her propensity for skipping meals derailed her thoughts and pulled them back to the book and the bowl of fresh fruit just beyond it in the center of the table. Again, her eyes swept back to the clock.

Five minutes of Maggie jumping rope . . .

Ten minutes of Spencer chasing bugs around the picnic area with his net . . .

Five minutes—tops—of Ava blowing bubbles alone . . .

Ten minutes of Spencer and Ava running around trying to catch the bubbles Maggie blew . . .

Ten, maybe fifteen minutes of all three playing hide-and-seek—

A quick vibration against her hip rerouted her hand from the fruit bowl to her pocket and the thumbnail image now illuminated on her phone's screen. Opening the message, Dani smiled down at the picture she'd all but demanded her mother send if Dani was going to heed the whole stay-home-and-take-a-little-time-for-yourself thing. In the captured moment, Maggie was trying desperately to blow a bubble but was having difficulty on account of the laugh she was clearly sharing with her brother and sister. In the background, behind Ava, Jeff, too, was laughing. Beneath the picture, a trio of moving dots let Dani know her mother was typing some accompanying commentary.

Sure enough, less than a minute later, her phone vibrated inside her hand with the arrival of another text, this one containing only words.

Kids loved the bubbles but now moving on to hide-and-seek. After that, Jeff mentioned feeding goats (?!?) and maybe making a quick stop at his office before heading home. Can't wait to hear what you think of the book.

She looked again at the picture, ran her finger across the faces of her children and husband, and swapped the phone for an apple.

Five-minute walk to petting zoo on southern edge of park . . .

Ten minutes of rooting around for quarters, inserting them into the feed machine, filling up three tiny hands, and then nonstop giggles over the feel of goat tongues . . .

Five minutes back to the parking lot . . .

Five minutes of bathroom trips . . .

Ten minutes to the office . . .

A few minutes to grab whatever Jeff forgot on Friday . . .

Ten minutes to get home . . .

Satisfied she had plenty of time to eat an apple and still make a sizeable dent on the rest of her to-do list, Dani opened the book and began to read. Page by page, and bite by bite, she made her way through chapter 1, and then chapter 2, the author's writing style sucking Dani into the main character's plight so fully she barely caught the dribble of juice from her apple before it dropped from her chin to her shirt. As she wiped it away with her thumb, the ever-increasing rumble in her stomach sent her to the pantry for a handful of pretzels and a chocolate-chip cookie she carried, along with the book, into the living room.

Chapter 3.

Chapter 4.

Chapter 5.

She stretched, pulled the meticulously folded afghan off the back of the couch and onto her shoulders, and then tucked her feet into the space between the armrest and the edge of her cushion . . .

Chapter 6.

Spurred on by the description of the coffeehouse in which Amanda now found herself looking up at a handsome stranger with ocean-blue eyes and a smile capable of powering the quaint riverside town, Dani returned to the kitchen for her own cup of coffee. With barely so much as a glance upward, she plucked a mug from the cabinet, turned on the kettle, rifled through the assorted instant coffees, settled on a packet of hot cocoa mix instead, and waited for the water to boil . . .

Chapter 7.

She poured the steaming liquid into her waiting cup, stirred, set the spoon beside the mug, and reached for the light switch . . .

Chapter 8.

Chapter 9.

She carried the now-empty mug to the sink, set it inside, and filled it with water to soak. Slowly, deliberately, she moved her head—if not her eyes—left and then right, the movement welcomed by her neck and shoulders . . .

Chapter 10.

The bounce of a car's head lamps across her book temporarily hijacked her attention first toward the stainless-steel refrigerator and then the window and its view of the driveway. She felt the pull of curiosity as to why Jeff hadn't pulled into the garage, but it didn't last as she quickly calculated how long it would take her to read the last two pages in the chapter before the door opened . . .

She dropped her eyes back down to the book and continued reading, a smile spreading across her lips as Amanda walked into the middle of a field of wildflowers, spread her arms wide, and—

A loud knock pulled Dani back into the moment, her smile morphing into a frown as the front porch light, set to come on somewhere between five and seven o'clock depending on the season, showed two adult-sized figures waiting on the other side of the door's stained-glass insert. Sighing, she set the book on the center island and hurried across the room, her mind's eye mentally inventorying the dinner she'd planned and whether there was enough for whatever unexpected guest Jeff had extended an invite to while at the park with the—

She looked from the porch light to the darkness beyond and then to the digital clock on the built-in microwave.

6:45.

"Six forty-five," she echoed aloud. "How on earth did it get to be six—"

Wrapping her hand around the muted copper knob, she yanked open the door. "So much for a quick stop at the office, mister—"

Her words bowed to a gasp as her gaze fell on the pair of state troopers standing, shoulder to shoulder, on the welcome mat, the porch light illuminating their drawn faces and hooded eyes. Confused, she looked past them to the driveway and the police car parked where her minivan usually sat.

"Danielle Parker?"

She leaned forward, craning her head just enough to afford a view of the rest of the driveway. Nothing . . .

"Ma'am?"

She abandoned her fruitless inspection and drew her attention back to the man on the left, his large dark eyes fixed on hers. The second man—his hair cut close against his ears—shifted his weight across his thick legs. "Yes . . . I'm Danielle Parker. Is there something—" Stopping mid-sentence, she looked outside a second time, her gaze drifting from her next-door neighbor's darkened windows to the troopers. "It's Roberta next door, isn't it? Something happened on her girls' trip to the city? Is-is she okay?"

The men exchanged glances.

"Oh no . . . Does Doug know yet?" she managed past the lump rising inside her throat.

Reaching up, the first trooper grabbed hold of his hat and pulled it from his head, revealing a mop of dark blond hair in the process. "Could we come inside?" he asked.

"Come inside?" she echoed. "But . . . Yes, yes, of course.

I'm sorry. I don't know where my manners are. I've been wait-ing for my husband and my mom to get back from the park with my kids and it seems I'm not the only one who has lost track of the time somehow."

She waited for them to step all the way in and then, after glancing down the road in the direction Jeff would surely come, she closed the door. The quieter cop's eyes dove to the floor, the tip of his tongue gliding across what she guessed to be dry lips.

"Can I get you something to drink?" she offered, gesturing toward the kitchen.

Shaking his head, the hat-holding trooper cleared his throat, his eyes leaving hers and traveling toward the kitchen table. "Perhaps you'd like to sit?"

"Right . . . Sure . . . Okay." She stopped halfway to the table and turned back to the men, the beat of her heart audi-ble inside her ears. "Did Doug take the kids to his parents' house? Do you know? Because if not, I can take them for a while if he wants. Or my husband or I can drive them wher-ever they need to go."

The trooper looked quickly at his partner, cleared his throat a second time. "Ma'am, we're not here about your neighbor."

She pulled back. "You're not?"

"No."

"Then . . ." The question died on her lips as the trooper stepped forward, his Adam's apple rising and falling with a hard swallow.

"Ma'am, there's been an accident."

My Day's To-Do List

- Reconfirm food arrival for 1 p.m. ✓

- Put out guest book. ✓

- Set out serving spoon holders. ✓

- Leave key under mat for Emily. ✓

- Service: 10 a.m. ✓

- Gratitude notes.

Chapter 2

It was as if she'd put up a sign outside each of the first-floor rooms, separating the various parts of her life into neat and manageable chunks. In the study, scattered about in twos and threes, were Jeff's business partners and employees, the rise and fall of their strident voices reminiscent of every summer gathering and holiday party she'd hosted for the company. Yet even amid the dull roar that had accompanied her every thought, her every move, since Sunday evening, the differences called out to her like flashing neon lights, searing themselves into the one part of her brain she couldn't seem to shut off.

Now the occasional slap of a hand on one another's shoulders lingered longer. Throats weren't cleared to gain attention, but rather to get a word or a thought past a rush of emotion. Eye contact bowed to glances at the floor, the ceiling, the smattering of plaques and framed awards lining the walls of the richly paneled room, and, of course, to Danielle herself.

She drew in a breath and forced herself to move on to the next group, to listen politely to stories about her husband, to field the sympathetic pecks on her ice-cold cheek, and to return the earnest embraces from those who had become treasured friends over the years.

Friends like Wayne Rodgers, Jeff's go-to guy for all things financial . . .

"One time, I literally used a bag of M&M's you sent in with Jeff for Valentine's Day one year to help him grasp a numbers thing he wasn't getting."

Oh yes, she remembered that Valentine's Day. She'd left bags of his favorite candy in his car, in his briefcase, in his gym bag, under his pillow, wedged inside his coffee mug, and even inside his slippers. She remembered, too, his *"found another one"* call after each discovery.

Friends like Kelly Collins, Jeff's assistant and second mom as he was prone to call her . . .

"Did you know he deliberately hung a picture of you and the children on the wall opposite his desk so that if he was on a call with a particularly trying client he could look at the four of you and breathe his way through it?"

Of course she'd known that. She'd been the one to track down his favorite picture, to purchase a frame that complemented the others in his office, and to move it *"an inch to the left"* and *"a half inch higher"* until he'd been completely satisfied with its placement.

Friends like Marty Jones, the once-homeless guy from the mailroom who was so grateful to Jeff for having given him a hand up in life . . .

"I will always wonder why me? Why was I the one fortunate enough to cross paths with someone so kind and so giving?"

Oh how she remembered that day. The gorgeous blue sky. The warmish temperatures. The smell of pizza and corn dogs and hot pretzels dotting the air. The way they'd wandered the city streets, slipping in and out of boutiques and pocket parks, talking about everything and anything like the newly in love. The fact that they had two under the age of five and another on the way just made the envious looks on the faces they passed all the more fun. And then, just as they were heading back to the car, they'd spotted Marty, sitting on the steps of a church, his clothes tired and ratty but his shoes spit-shined to perfection. It was those shoes that had led her to whisper, *"Let's talk to him,"* in Jeff's ear.

And friends like Tom Gavigan, Jeff's best friend from college and his partner at the marketing firm . . .

"I never could have made this place the success it is without Jeff. Clients took to him right off the bat, you know?"

Yes, actually, she did know. Because she, too, had taken to Jeff like *"Pooh Bear to honey,"* as she loved to tell the kids whenever they asked about the moment she'd met their dad. Something about his strength—wrapped around an almost boyishly innocent optimism—had let her know before their first official date was even completely over that he was the man she would one day marry.

Friends like—

"Dani?"

Pausing, mid-step, she turned back to Tom in time to see him glance at the floor and swallow. "I don't know what we'll do without you, Dani; I really don't. Your encouragement of Jeff and the company as a whole has been a light for all of us at Parker & Gavigan. And your Friday cookie plates? Your holiday parties? Your gentle touch with the new spouses? Your charm with the prospective clients? The way you did all of those things while somehow still keeping up with everything here at the house, and with your volunteering, and, of course, with—"

She felt his fingers release her arm in favor of an awkward sweeping gesture, but when her gaze followed she saw only the empty glass in Marty's hand that needed to be filled, the used napkin Kelly was awkwardly holding, the fingerprints being left on Jeff's many plaques, and the discarded plate atop his desk . . .

"The kids." Tom slipped his hands into the front pockets of his suit pants, his shoulders hunched forward. "You handled everything so perfectly all the time."

She looked again at Marty's glass, Kelly's napkin, the smudged nameplates on the bottoms of the plaques, and the abandoned plate on her husband's desk, and gave in to the mirthless laugh bubbling its way up from deep inside her chest. "Do you see that glass in Marty's hand?" she asked, pointing Tom's attention, and that of everyone else who was trying so hard not to eavesdrop, toward the beloved mailroom employee. "If I really handled everything perfectly, as you say, his glass wouldn't be empty. And that plate"—she gestured toward the desk she'd skimped and saved to get Jeff for his fortieth birthday—"would be in the dishwasher, instead of sitting there like the eyesore it is."

Tom drew back, the pain he'd worn just seconds earlier replaced first with discomfort and then, when Kelly scurried over like the mother hen she was, relief as he quietly stepped away.

"Danielle, sweetie, do you want me to take you upstairs so you can lie down for a little while? A little alone time might do you some good. I can handle things down here while everyone finishes and—"

"No. I've got it." Again, her gaze returned to Marty only to find him no longer holding his glass. Likewise, when she glanced at the desk, the plate was gone, as well. Stepping back, she mentally inventoried the faces and, when she was satisfied she'd spoken with everyone from the firm, wiped her sweaty palms down the sides of her simple black dress and hooked her thumb in the direction of the hallway. "I really need to check in on everyone else, make sure everyone has had enough to eat, and to thank them for coming."

Kelly stopped Dani's forward movement with a gentle hand to the arm. "Your friends from the neighborhood have everything under control with the food, and everyone will understand if you need to rest for a while."

There was something about the woman's words and the way everyone in the room kept looking at her even when they were pretending not to that was making it difficult to breathe. She could see some of their mouths moving, knew they were talking about Jeff, about her, about the—

Murmuring something she hoped fell somewhere on the spectrum between polite and coherent, Dani strode out of the

room and into the hallway, the need to be somewhere, anywhere, else giving her feet purpose if not a clear-cut destination.

Breathe in . . .

Breathe out . . .

Breathe in—

From behind her she heard Tom's voice . . . A quick laugh . . .
A weighted silence . . . Conversations resuming . . . Sounds that
propelled her farther and farther away from the study, down
the same hardwood floor she'd walked a million times with
forgotten shoes, extra pairs of socks, baskets of laundry, grocery bags, and sleeping children.

Her sleeping children.

Squeezing her eyes closed until the image had passed, she
willed herself to keep breathing, to keep moving, past the laundry room, past the guest bathroom, past the door to the mud-
room and the garage, until finally, mercifully, the dull roar in
her head parted in favor of the dishwasher's steady yet oddly
comforting hum. Soon, it was joined by the *whump whump*
of the pantry door hinge as it opened and then closed . . .

"Every single time I hear that awful sound, I'm reminded
of how badly I need to tighten those screws. But then"—she
stepped into the kitchen—"I get sidetracked and it doesn't
get done."

"Dani!" Roberta set the empty lasagna pan in the sink,
waved off the advances of the other women in the room, and
hurried around the center island like the neighborhood queen
she only half kiddingly professed to be. "I made a plate for
you to eat now, and I also made up a few containers for the
freezer that you can take out and reheat as you see fit."

She nodded, or at least thought she did, her thoughts already on to the parade of foil serving dishes lined up, one beside the other, across the center island. "Did I order enough of
everything?" she asked, glancing back at Roberta. "I wasn't
sure how many people were going to come back to the house,
so I had to do a little guesswork with the caterer."

Roberta's large doe-like eyes moved back across the kitchen to the other women before returning, once again, to Danielle. "You did . . . fine. There was plenty of everything."

"Good." She stepped closer to the foil platters and, seeing several were empty, began stacking them inside one another for the inevitable trip out to the trash can in the garage.

Suze, the neighbor on the other side of Roberta, stepped between Danielle and the next empty tray. "Dani, stop. We've got this. Why don't you let Emily warm up your plate of food for you now and I'll get rid of these, okay?"

"No. I'm fine. I-I'm really not hungry."

"Are you sure?" Emily chimed in from her spot by the bay window and its view of her own home across the street. "Because I can do that if you want me to. Or if you'd rather something a bit lighter, there's still some salad left. I can even put one together for you with extra *toe*-matoes and cu-*mum*-bers just the way you—"

Emily's quiet gasp was drowned out by the louder, collective exhale of Roberta and the others. Covering her face with her hands, the petite brunette who was Dani's closest friend on the street dropped onto a kitchen chair and doubled over. "Oh, Dani, I'm . . . so . . . *sorry*. I-I didn't mean to-to say it the way that Ava—"

The door to the sun porch opened, pulling Dani's attention off her grief-stricken friend and fixing it, instead, on Lila Roberts, her co–room mother in both Spencer's and Maggie's classrooms. In the woman's hands were two large black trash bags that were quickly shoved back inside the sun porch at the sight of Dani.

"Oh. Dani. I didn't know you were in the kitchen."

"I didn't know you were here, Lila."

"Where else would I be?"

"Are the kids with you?"

Lila nodded—once, twice.

Dani pointed to the now-closed sun-porch door. "What were in those bags just now?" she asked as she followed Lila's

widening eyes to Roberta, and then Suze, before they returned, more sheepishly, to Dani.

"I-I just wanted to help out a little," Lila said, her voice
raspy.

"Help out?" Dani repeated. "With what?"

This time, when Lila's eyes moved to the others, they no
longer conveyed discomfort but, rather, panic.

"We just thought we'd help clean up from Saturday,"
Roberta offered, leaning against the island. "So you wouldn't
have to keep looking at it and remembering."

"Keep looking at what?" Dani swung her gaze off Roberta
and onto the pair of French doors just beyond Lila's shoulder.
The four-season addition was everything she'd hoped it would
be with sheer white curtains that billowed in the lightest of
breezes, white wicker furniture with sand-colored cushions,
the cute end table fashioned from an old ship's steering
wheel, and the walls' ocean-blue hue that—

Ocean . . .

Pressing her forehead to the glass, Dani stared into the
room, her mind's eye filling in what was now missing.

The royal-blue streamers she'd painstakingly hung from
the ceiling with a colorful fish attached to the end of each
and every piece . . .

The sea of light and dark blue balloons that had covered the
floor so deftly it was virtually impossible to see the carpet . . .

The chest she'd found in an old thrift store and refinished
to look like one fit to hold a myriad of treasures—dress-up
rings and tiaras, beaded necklaces and sparkly faux jewels—

"Where is everything?" she managed past the queasiness.
"The treasure chest? The streamers? The . . . *balloons?*"

When her questions were met with silence, she fixed her
gaze on Lila only to have Lila's lead it back to the neatened
room with its uninhibited view of the carpet, the trio of black
garbage bags just inside the door, the blue latex mound stick-
ing out from the bag in the middle—

She heard herself gasp, heard it fade to nothing against the equally distinct latch of the treasure chest, the rustle of the fish-adorned streamers, the shrieks of excitement at the thought of "swimming" in an ocean of balloons, and Ava's giggles rising above everything else.

Ava's giggles.

"Dani? Are-are you okay?"

Lifting her hand, she tried to keep Lila's voice from drowning out the flash of joy in her ears, but it was no use. Just as every remnant of her daughter's third birthday party was now gone, so, too, were Ava's giggles.

"I didn't mean to upset you, Dani," Lila rasped. "I just wanted to help. To make it hurt a little less. To do something—to *fix* something for you."

The words reverberated in her thoughts, fading in and out against the thudding in her head. There would be no fourth birthday for Ava. There would be no more soccer goals or base hits for Spencer.

Whump. Whump.

There would be no new badge ceremonies or sleepover parties for Maggie. There would be no new clients to woo or deals to celebrate for Jeff. There would be no—

Whump. Whump.

Whirling around, she looked from the pantry to Suze and back again, her hands clenching into fists at her sides.

"Dani, please . . . I can put everything back the way it was if you want."

She didn't mean to laugh, if that noise bubbling out of her at the moment could even be construed as a laugh . . .

Was it? She wasn't sure.

Pulling her arm free of Lila's grasp, Dani crossed to her desk, yanked open the top drawer, and felt her way past the tin of sharpened number two pencils, the bin of big block erasers, the box of crayons, and the cute little grocery store list she'd yet to use.

She moved on to the middle drawer, pushing aside the family address book, the latest issue of *MOM Magazine*, and the box of animal stickers she kept at the ready for rainy days . . .

"Dani, can I help you find something?" Emily asked, coming up behind her.

"No, it's here; I know it is." She shoved the drawer closed and moved on to the bottom one, lowering herself to the chair as she did.

The town's recreation calendar . . .

The school's information binder . . .

The room mother folders for both Maggie's and Spencer's classes . . .

"Finally," she muttered, grabbing hold of the miniature tool kit and pulling it onto her lap. With her thumb and forefinger on the zipper, she began to pull, her gaze returning to the drawer, the binder, the folders, the sleek color brochure for the—

"Are you wanting to tighten that hinge on the pantry?" Emily squatted down beside the chair and lowered her voice so only Dani could hear. "Because it's okay to leave it for another day, sweetie."

She squeezed her eyes closed against the parade of images she didn't need to see to know. She'd memorized every detail a million times over.

The glass of wine waiting on a nearby table . . .

The thick white robe draped over a nearby chair and the matching slippers waiting beneath . . .

The outdoor massage tent with its scenic view of award-winning vineyards . . .

The stone patio with the twinkling lights that looked like stars . . .

The—

"Talk to me, Dani. Just tell me what I can do for you and I'll do it. Please."

Stilling her fingers atop the tool kit, Dani looked back at

her friend; the same worry she saw etched into the skin beside Emily's brown eyes now trembled the woman's lips, too. It was a worry Dani could feel just as surely as she could Emily's hand going round and round on her back. It was also a worry she knew she didn't even come close to deserving.

"I need you to get everyone out of here, Emily. *Now.*"

Chapter 3

It took every ounce of energy she had to keep her eyes open, to swing her legs over the edge of the bed, to slip her feet into her slippers. The swath of sunlight creeping its way around the edges of the window shade told her it was morning. So, too, did the rumble of the garbage can as Jeff wheeled it down to—

Rocketing forward, she pushed the corner of the shade to the side in time to see Emily wheel the can to a stop against the curb before heading back across the street, her gait void of its usual zip.

Emily.

She'd known it couldn't be Jeff. Yet, for one disoriented second, she'd almost let herself believe the past five days had been some sort of heinous nightmare rather than her new reality. The echoed slap of the shade against the windowsill as she sat back in the otherwise silent room said otherwise. So, too, did the undisturbed sheets on the other side of the bed . . .

Reaching back, she pulled Jeff's pillow against her nose and chest. There, in the tear-dampened folds of the feather-soft fabric, she could smell him—his shampoo, the faintest hint of his cologne, his *very being.*

For hours after everyone had finally left the repast, she'd buried her face in the same softness, her sobs broken only by

her repeated requests—each one hoarser than the one before—for a single do-over from the same God Pastor Pete
had always said could do anything.

But He hadn't.

Jeff was gone . . . The kids were gone . . . Her mom was
gone . . . And she—

The vibration of her phone against the top of the nightstand startled Dani into wiping the latest round of tears from
her cheeks with one clumsy swipe of her non-pillow-hugging
hand. A glance at the screen had her reversing her initial vow
to let it go to voicemail.

Still, when she lifted the device to her ear, she found she
had nothing to say.

"Dani? Are you there?"

She made herself nod.

"Dani?"

Realizing her mistake, she lowered her chin to the top edge
of the pillow and closed her eyes. "I . . . I'm here."

"Oh, thank God," Emily said on the heels of an audible
whoosh. "I was worried when I didn't see you at all yesterday, but Rob said I needed to give you a little time."

She lifted her head, kneaded the skin beside her eyes with
her thumb and forefinger. "You saw me yesterday," she whispered. "And, about that . . . Thank you. Thank you for getting everyone out the way you did. I just couldn't do it all
anymore—the stories, the awkward hugs, the pity. It was too
much."

"It's *Friday*, Dani. That was Wednesday." Emily paused,
coughed. "I took your garbage out to the curb for you just a
few minutes ago. I didn't want you to miss it with all the
empty tins and stuff from the caterer still in the can. But
don't worry, Rob or I will put it back inside the garage after
they come and empty—"

"Wait. What?" She inhaled against the pillow one more

time and then gently shifted it back into its place beside her own, Emily's words looping round and round in her thoughts. "I think you're off a day, Em. It's only Thursday."

"No. It's Friday. The Friday paper is sitting in front of me on the table right now."

"What happened to Thursday?" she asked, rising to a stand.

The silence that met her question lasted a beat, maybe two. "Do you want me to come over? I don't have to pick Bobby up at school until eleven thirty."

She knew Emily was still talking. She could hear the rise and fall of her friend's voice just as surely as she could feel the rise and fall of her own breath. Only her breath was coming faster, her chest beginning to pound.

If Emily was right, and it was Friday, *Dani* was supposed to make the run to pick up the boys from morning kindergarten. It was her turn. *Next* week it would be Emily's. She'd arranged it that way so she wouldn't have to drag Ava—

"Emily, I'm sorry, I have to go. I don't feel very well."

It was true; she didn't. The same queasiness that had driven her from bed a few times during the night was back, hovering, threatening.

"Have you eaten?" Emily asked.

Had she? She didn't think so. But then again, if Emily was right about it being Friday, she'd lost track of an entire day somehow. Just like she had when—

"Because if you look in your freezer," Emily continued, almost breathless, "you'll find all sorts of things you can warm up in the microwave. I could even do it for you, when I come over."

"Please don't come," Dani managed past the tightening in her throat. "I'm not hungry."

"Then we can talk or just sit together if you'd rather. Whatever you need."

"Whatever *I* need?"

"Yes, whatever you need."

"Can you pick Spencer up when you get Bobby?" Dani asked. "Can you take a picture of me and Maggie painting the mailbox together so I can send it to my mom?"

Now that she had started, she couldn't stop the words or their shrillness any more than she could the tears she felt streaming down her cheeks and into her mouth, each question, each image, hitching her shallow breaths. "Can you scoop Ava off the ground and put her into my arms so I can take her up to her room and read her favorite book to her again and again? Can you have Jeff stop on the second step from the top in the garage so I can wrap my arms around his neck and be at the exact right height to kiss him full on the mouth?"

The silence in her ear was back, but still, she pressed on, her words giving way to broken sobs. "And while you're doing *whatever I need* . . . can you . . . can you rewind my life back to that morning . . . and make me keep them home . . . *with me*? Or . . . have me go with them . . . so none of this would've happened . . . or . . . so . . . I could be with them now . . . instead of here—*alone*?"

"Oh, Dani, I'm so sorry you're going through this. I'd take it all away if I could; you have to know that."

She knew Emily was crying. She could hear her friend's sniffles intermingled with her own. But when everything about her was literally numb, it held little effect. "Emily, I have to go."

"Go? Go where?"

"Off the phone. I just can't do this anymore."

"I could come over later if that's better. Maybe when Rob is home and he can be here with the—" Emily's words fell away.

Dani picked them up. "*You* need to be with your kids, Emily. And with Rob. *That's* where you should be—where you should *want* to be. Always. Not looking for time alone so you can come over here, or get your hair done, or-or"— she pressed her fingers to her lips in a futile attempt to stop their trembling—"get a massage, or sit at a bistro table staring out at *grapes* of all things. Because those thoughts? Those wishes? *That time* you think you need so badly? You just might actually get it."

She sat on the bottom edge of the twin-sized bed and pulled the discarded sock to her cheek. Was it just six months ago they'd redecorated Maggie's room, taking it from the teddy bear motif of her kindergarten days to the more frilly and fanciful space of a still sweet and innocent third grader?

The wall color had been easy: princess blue—the same princess blue as the comforter. The trim had been painted a crisp white that popped against the wall just as the white and silver dust ruffle and pillow sham did against the bedding. The window seat where Maggie loved to sit and read boasted a slew of throw pillows in blues, whites, and silvers. And the floating shelves the contractor had built for the wall across from the bed helped put the exclamation point on the room's underlying theme with a place to tuck a tiara, a magic wand, and the jar of pixie dust Dani had made with silver glitter.

Closing her eyes, she let herself remember the moment she and Jeff had led Maggie up the stairs to see her newly finished space. Maggie had been so excited to see it she'd bounced up and down on her feet, waiting for Dani and Jeff to open the door. And when they had? The child's pure joy had been so real, so heartfelt, the mist that always seemed to find its way into Dani's eyes during such moments had been reflected in Jeff's, as well.

Soon, the moms of Maggie's friends had begun calling, asking to stop by and see the room they'd heard so much about, with more than a few who did saying it belonged in a magazine. Yet now, as Dani took in the desk and the shelves

Maggie could reach, she began to notice things she hadn't put there during the decorating phase.

A Barbie doll, dressed in a princess-like dress, sitting on the edge of one of the floating shelves . . .

A seashell Dani recognized from their last trip to the beach . . .

A—

Clutching the sock to her chest with her left hand, Dani stood and made her way over to Maggie's desk, her gaze riveted on a drawing taped to the wall. Behind, and slightly to the right of the princess desk clock, the artwork depicted a little girl with brown wavy hair Dani knew to be Maggie, sitting at a table with a rolling pin in one hand and a flower-shaped cookie cutter in the other. The light brown circle on the table in front of her was clearly rolled-out dough. On the round face was a smile that stretched from ear to ear. Behind the drawn Maggie was a drawn Dani, her brown hair sitting atop her shoulders, her cheeks rosy, her smile a near perfect match of her daughter's.

She lingered her gaze on the drawing through a few more thumps of her heart and then wandered over to the window seat and its view of the backyard. How many times had she come into this room and found Maggie reading in this very spot?

Hundreds . . .

How many times had she watched Ava or Spencer climb up next to their big sister for cuddles and a story?

Hundreds . . .

How many times had Maggie begged to wish on stars with her before bedtime only to give up and make one by herself when Dani said she already had everything she wanted?

Hundreds . . .

She tried to stifle her answering sob with the sock, but it was futile. Maggie would never read in this spot again. Ava and Spencer would never again wander into this room in search of their sister. And all those wish-making requests she'd turned down? They, too, were gone. Forever.

"Oh, my sweet, sweet Maggie, I have a wish now," she managed between strangled sobs. "I wish I could have all of you back."

Chapter 4

Using her shoulder and the wall as a guide, Dani made her way down to the first floor, her legs quaking between steps. Sometime during the night, the slow, steady beat of dread had switched into warp drive, expanding its way beyond her ears and into her chest. But even as she'd prayed it was a sign of the heart attack she'd begged God to give her, she knew better.

Beyond the occasional sip of water, and the two crackers she'd found in Jeff's suit pocket that had taken her nearly four days to consume, she hadn't eaten since the repast. Longer, if she didn't count the single, solitary crouton she hadn't been able to keep down, anyway.

She'd tried to ignore the rapid heartbeat, the clammy hands, her nearly paper-dry throat, but to do so meant continuing to stay upstairs where every sound, every sight, made the emptiness in her heart all the more crushing. No, she needed a chance to catch her breath no matter how shallow and fleeting it might be . . .

At the bottom of the steps, she stopped, collected her balance, and reveled, momentarily, in the sameness of the noises that had greeted her in this same spot every morning for nearly a decade. There was the quiet yet steady ticking of the kitchen clock, the faint hum of the ice maker, and the distant bark of

the Andersons' dog as it spotted the Ridgeways' cantanker-
ous cat heading home after yet another night of carousing.

It was all so normal, in fact, that for a few quick strides
she actually found herself mentally inventorying the pantry
as she wavered between making pancakes or French toast.
But it didn't last. Because as normal as those first few sounds
had been, the absence of Ava's sweet *"good morning,
Mommy,"* and Spencer's running feet on the stairs compared
to Maggie's more methodical pace told her everything was
different.

Grabbing hold of the edge of the center island, Dani closed
her eyes through the sudden yet powerful wave of nausea.
When it passed, she crossed to the refrigerator and made herself pull it open.

Sure enough, the milk she would normally have picked up
on a Friday afternoon wasn't there. Neither was Jeff's favorite brand of orange juice. Instead, in the places where she
would have put them, there were stacks of Tupperware in assorted shapes, sizes, and lid colors. The stack of red-lidded
containers, according to the sticky note on top, was from the
Andersons and included a tuna casserole, a side salad, and a
homemade biscuit. The blue-lidded containers were from the
Ridgeways and included the various components of their
family's favorite comfort meal.

Dropping her hand to her side, she stared at the containers
in front of her even as her mind's eye wandered to the freezer
and the packed shelves she didn't need to see to know were
filled. It was what she and her neighbors did for one another
when someone's parent passed, or the season's creeping crud
rendered a mom too sick to feed her family. In fact, not more
than six months earlier, while battling a flu she'd picked up
in Spencer's classroom, she'd opened the refrigerator to these
same colored lids with the very same contents. Only that
time, the containers were bigger, their contents intended to
feed five people . . .

Jeff.

Maggie.

Spencer.

Ava.

And herself.

But now, despite the same families using the same colored lids, the containers were smaller, their limited contents reflecting the single mouth left to feed.

The quaking in her legs was back. So, too, was the nausea that had her closing the refrigerator door on food she needed yet had no desire to eat. Instead, she grabbed a glass from the cabinet, filled it halfway with water from the sink, and carried it over to her spot at the kitchen table. It wasn't that she wanted to sit there, surrounded by four empty chairs, but it was getting harder and harder to stay standing without feeling like she was going to faint.

She needed to eat. She knew that. But knowing it and doing it were two different things.

"Baby steps get you to the same place, Dani . . ."

Startled as much by her own gasp as the clarity of her mother's voice in her head, Dani rushed to right her glass before she spilled its water down her chin and neck. She knew her mother wasn't there, knew it just as surely as she knew her own name, but still she looked toward the hall . . . the pantry . . . the sixth chair at the table, and held her breath for half a beat just in case she was wrong.

She wasn't.

The voice, the words, had been so real, so true to what her mother would have said in that moment, she dropped her head into her hands and hitched out a sigh. "I don't know how to do this, Mom," she whispered. "How to do *any* of this.

"Jeff and the kids—they . . . they were *my world*, Mom. *My everything*." She tried to clear the rasp from her throat but to no avail. "You *all* were."

Lifting her chin, she wiped the growing wetness from her cheeks. "*That's* why I didn't take time for me. Why I didn't want you *pushing me* to stay behind.

"But you did!" She shoved back from the table so hard the chair smacked into the corner of the island. "Why? Why did you do that? Things were fine the way they were—*I* was fine. I was great!" she spat through clenched teeth. "I was whole! And now?

"*Now?*" she repeated, shrieking. "Now Jeff is gone . . . Maggie is gone . . . Spencer is gone . . . Ava is gone . . . *You*'re gone . . . And I'm here—here without them, and without you! And why?"

She scanned the island, the countertops, and the table before settling, finally, on her desk and the hardback book in its center. "So I *could read a book?*" she screamed. "*A book?*"

Racing across the room, she grabbed the book, looked down at the same cover that had once enticed yet now repelled, and threw it across the hall so hard it left a mark on the wall where it hit. "I was *reading a book* when my family needed me most!"

The anger that had propelled her across the room bowed to a wave of grief so strong her knees buckled her onto the edge of her desk chair.

"*The other vehicle jumped the median at such speed, your husband's attempt to swerve out of the way was futile.*"

She held her hands to her ears in an attempt to block out the trooper's description of the accident, but it, too, was futile. Jeff had tried to swerve. That meant he'd seen the car coming at them.

Had he yelled?

Had Mom looked back at the kids?

Did the kids see the car?

Did they call out for her in their fear?

Did they wonder, in those last moments, why she'd chosen to stay behind, why she wasn't there to hold them . . . to comfort them . . . to protect them . . . to tell them she loved them?

Or did Maggie think about the brochure she'd caught Dani looking at that morning—the one for the spa and its promise of peace and quiet without the kids?

Extending her hands, Dani gripped on to her roots and pulled, her teeth clenching in anger even as a fresh set of tears spilled down her cheeks. "How could you stay behind? How could you leave them to go through that alone? How could you lose track of everything about them because of *a book*?"

Slowly at first, and then with gathering speed, she tore into herself, her throat growing rawer and rawer with each accusation she was unable to hold back.

"How could you not know they needed you? That they were scared? That they were hurt? That they were screaming your name? How could you"—she let loose a guttural noise from somewhere deep inside her chest—"not know your family was *dying*? How could you not know *they were dead*?"

She heard the words as they left her lips, heard them echo through the empty room, but for just a moment, it was as if they belonged to someone else. Someone she didn't want to know. Someone awful and selfish and—

The ring of the desk phone stole her thoughts and sent them toward the caller ID screen and the out-of-state number she didn't recognize. She knew the likelihood that it was a solicitor was high, but for just a moment she wanted someone to yell at, someone to unleash her anger on besides herself.

But when she reached for the phone, her fingers hit the button on the answering machine instead, unleashing a trio of giggles that stole her breath from her lungs. As she worked to catch it, Maggie's sweet voice emerged in the greeting they'd painstakingly rehearsed together.

"Hi! You've reached the Parkers' res-i-dence. We are not home right now, but if you tell us your name and your phone number, Mommy or Daddy, but probably Mommy, will call you back very"—Maggie's voice bowed to a flurry of whispers, a loud yet quick "very" from Spencer, a softer and not-so-quick "very, very" from Ava, before returning—"soon! Bye!"

Lunging forward, Dani grabbed the phone. "No! No! Don't go yet, please! Don't . . . go," she rasped. "Please . . . I'm sorry! I-I didn't need time."

There was no use; she simply couldn't hold back the sobs that rattled her body from head to toe. Maggie's voice was gone, taking with it the confusion that had let her believe, for the most wonderful of moments, that their presence was in real time, rather than a recording of the past.

A recording—a recording she could listen to again . . .

Tightening her grip on the phone, she reached for the machine's play button only to pull her hand away as a different voice, a hesitant murmur really, cut through her sniffles.

"Danielle?"

She pulled in a breath, held it for a beat. "Yes . . . Who is this?"

"This is Lydia. Lydia Schlabach."

The familiar name pulled her shoulders up and then sank them back against the chair. "Lydia?"

"Yah. It is me."

Her mind's eye rewound back to her own childhood and the trip she'd taken to Lancaster County, Pennsylvania, with her parents when she was Maggie's age.

Maggie . . .

Squeezing her eyes closed, Dani willed herself to breathe. To focus. To—

"Wait," she rasped. "You're *calling* . . . On a telephone . . ."

"Yah. It is the phone between our farm and the Zooks'."

She rested her elbow on the desk and, using her thumb and index finger, kneaded the area near the outer corner of her eye. "I-I didn't know you could call like this. I thought it was just letters—like the ones we send each other at Christmas."

"I could not send just a letter for this."

And then she knew. Somehow, someway, the eight-year-old Amish girl she'd befriended nearly a lifetime earlier had heard the news about Jeff and the kids. A chill that began in her chest inched its way outward toward her limbs . . .

"Danielle, I am sorry to hear of the loss of your family."

She stopped kneading and, instead, dropped her free hand onto the desk. "How? How did you know?"

"It was Abram Zook's wife, Katie. Her twin sister, Hannah, phoned to speak of the accident."

"But I don't know anyone named Hannah who is Amish," she murmured.

"Hannah was not baptized. She lives an English life now in the big city. She takes care of a little boy—Jack."

Jack . . . Jack . . .

Was there a Jack in Spencer's—

"Hannah told Katie that Jack's kin live next door to you," said Lydia.

Dani lifted her gaze to the window as the woman's words rang true. "Wait. I think I remember this now. Hannah grew up by you—in Blue Ball. Roberta's sister is a bit of a socialite and this Hannah—your friend—is her son's nanny. Roberta mentioned her one day when I was talking about you and how we've been pen pals since we were eight. I made a mental note to ask you if you knew her when we next exchanged letters, but I guess I got busy with the kids and . . ."

The explanation died on her lips as her eyes, her thoughts, returned to the answering machine and the voices she knew it held. "Lydia, I . . . I have to go. Thank you for calling. It means a lot."

"Please do not go yet," Lydia asserted, shyly. "There is more I want to say."

"You're sorry. For my loss. I-I get it; I do. And I'm grateful for the call, truly. It's just that"—she stopped, gathered her breath, and then released it slowly—"sorry doesn't bring them back. I . . . I-I wish it did."

"Sometimes it is difficult to understand God's will. It—"

She jerked upright in her chair. *"God's will?"*

"Yah."

"Wait." Gritting her teeth, she pulled the phone so tight to her face it hurt. "You're telling me it was *God's will* to have my husband's car at the exact spot where another one could hit it with such force it killed my entire family in one shot? That was *His* will?"

Her question, her tone, was met with a heavy silence.

"Lydia?" she prodded, her anger audible. "Is that what you're saying?"

"It is not *I* who says such things, Danielle. The Bible says: 'Thy kingdom come. Thy will be done on earth, as it is in heaven.'"

"And that is supposed to make me feel better?" she asked, shrieking. "That God *chose* to do this to a man like Jeff, who was kind and thoughtful and smart and true? That God *chose* to do this to my eight-year-old daughter, who loved helping people? That God *chose* to do this to my five-year-old son, who was going to move mountains one day? That God *chose* to do this to my little one, whose smile rivaled the sun? And that God *chose* to do this to my mom, who loved them all—*and me*—so fiercely? That's supposed to make me feel better somehow?"

"It will not, at first. But, in time, it will . . . *help*. For the Bible also says: 'Trust in the Lord with all thine heart; and lean not unto thine own understanding.'"

"Lydia, *please*. This isn't helping."

"It is not my wish to upset you."

"Then what *is* your wish?" she said, her throat tight.

"For you to know *I* know. And for you to know that Elijah and I have spoken and there is room for you if you would like to get away for a little while."

Like clockwork, her gaze dropped to the bottom drawer and the brochure that taunted her thoughts around the clock. "Trust me, Lydia, the last thing in this world I want or need is a getaway."

"But perhaps, if you come, you can begin to heal, too."

"Heal?" Dani echoed, her anger draining into a heavy, choking sadness. "You don't *heal* from something like this. You"—she looked up at the ceiling and then back at the answering machine—"you just wait. Until you get to die, too."

"Yah. But until you do, you must learn to keep living."

Keep living . . .

It sounded like a death sentence.

"Danielle, I must go. Elijah will be wondering where I am if I am not back soon. But please know that when you are ready, you do not need to send word. Just come. There is room and friendship for you here."

Chapter 5

Dani was waiting when the morning sun finally poked its way around the edges of the blinds to project its presence onto the far wall. The first day she'd been aware of its intrusion, she'd pulled her pillow over her eyes and fallen back into yet another dream-filled sleep in which Maggie, and then Spencer, and then Ava had called out to her again and again, her own desperate attempt to find them repeatedly foiled. On each of the next six mornings, she'd held that dream at bay by closing her eyes but remaining awake, the promise of yet another twenty-four hours alone igniting a fresh new round of tears. But this time, when she turned her cheek against the still-damp pillow, she followed the vertical lines back and forth across the wall and fancied herself standing behind them, looking out, waiting for someone to release her from their confines.

But there would be no release, no grace awarded for time served.

"My jail," she murmured, changing her view first to the ceiling and then to the stack of crackers on her nightstand that didn't look a whole lot different than it had the previous night.

She'd forced herself to eat one, and then two, chasing each and every nibble down with water to keep it from getting stuck in a throat that was at once dry from intermittent bouts of screaming and then raw from the tear-induced nausea that often followed. Yet as pathetic as it was, it had become part of her new routine . . .

Lie in bed.

Scream.

Cry.

Run for the restroom.

Emerge, shaky and spent.

Sleep.

Go downstairs.

Open freezer.

Contemplate one of the dozen or so containers of food from her well-meaning neighbors.

Close freezer.

Grab a half dozen crackers and a glass of water.

Go back upstairs.

Eat one, maybe two crackers.

Drink water.

Spend time in one of the kids' rooms.

Scream.

Cry.

Run for the restroom.

Emerge, shaky and spent.

Sleep.

Rinse and repeat. Day, by day, by day, until somehow two weeks had gone by since—

Biting back the urge to scream, Dani turned back to the slatted square on the wall and willed herself to breathe. Slowly. Deeply.

Breath by breath the prison bars gave way to the light until, struggling up onto her elbow, she found herself looking at the actual window and the light forcing its way into the otherwise darkened room. She didn't need to open the blinds to know the sun was there, that another twenty-four hours had dawned, but for the first time in two weeks, she wanted air, *needed* air.

She flung back the sheet, pushed herself up onto her elbow, waited for the dizziness that had become her morning norm to fade, and then swung her legs over the edge of the bed. For a fleeting moment, she considered opening the window around the blinds, but instead, she wrapped her hand around the cord and pulled, the answering blast of light lifting her shoulders and chin of their own accord.

Oh yes . . .

Seated there on the bed, bathed in the sun's strengthening light, the chill that had taken up residence in a place no blanket seemed to reach finally loosened its grip. She reached for the latch, spun it to the open position, and slid open the window.

Somehow, despite her pleas for time to rewind back to that fateful morning, or to fast-forward until she, too, could be gone, time had moved at its own pace. Now, based on the sights and sounds filtering through her screen, spring had dispensed with its annual game of cat and mouse in favor of strutting around in all its glory.

Gazing down at the yard, she spied a female cardinal hopping around on the ground, happily partaking in a thawing earth's feast. She heard another bird, not too far off, trying out a voice that had been virtually silent throughout the winter. A flowery scent in the air stole her attention from the feathery concert and sent it racing toward the back patio and the—

She sucked in her breath so hard, all sounds outside the window ceased. There, just beyond the blooming Bradford pear tree and atop the little patch of earth she'd cleared in the fall, was a mass of tulips in a sea of bold, brilliant colors— reds, yellows, purples, and pinks. And in the center of them all, nestled amid a distinctive circle of pink, was a happy face made of two yellow tulips for the eyes, one yellow tulip for the nose, and a slightly curved line of four yellow tulips for the mouth.

"What on earth?" she whispered, only to press her fist to her mouth as Ava's voice filled her ears.

"I made a surpwise for you, Mommy! A weally, weally special surpwise! It's a happy face! With the pwetty fwowers!"

Rocking forward, Dani rested her forehead against the glass, her eyes riveted on the fruits of an afternoon that had entailed dirt, water, endless questions, lots of giggles, wide-eyed plans, a carton of bulbs, and, finally, a mad dash to pick Maggie up at school and get her to a scout event.

"They are going to be wewy, wewy bootiful."

Suddenly, she was back there, on that day—in that moment when she'd looked at her phone and realized it was later than she'd realized. Like a whirling dervish, she'd grabbed the dirt and the watering can and run them over to the shed. When she'd returned for the little shovel, she'd found Ava hastily digging holes in the center of the flower bed and begging for just *"fwee more minutes . . . pwease, Mommy."*

Of course, three minutes had become ten, but—

Blinking against the day's latest round of tears, she again took in the flowers that marked the eyes . . . the nose . . . the smile . . . "Oh, Ava, you did it . . . You made a happy face just like you said," she managed through her trembling smile. "And it is absolutely *boo*tiful, my precious angel."

She wasn't sure how long she stayed there, staring out at those flowers, but, eventually, the sun on her cheek became the sun on her forehead and kicked off the first real rumble of hunger she'd had in two weeks. Slowly, she backed away from the window and made her way from the room. At the top of the stairs, she waited a few seconds to see if the rumble was, in fact, a sign she was about to get sick, but when it remained, and even strengthened, she headed downstairs to the kitchen and the mountain of meal choices that awaited her inside the freezer.

Tetrazzini . . .

Ziti . . .

Beef tips and noodles . . .

Shepherd's pie . . .

One by one she sifted through each stack before settling on Emily's chicken casserole. Pulling it out, she carried it over to the counter, peeled off the sticky note with heating instructions, and popped it into the microwave for the first two-minute segment. While it cooked, she liberated a fork and knife from the drawer, set them on the counter, and opened the front window to the same gentle spring breeze that had greeted her upstairs.

When her meal was ready, she headed toward her spot at the six-person table only to change course in favor of her desk and the single chair it boasted. There, surrounded by all things Dani, she took one bite, and then another, the simple act of eating both foreign and familiar all at the same time.

Soon, two bites became three, and four, and soon, it was all gone, her friend's simple yet tasty casserole the perfect choice for her first non-cracker meal.

Pushing the plate to the side, Dani opened the top drawer, retrieved the package of thank-you notes she always kept on hand, and began to write notes to correlate with the names she'd seen in the freezer—Emily, Roberta, Suze, Nancy, David, and on and on she went, the routineness of the task calming. When the notes were done, she set about the task of stuffing them into envelopes she addressed, stamped, and placed into the growing pile at her elbow.

When the last stamp was placed, she returned the packet of unused notes to the drawer and sank back against the chair, her gaze moving from the pile, to the clock, to the pen she needed to cap, and, finally, to the wall calendar and the multi-colored notations that filled each and every square—purple ink for Maggie, blue ink for Spencer, pink ink for Ava, and green for Jeff. Grabbing her glass, she tried to offset the sudden dryness in her throat with what was left of her water, but really, all she could do was stare at the days that had come and gone since the accident.

Maggie had missed a scout meeting, a classmate's party at the new paint-your-own-pottery shop in Westfield, two dance classes, three playdates, and tryouts for *Annie* at the local theater . . .

Spencer had missed three soccer practices, three baseball practices, one game of each, two sessions of karate, a play-date with Bobby, a party at the rec center, and a swimming lesson . . .

Ava had missed two story hours at the library, four sessions of gym time for three-year-olds at the rec center, two beginner ballet and tap classes, a mom-and-me trip to the zoo with their church friends, and her three-year-old birthday portrait . . .

Jeff had missed a client dinner, a golf outing with his partners, and the second of their two planned date nights during Mom's visit . . .

From a distance, the mishmash of colors was almost rainbow-like with the addition of things like parties and dinners being squeezed in alongside the staples like games and practices and classes. But up close, as it was at that moment, it wasn't rainbow-like at all. Rather, it was crazy and chaotic and—

Desperate for air, she slid back her chair, grabbed the stack of stamped thank-you notes, and stepped out onto the front porch, her gaze, if not her thoughts, firmly rooted on the mailbox at the end of the driveway.

By muscle memory more than anything else, she crossed the front porch, made her way down the trio of steps onto the flagstone walkway, and then stopped dead in her tracks as a series of sounds broke through the haze in her brain and forced her to look up.

Across the street, Bobby and a little boy from his soccer team were running around the yard playing army men. Next door, Roberta's daughter was playing Barbies with Suze's daughter, their sweet, almost singsong voices trying desperately to adopt a more appropriate tone for their adult-age dolls. And between both groups, in the middle of the road, were Dani's friends and fellow moms, their laughter-infused chatter like ice water against bare skin.

She didn't mean to gasp or breathe or step backward or swallow or do whatever it was that made everything in front of her stop in one swipe of an invisible conductor's baton, but she did.

The *pow-pows* of the army men's weaponry ceased . . .

Barbie's trip to the cardboard mall in her bright pink coupe stopped . . .

And the laughter-filled chatter of her peers drifted away into a suffocating silence.

Clearing her throat, Dani motioned toward the mailbox with the stack of thank-you notes. "Don't mind me. I-I just need to put some things in the box real quick."

The boys' eyes widened across the tops of their empty water guns, the girls pulled their Barbie dolls onto their pastel-clad laps, and the moms exchanged knowing glances before heading, as a unified group, in her direction.

"I didn't mean to interrupt," she said, holding up her free hand. "Just wanted to mail these, that's all."

Roberta and Suze stopped. Emily didn't.

"It's good to see you outside," Emily said, hurrying in her direction.

Unsure of what to say, Dani stuffed the envelopes into the mailbox and mentally calculated how fast she could make it back inside.

Thirty seconds? Maybe forty?

Of course, with Emily now standing in the middle of the walkway, blocking her path, all bets were off.

"It's really, really good to see you out here, Dani. Like *real* good."

In lieu of the words that still seemed to have abandoned her, she tried to offer a smile. But even without the benefit of a mirror she could tell the effort yielded something far more grimace-like than intended.

"We"—Emily swept her hand toward Roberta and Suze— "miss having you out here with us, Dani."

"Emily is right!" Roberta called. "We really do!"

Dani shifted her weight across her legs and swallowed.

"In fact, Emily was just bringing us up to speed on the latest escapades involving that lunatic mother in Bobby and Spencer's—" Suze's perfectly manicured hand came down on Roberta's arm, silencing the rest of the story and sending both women's eyes down to the pavement in near perfect unison.

"Oh, Dani," Emily whispered. "They didn't mean it. Roberta and Suze—they must have just forgotten what they were saying, and who they were saying it in front of for a moment. I mean, *this*"—Emily motioned toward Dani's house—"is just still so hard for everyone to wrap their head around, you know?"

Her answering laugh held no humor.

Emily's cheeks reddened along with her neck. "I mean, of course *you* know. You're living it every single day. But we feel it, too."

She could feel her throat tightening, her eyes beginning to burn, but still, she stood there, unable to move, unable to even really breathe.

"Stay outside with us for a little while, Dani, please. It'll be good for you—for all of us." Emily's eyes led her own to the boys on the other side of the street, and then across her own yard to Roberta's and the girls quietly holding their Barbie dolls. "I could put on a movie for the kids so they're not out here where you have to see them. Or-or I could ask Roberta and Suze to keep an eye on Bobby and his friend for me for a little while so I can go inside with you for a cup of coffee or whatever. That way we could talk in private or I could just shut up and listen. I just want to do whatever you want, Dani. Whatever you need."

Whatever she wanted.

Whatever she needed.

She looked beyond Emily to Roberta and Suze, noted the way they toed the ground, picked pretend lint off their clothes, and turned toward imaginary sounds in the distance lest Dani think they were watching her every move, her every facial expression . . .

Twenty paces to their right, and still clutching their dolls with uncertainty, the pair of eight-year-olds who had been Maggie's closest neighborhood friends looked as if they were afraid to move, afraid to speak, afraid to keep playing . . .

And Bobby? Spencer's best friend? He slowly tugged the army-green bandana off his head and sat down in the middle of the grass much to his teammate's chagrin . . .

Emily's gentle hand on her arm brought her back to the conversation she didn't really want to be having. Not now. Not there. If at all. "Please, Dani. Let me do something to help."

Again, she looked from Roberta and Suze, to the girls, to Bobby and his friend, and, finally, back to Emily. "Actually, there is something you could help with if that's okay."

"Anything! Just name it!"

"Can you look after things for me for a while?" she asked.

"Of course."

"Bring in the mail? Water the flowers? Make sure everything is okay from time to time?"

"Of course," Emily said again. "And if you're not downstairs when I bring in the mail, should I leave it on your desk in the kitchen or bring it all the way up to you?"

"Just put it on my desk and I'll deal with it when I get home."

Emily drew back. "When you *get home*? Does-does that mean you're *going* somewhere?"

"It does."

"But . . . *when*? And *to where*?"

"First thing in the morning." Dani stepped around the mailbox and headed up the walkway, glancing back at Emily as she reached the base of the porch steps. "I'm going to Pennsylvania. To stay with a friend."

Chapter 6

She tried to concentrate on the traffic, the scenery whizzing by, even the periodic instructions from the built-in GPS, but like the house, there were reminders of her family and the accident everywhere she turned. In fact, two different times before she'd even reached the end of the driveway she'd wrestled with going back inside, but she'd pressed on, her fear of going rivaled only by the pain of staying.

Tightening her fingers around the leather-wrapped steering wheel of Jeff's sedan, she saw little of the passing countryside to her left and right. Instead, she visited and revisited the moment she'd wheeled her suitcase into the garage and seen the empty spot where her minivan should have been. It had felt oddly normal at first, as if it were any other Saturday morning and Jeff would soon be pulling in with the kids, their mouths already messy from the donuts they were supposed to wait to eat until they were back home. But it wasn't any other Saturday morning and it never would be again . . .

She glanced in the rearview mirror at the back seat, her thoughts immediately wandering to the same view in her minivan—Spencer's booster seat behind the passenger seat, Ava's car seat strapped into the middle, and the spot behind her own seat where Maggie proudly sat *like a big person*. On the floor in front of Maggie was the car toy bag, and its plethora of books, dolls, and cars capable of staving off boredom.

Was Ava holding the little stuffed pink dog when it happened?

Or was she playing with the mermaid doll?

Shaking her head, she grabbed the water bottle she'd placed in the center console and forced herself to take a sip.

Was Maggie looking out the window? Did she see the car hurtling across the median in their direction? Did she understand what she was seeing enough to feel fear?

She tried to take another sip, but her hand was shaking so bad she simply returned it to the holder and willed herself to focus on the license plate in front of her—Connecticut. When the car moved into the exit lane, she looked over just long enough to take in the child sleeping in the back seat, his head resting against the windowsill, his mouth open.

Was Spencer dozing off like that? Had his head been pressed against the window, too, or was it resting on the edge of Ava's car seat? Did he wake up when he heard the crash?

The sound of a horn to her immediate left pulled her back into the present in time to see a car whiz around her, the driver's shaking fist and passenger's evil stare down serving as a reminder of where she was, and where she wasn't.

Had the driver who killed her family been distracted? Had he been talking on the phone? Texting? Dozing? Reading? Thinking about something other than the road in front of him?

A second horn, this time to her right, had her glancing over in time to see a woman, about her age, eyeing her warily from the driver's seat of a dark green minivan. Seated behind the woman and peering through the side window at Dani was a little boy, drinking from a sippy cup with one hand while making a stuffed dog jump up and down on his leg with the other.

If she had to take a guess, the little boy was probably a little younger than Ava, although not by much. Either way, he looked like a happy kid, someone Ava would have gravitated toward if they'd crossed paths at the park or while sitting on the bleachers at an older sibling's game.

She tried to see if there were any other kids in the car, but when she started to drift out of her lane in the process, the minivan sped up, the child's mother clearly trying to put as much distance between herself and Dani as possible.

Would Jeff and Mom and the kids still be alive if he'd sped up instead of swerving? Would—

"In two miles, take the exit for Route 322 toward Blue Ball."

Startled, she looked at the dashboard screen and peeked at the estimated time of arrival on the bottom corner of the display: 1:25 p.m. Twelve minutes away.

For the first time since her spur-of-the-moment decision to take Lydia up on the offer of an escape, she found herself beginning to squirm. After all, their contact with each other had been strictly pen and paper since they'd met as children twenty-seven years earlier. And while those earliest letters had been exchanged once a month into their respective teen years, they'd petered out to an annual Christmas letter with an occasional *just because* thrown in over the summer.

What did Dani really know about the Lydia Yoder of today besides the fact that she was now Lydia Schlabach and had been for close to fourteen years?

"Not much," she whispered. "Not enough to be showing up on her doorstep like—"

"Take a left onto Route 322 and proceed for eight miles."

Like a dutiful child, she turned left, her gaze taking in the gas station on the corner, the grocery store on her left, and the fast-food restaurant in her rearview mirror. Soon, the standard commercial trappings gave way to large tracts of land on which cows grazed, farmhouses were nestled, shirts and dresses blew and snapped on clotheslines, and grain silos broke the seamless line between earth and sky.

She took in the dark green shades in the second-floor windows and tried to remember what it was about that detail she'd learned while visiting the area as a child. Letting up on the gas pedal, she rounded a slight bend in the road and sucked in her breath at the sight of the gunmetal-gray buggy and its chestnut-colored mare traveling toward her on the opposite side of the road. A quick glance to her left as it passed revealed an elderly couple seated on the driver's bench, the end of the man's beard reaching the mid-point of his chest.

Being there, surrounded by farmland and horse-drawn buggies, it was, as she remembered from her youth, like stepping into a story whose characters lived in another century— a life that was so different from her own, yet alluring for the same reason. But perhaps what struck her most was how her own heartbeat seemed to slow, how her fingers loosened on the steering wheel, how the music she'd been playing as a mind-numbing distraction the whole time suddenly seemed so jarring, so unnecessary.

Maybe some of that was nothing more than the miles she'd put between herself and a house that no longer felt like home. But that wasn't all of it. There was something about the wide-open fields and the slower, simpler pace that had resonated with her all those years earlier in a way she'd never truly understood or ever quite forgotten. She just knew it had and, apparently, still did.

"Take the next right onto Weaverland Road."

She glanced at the screen, noted the remaining half mile left in her drive, and slowed still more as the street name she'd been writing on envelopes for years revealed itself on a faded sign tucked back from the main road. Still, she pulled onto the shoulder, double- and triple-checked the open address book on the passenger seat, and then turned onto the sparsely graveled road bookended by grazing cows to her left and rows of what looked to be barley to her right.

"Your destination—404 Weaverland Road, Blue Ball—is .5 miles away."

Beyond the cows, in a wide field, she could make out a team of horses pulling some sort of farming equipment. Atop the back of the machine, an Amish man stood, overseeing the horses. A young boy walked ahead of the team, occasionally stopping to pick something up. Inching forward, Dani slid her gaze right, to the white farmhouse she could see on the other side of the road. There, a woman clad in a prayer kapp and aproned dress was sweeping the front porch while a younger girl pulled laundry from a clothesline and set it into a basket at her feet.

Here, as had been the case with her first buggy sighting of the trip so far, she reveled in the quiet calm of the air—a quiet calm she breathed in and held before letting it go in a much-needed sigh.

"You have arrived at your destination. Arrived."

Abandoning her view of the woman and her daughter, Dani looked to the left again, the slight bend in the road making the cows and tractor she'd seen just moments earlier visible only through the rearview mirror. Now the view from the driver's side window was one of sheep munching on grass, a wood and wire fence that ran alongside a dirt lane, and a black mailbox bearing the name Schlabach.

Like clockwork, the rapid breathing was back, this time accompanied by a sudden clamminess in her hands that necessitated a quick wipe of each down the sides of her jeans. "Relax," she murmured. "Lydia asked you to come."

She knew it was true, yet sitting there, staring across the road at Lydia's driveway, she couldn't help but feel as if she'd made a huge mistake. Yes, she and Lydia had struck up a friendship decades earlier, but they'd been kids. And while they'd kept in touch throughout the years, their lives couldn't be any more different. Connections no longer came down to whether someone liked to play dolls or run and jump the way you did. For adults, commonalities were more about jobs and hobbies and where you lived. She had none of that with Lydia any longer. They were strangers, really. Strangers who just happened to have each other's name in their address books.

A soft whir from somewhere close by broke through her woolgathering and pulled her attention back to the rearview mirror in time to see an Amish boy, in a straw hat, coming toward her on what looked like a half bicycle, half scooter. Before she could process anything else, he was beside her, his curious blue eyes meeting hers through the partially open window.

"Are you stuck?" he asked, pointing at the front of her car.

An odd sensation of familiarity kept her gaze firmly rooted on the young boy she guessed to be a year or so older than Maggie. "I . . . um . . . no. Not really. Just trying to decide what to do."

"You looking for a birdhouse?"

"A birdhouse?" she echoed.

"Yah. I help Dat build them and Mamm paints them." The boy pulled his right hand from the handlebar of his scooter bike and pointed toward a wooden stand about ten yards away. "If you see one you want, just take it and put the money in the yellow-painted box. There's a hole at the top where you can push it in. Dat will get it out later, before dinner."

Using her hand as a shield against the early afternoon sun, she studied the stand and the hand-painted sign in front of it: Birdhouses for Sale. Even from her vantage point, she could see the craftsmanship present in the little wooden houses. Some were the more standard square birdhouse with a hole in the center. Others appeared to be mounted to poles and ran the gamut from miniature Victorian homes with turrets to the more garden-variety apartment building. "You made those?"

The boy nodded. "Yah. Dat and me did."

"Wow. You're very talented."

Instead of the broad smile she would have expected her praise to bring, the boy's gaze dropped to the road, where it remained for several beats. Then, "I must go. Mamm asked me to bring some bread to my grossmudder after school and then hurry home to help Dat and my uncle in the barn. Soon, Molly will have her baby. Maybe today."

"Is Molly your sister?" she asked.

A smile pushed his cheeks practically into his eyes. "My sister is Nettie. She is only three. Molly is Dat's cow."

"Oh. Sorry." She met his smile with a more sheepish one of her own and then dropped her focus to the boy's mode of transportation. "I imagine you'll get home pretty fast on that."

"I *am* home." Nudging his chin across his shoulder, he tucked his thumb beneath one of the suspenders that sat atop his pale blue shirt. "And faster than I did it yesterday, I think."

She recovered the brief gape of her mouth and, instead, looked back at the boy. "You live there?" she asked, nudging her own chin at the mailbox.

"Yah."

Lydia's son . . .

Again, she took in the boy, her earlier assessment as to his age now bringing with it a name she'd been seeing in Lydia's holiday letters since before Maggie was born.

"So you must be Luke," she said. "The oldest."

The boy's eyes widened. "Yah. I am Luke. How do you know my name?"

"Because I've been friends with your mom since we were almost as old as you are."

"I am almost ten."

"And your mother and I were eight when we met and became friends."

Luke took a half step closer toward the car, then recovered it with a quizzical look. "But you are English."

"You're right; I am."

"I do not remember seeing you before."

"That's because you haven't. Your mom and I are more pen pal friends; we've stayed friends through the letters we write one another."

Luke righted his scooter bike beside him but refrained from actually stepping onto the riding shelf. "Sometimes Mamm reads us the letters she gets in the mailbox. My favorite are the ones from Mamm's sister. She lives in Ohio." He looked from Dani to the bike and back again. "They had a very bad storm in the fall and lost all their corn! When Mamm read that part after dinner, Dat said it sounded like a hailstorm! He said such a storm took Grossdawdy's corn one year when Dat was my age. He said he still remembers waking up and looking out his window to see the broken stalks scattered across the field."

She looked past him again, this time taking in the fields she could just make out beyond the sheep. "Is that what is growing there?" she asked, pointing. "Corn?"

"No, that is wheat. We will plant corn soon." He stepped onto his scooter bike, but again, he did not move. "Where are you from? Maybe Mamm has read us some of your letters, too."

"I live in New York."

"New York," he repeated quietly as if trying to place the name in relation to a memory he couldn't quite capture. "What is your name? Maybe I will remember that."

"My name is Dani—Danielle, actually. But your mom and I really only exchange letters once a year, around the holidays mostly. Though, now that I'm thinking about it, I don't re-member getting one from her this year."

"Do your letters make her smile?" he asked, his own ex-pression growing serious.

Caught off guard by both the question and the boy's di-minished smile, she considered her words more carefully than she might have otherwise. "I-I hope so. I know her let-ters always make *me* smile."

And it was true. Seeing the standard white envelope with its Pennsylvania postmark nestled amid the stack of bills and solicitations each December was always a quiet thrill. It didn't matter what she was doing when she saw Lydia's letter, be-cause the moment she did, all else stopped for the time it took to read each and every word from the *Dear Danielle* at the top of the page all the way to the *Your friend, Lydia* at the bottom.

"Perhaps you are like the rainbow Grossmudder speaks of."

"Rainbow?"

"Yah. Grossmudder says a friend is like a rainbow that comes after a storm."

She tried to make sense of what the boy was saying, but she came up empty. "I don't understand . . . Has something happened?"

"You must come. Inside." Luke motioned for Dani to fol-low him toward the driveway. "You can park your car next to the barn, and I will tell Mamm you are here."

"Perhaps it will be better if I come back another time, on another day. When things are not so busy."

"It is not so busy."

"You said there will be a new calf soon. Maybe today."

"Yah."

"*That's* busy. And if you've only been out of school a little while"—Dani glanced at the dashboard clock—"your mom might be helping one of your siblings with homework or something before dinner."

"You said Mamm's letters make you smile, yah?"

She met his big blue eyes once again. "I did, because they do. All the time."

"Then I am sure a visit with you will make *Mamm* smile, too." This time, instead of just motioning her toward the driveway, he pushed off the ground with his left foot, scootered to the other side of the road, and then glanced back at her over his suspender-clad shoulder. "Come."

Chapter 7

She pulled to a stop behind Luke's scooter and watched as the hatted towhead ran across the side lawn, up the porch steps, and through the front door of the basic two-story white farmhouse. Shifting the car into park, Dani made herself cut the engine even though her every instinct told her to turn around and head back to the highway.

There had been a few seconds, as Luke was heading down the driveway, glancing back every few feet to make sure she was following, when she actually found herself calculating whether she could make a clean U-turn on the narrow road. When she was pretty sure she could, she inched forward, turned the steering wheel to the left, and then locked eyes with Luke—

In that instant, she knew she couldn't just leave. Not without being rude, anyway. And so she'd followed . . . She'd taken in the cows and the horses and the barn she'd passed . . . She'd stopped in the spot he'd pointed to just before he abandoned his scooter . . . And now she sat, looking up at the door, waiting for her first sighting of a woman she really didn't know—a woman who'd offered her home as a place to heal.

As if that could ever happen.

Blinking back the tears she refused to shed at that moment, Dani swung her gaze back to the side yard and two more scooters—one large, one small—she hadn't noticed until that moment. Beyond them, on a swath of hard-packed dirt, was a buggy parked next to a nondescript-looking black pickup truck.

A long moo from the vicinity of the barn pulled her focus there, only to have it stolen back toward the house by the sound of hurried footsteps across the front porch.

"See, Mamm?" Luke said, dividing his attention between pointing at Dani and looking back at the door from which he'd just come. "She is there, in the car."

Then, nudging his chin in the direction of the barn, he clambered down the steps, his words still directed toward the house. "I will go help Dat and Uncle Caleb with Molly now."

Dani followed him with her eyes as he made his way across the yard and past the passenger side window, his gait one of anticipation and—

A slow creak, followed by the telltale bang of a screen door, yanked her gaze back toward the front porch and the woman now standing at the top of the steps looking in Dani's direction. Clad in a dark green dress and white prayer kapp, the woman lifted her hand as a shield against the afternoon sun, slanted her head to the left, and then, on the heels of a soft squeal, hurried down the steps and straight for the car.

Dani, in turn, simply stared at the approaching face as her mind's eye mentally cataloged the differences between eight-year-old Lydia and present-day Lydia. So much was the same—the warm honey-blond hair just barely visible along the edges of the kapp, the high cheekbones that pushed still higher with a smile, the daintily defined chin, the emerald-green eyes that—

"Danielle! You have come!"

Pushing open the driver's side door, Dani stepped onto the hard-packed dirt and braced herself for the warm and welcoming embrace that came next. "You-you look exactly as I remember, Lydia," she managed past the sudden tightness in her throat. "Exactly."

Lydia's answering laugh echoed around them as the woman

gave Dani one last squeeze and then released her for a once-
over of her own. "Yah. Just taller, and wider, and older. But
you—let me see what far too long has done to you."

"Are you Mamm's special friend?"

Dani glanced down at the small, round face that stopped just
shy of her hip and felt an instant wave of light-headedness.
Lydia, in turn, rushed forward, grabbed hold of Dani's arm,
and gently guided her backward until she was flush against
the car. "Danielle? Are you okay?"

"Yes, I-I . . ." The words drifted away as she lowered her
gaze again to the little girl standing beside Lydia. Like her
mother, the child Dani guessed to be about three, maybe four
years old wore a white prayer kapp over hair that was even
blonder. Her eyes weren't green at all, though. Instead, they
were a cornflower blue. Her pale green dress reached midway down her calves, revealing bare feet. "Who is—"

A flood of emotion made it so she couldn't finish the sentence Lydia rushed to answer. "This is Nettie."

Closing the gap between them, Nettie reached up, wrapped
her soft hand around three of Dani's fingers, and gave a little
tug. "Molly is going to have a baby soon. Dat says if it is God's
will I can play with *that* baby."

Dani felt Lydia's grip on her arm release, even heard what
sounded like a soft if not slightly strangled gasp in the process,
but she couldn't take her eyes off the child now hopping from
foot to foot with unrestrained joy. "And there are new bunnies,
too. Two of them! Their eyes are like this"—Nettie squinted
her eyes into slits—"right now, but soon Mamm says they will
open big like Hopper's."

"Hopper's?"

"Their mamm!" Nettie let go of Dani's hand just long
enough to point at her dress. "Mamm made my dress. She
has one that matches, but she does not wear hers today. Hers
is *there*. See?" She moved her finger to indicate the clothesline
and the matching dress flapping in the soft breeze between a
pair of black pants on one side and a soft blue Nettie-sized

dress on the other. "Hers is getting dry. One day I will be big enough to hang dresses, too."

Then, rising up on her tippy-toes, the child released Dani's hand again and took off in a run toward the barn. "I must check the bunnies."

The soft patter of feet against dirt gave way to an all too familiar roar in Dani's ears—a roar she broke with her own rasped and broken voice. "She's . . . three, right?"

"Yah. But she will be four next month."

She knew she should say something or, at the very least, smile and nod, but all she could do was stare at the barn door through which Lydia's daughter had disappeared.

Three years old . . .

Pressing her fingers to her lips, she tried to catch her breath, to remind herself that lots of little girls were three years old, but the light-headedness was back. "Lydia . . . I . . . I'm sorry . . . I-I don't think I . . . I don't think I can do this. I-I don't think I can be here . . . It's too soon. Too—"

And just like that, the tears she'd managed to keep contained behind closed doors made their way down her cheeks and onto her lips.

"Oh, Danielle." Lydia pulled her close once again, gently guiding Dani's face to her shoulder as she did. "Please stay. It is not good to be alone with such sadness. It does not get better that way."

Lydia's words pushed her back a step. "Better?" she rasped. "There will be no better—ever. Don't you get that?"

"Today, it may seem that way. Tomorrow, too. And for many tomorrows after that, I am afraid. But one day it will get better."

"When I die, maybe. When I finally get to be *with them* again." She knew her voice was growing shrill, but it was that or start screaming in a place where such an outburst fit even less than she did. "Because that is the only way this loneliness, *this pain*, will go away."

Lydia's swallow was audible in the otherwise still air. "I

did not say your pain will go away. Because it won't. It will live inside you forever. But I also know that it won't take up your whole heart as it does now. One day, when you are ready, there will be room for joy, too."

"I don't believe that."

"I know you don't. And that is okay. I will know it for you when I can. Until you are ready to know it for yourself."

She broke eye contact long enough to note the wet spot her tears had left on her friend's shoulder. "Lydia, I don't belong here, in your home, with"—she swept a limp hand toward the barn—"your children."

"You do not have to stay in the house if you do not wish to. You can stay in the grossdawdy house, instead." Lydia pointed toward the farmhouse. "You cannot see it from here, but it is there, just around the corner, and it has been empty since Elijah's dat and mamm passed in the fall. You will have your own bedroom, your own small kitchen, and places to sit outside when you want to be by yourself. I will even put a chair under my favorite tree for you."

"Lydia, I can't. You really don't know me well enough to—"

"You are my friend, Danielle. You have been for a very long time."

"In letters, sure. After seeing each other a few times over the course of a single week almost three decades ago . . ."

"You are my friend in *here*," Lydia said, touching her heart. "That is enough for me, and it is enough for Elijah."

"But—"

"It was Elijah's idea to let you use the grossdawdy house. And I will see to it that the children do not bother you."

She let her gaze drift to the house, the barn, and the fields in the distance, and then allowed herself the long, slow inhale that came with the calm that surrounded it all. "Oh, Lydia, I don't know what to say."

"I know such a place must be very different from what you know and from where you live."

"It's like night and day," Dani said, her voice hushed. "Here, the only sounds beyond our voices are birds and chickens and"—she paused as a long moo rang out—"cows. At home there are birds, sure. But there are also delivery trucks, and garbage trucks, and horns honking, and the kids' friends playing outside, and . . ."

She looked again at the quiet fields, and the laundry flapping in the breeze, and, finally, back to Lydia. "Are you sure? I mean, really, really sure it would be okay for me to stay for a few days?"

Lydia's eyes flashed bright just before she gathered Dani's hands inside her own. "The only thing that would be more okay would be for you to stay *many* days. But I will not push. Yet." Then, releasing her hold, Lydia motioned toward the house. "Come. Let me show you where you will stay."

Dani heard the door click closed and slowly sank onto the wooden chair closest to the small sitting room window. Outside, just beyond a simple row of hedges, she could see the well-worn path Lydia had mentioned in her quick yet efficient tour of her late in-laws' home. The path, she'd said, led to the chicken coop and the rooster who would likely wake Dani at sunrise each morning. Beyond that, growing in long rows across a nearly football-sized field, was Elijah's barley crop.

She took it all in for a few long moments and then pulled her focus back inside the room. Besides the chair in which she was sitting, there was a second, cushioned chair and a rolling wooden cabinet that held a small propane tank capable of running the lamp affixed to the top. The light, Lydia had explained, could be wheeled from the sitting room into the kitchen and, finally, into the bedroom—basically anywhere Dani might need light once the sun slipped below the horizon.

The kitchen, like everything else in the house, was basic

yet sufficient with a propane-powered refrigerator and stove, a small table with bench seating, and just enough counter space to make a meal and prepare a plate.

Rising to her feet, she wandered into the bedroom. Here, like everywhere else, furnishings were sparse: a full-sized bed topped with a quilt made by Lydia; hooks for hanging clothes; and a four-drawer upright dresser with a washbasin and pitcher. She crossed to the window and the view it offered of the driveway and barn as her thoughts moved to the suitcase she knew she should unpack before Lydia returned with the insisted-upon dinner plate Dani had tried valiantly to duck.

It was probably silly to unpack what amounted to roughly a week's worth of clothes for what would likely be a single overnight stay, but, if nothing else, the act of putting things into drawers might be the perfect way to quiet the growing case of nerves that made it so even the simplest decisions—like whether to sit or stand, or keep the shades open—were just too overwhelming to entertain, let alone actually make.

With much effort, she hoisted her bag onto the bed, unzipped it open, and stared down at the pairs of underwear and socks haphazardly tucked alongside a single pair of jeans, a pair of dress slacks, a satin blouse, a long-sleeved paisley top, a short-sleeved solid-colored shirt, and a pajama set that still had the price tag affixed to the fabric. The jeans and the top made sense, but the dress slacks and satin blouse? On a farm? What on earth had she been thinking?

A soft knock at the door was followed by a slow, steady creak and Lydia's hushed voice. "Danielle? It is me—Lydia."

"I'm back here. In the bedroom."

"May I come in?"

"Of course." She turned toward the open doorway between the bedroom and the kitchen and tried to find the smile she knew the Amish woman deserved. But even without a mirror, she knew it was lacking.

"You are unpacking! That is good," Lydia said.

"It would be if I'd actually thought about where I was going when I packed." Dani pulled out the blouse and gave it a quick wave. "But when I was throwing everything into my bag this morning, I was just grabbing and shoving with no rhyme or reason. I just needed to get out—get away."

She sank onto the bed, the blouse clutched to her chest. "That sounds horrible, doesn't it?"

Lydia inched her way into the room. "I do not think that sounds horrible."

"You don't think it sounds horrible that I couldn't wait to get out of the last place I saw my family alive?"

"Perhaps, if that was true, yah. But it is not. You must breathe, that is all."

She stared at her childhood friend. "Lydia, I'm here because I had to get away—from the kids' rooms, from the bed I slept in with Jeff, from my mom's picture on my desk, from the people who know me only as Jeff's wife and the kids' mom. From all of it."

"You brought something from him, yah?"

Following the path forged by Lydia's pointed finger, she looked into her bag. There, beneath her folded jeans and pajamas, she spotted a familiar dark blue jacket. She reached in, pulled it out, and held it to her face, inhaling deeply as she did.

Oh, Jeff . . .

"I-I don't even remember packing this," she whispered around the soft fabric. "I just opened some drawers and threw stuff in my bag."

Lydia lowered herself onto the bed beside Dani. "Sometimes the heart knows things the head does not."

"I can still smell him in the fabric . . ."

"Yah."

She breathed in Jeff's lingering scent and then, pressing the jacket to her chest, she peeked inside the bag once again. Sure enough, in the side pocket usually set aside for the socks she'd tossed into the main compartment, she spotted her mother's small book and the drawing from Maggie's room—the one of them making cookies together . . .

"This book was in my mother's suitcase," she said, running her fingers along the pale pink cover and its embossed flowers. "I gave it to her as a gift a few years ago. I didn't know she took it along when she traveled. And this—my Maggie made this." Dani swapped the book for the drawing, her throat tight. "It was taped to the wall in her room."

"Perhaps you can tape it to the wall here, in *your* room. That way you can see it whenever you want to see it."

Reaching still farther into the compartment, Dani pulled out the wooden pencil case with Spencer's name spelled out across the top in tiny pictures. "This was my son's. I made this for him to take to kindergarten. So he would be able to see Jeff and his sisters and his friends whenever he felt homesick."

"That will look lovely *there*, don't you think?" Lydia asked, pointing to the empty spot on the dresser beside the washbasin and pitcher. "That way you can see it when you open your eyes in the morning, and before you must close them at night."

Dani reached into the compartment again, felt around, and then slowly pulled her empty hand back out. "I-I don't have anything of Ava's," she whispered. "How could I not have grabbed something of—Wait! Wait! Yes I do!"

Pushing off the bed, she practically ran to the kitchen only to return, seconds later, with her phone. "I took a picture of the happy-face flowers she planted for me."

"Happy-face flowers?" Lydia echoed.

"Yes, they're right—" She stopped, looked at the picture, and then back at her friend. "You can't look at pictures, can you?"

Lydia's answering laugh filled the space between them. "Amish can look at pictures. We just do not want ours to be taken."

Dani reclaimed her spot beside her friend and quickly pulled up the image of the tulips she'd taken the previous day. "Ava planted them like that. Like a happy face. She made them that way for *me*." Turning the phone for Lydia to see, she felt her lips begin to tremble. "When I . . . When I looked out my bedroom window, yesterday, I-I saw the face straightaway. It was just there. Looking back up at me. The second I saw it, I knew it was from Ava, and it made me smile and cry all at the same time. I felt her loss, of course, but it was like"—she drew the phone close to herself—"she was still here for a few minutes. Like my sweet, always happy, bright, creative, kind little angel was *there*."

"I am glad you knew to look," Lydia said, drawing Dani close in a side arm hug.

"I-I didn't. I mean I should have known; she told me she'd done it. But I didn't. Not really. Not the way I should have— not enough to know to look for them." Dani dropped her gaze to the picture and smiled despite the pain in her truth. "I only saw it at all because I was desperate for a little fresh air. And when I opened the blinds, there it was, looking up at me. For a second, I could actually see her standing next to her surprise, grinning up at me, so proud of herself for what she'd done."

Lydia withdrew her arm and stood, her movements weary. "I should probably leave you to the privacy I promised you would have if you stayed."

"You think I'm crazy, don't you?" she said, lowering the phone to her lap, her words peppered with emotion-laden breaths. "Crazy for saying I saw her standing there next to a happy face of tulips?"

At the doorway to the kitchen, Lydia stopped, glanced over her shoulder at Dani, and then looked away. "No. It makes me think that perhaps I am not."

Something about her wistful tone stirred a fresh round of tears to Dani's eyes—tears she tried valiantly to blink away as Lydia disappeared from view altogether. Wiping a rebellious one from the top of her cheek, she slid off the bed and made her way toward the now-empty doorway. "Lydia?"

The woman paused her hand on the exterior door, her slight, narrow shoulders rising with what seemed like an intentional breath. "Yah?"

"Thank you. For . . . For letting me stay here tonight."

"I hope it will be for many nights." Opening the door, Lydia, once again, met Dani's eye. "Soon, when Elijah is ready to eat, I will make up a supper plate for you and bring it over. I will set it outside on the porch and then knock so you know it is there."

She waved her hand in protest. "No, really, you don't need to do that. I'm not hungry."

"I know. I still feel the same, sometimes. But I know that if I do not, there is worry to be had by others."

"Others?"

"The people who love you."

"Ahhhh . . . Yes . . . *Those* people . . ." Dani drew in a deep breath. "Yeah, I don't have any of those left."

"You have me."

Chapter 8

It was sometime after three in the morning when, exhausted from crying, Dani finally drifted off into the kind of sleep where every dream felt real.

The walk along a sandy shoreline with Jeff, their fingers interlaced . . .

Sitting across the coffee shop table from Mom . . .

Tiptoeing around the kitchen with Maggie as they put the finishing touches on the secret dessert buffet they'd planned for the rest of the family . . .

Covering her mouth to keep from giving herself away during a game of hide-and-seek with Spencer . . .

Playing mermaids with Ava in the rec center swimming pool . . .

She could feel Jeff's hand, hear Mom's gentle laugh across her coffee mug, taste the white chocolate drizzle on Maggie's brownies, see Spencer's shadow as he crept by, and smell the suntan lotion on Ava's wet skin. Yet as real and as vivid as those moments, those sensations, seemed, they all scattered and disappeared at the ill-fitting sound that had her rubbing her eyes and then struggling up onto her elbow, confused.

"What on earth?" she mumbled as the fog in her head cleared enough to reveal a stark white wall and the faintest hint of light making its way around the edge of a dark green shade.

White wall?

Dark green shade?

Where did the sand go? The coffee mugs? The plates mounded high with everyone's favorite desserts? The bush she was kneeling behind? The ripple of the blue water—

And then she remembered.

She wasn't at the beach.

She wasn't in a café.

She was lying in an unfamiliar bed, in an unfamiliar house, in an unfamiliar town. And everything that had seemed so real just moments earlier was, in fact, not.

Squeezing her eyes closed against the familiar prick of tears, she willed herself to breathe. To count to ten in her head. To bite her lip. To steel herself for yet another day without Jeff . . . without Maggie . . . without Spencer . . . without Ava . . . without Mom.

"Why?" she rasped past the hard knot in her throat. "Why? What did I—"

Again she heard it: the same exact noise that had pulled her from her dreams in favor of her day-to-day nightmare. Only this time, she knew what it was.

It was Lydia's rooster alerting her to the start of yet another day without her family—another day she'd prayed wouldn't come yet clearly had. Sliding her legs off the edge of the bed, Dani sat up, rubbed her tear-dappled lashes, and then froze as another sound—this one more of a quiet thud, followed by footsteps on wood planks—took over for the now-silent rooster.

She waited for the silence to return and, when it did, she stood, crossed to the window, and pulled back the shade just enough to afford a view of the narrow porch that wrapped around the front of the house. With the help of the rising sun that streaked the sky in a yellowy pink, she spotted a basket that hadn't been there the previous night. Attached to the woven handle was a piece of what looked to be blue yarn and a slip of paper.

Curious, she let the shade drift back into position against the window and then headed across the kitchen to the front door. A peek outside showed the slip of paper contained her name as well as a series of words she couldn't make out from where she stood.

When the basket was inside and on the table, she bypassed the contents in favor of the note she was able to read with the light coming in from the kitchen window.

> *Danielle,*
> *I did not know how many eggs you would eat, so I have sent two. The milk came straight from the barn this morning. The loaf of bread is one I was making when you arrived yesterday. The cinnamon butter is Elijah's favorite. I hope you will enjoy it, too.*
> *We will be leaving for church service at eight and will return before dusk. Since I am to bring sandwiches to share for the meal today, I will leave an extra behind for you. It is important to eat.*
> *Your friend,*
> *Lydia.*

Slowly, she refolded the note and carried it back to the table. With a quick swipe of her hand, she parted the blue-and-white-checkered cloth that served as a makeshift lid of sorts and peered inside to find the eggs, the butter, the small bottle of fresh cow's milk, and the most perfect loaf of bread she'd ever seen.

The thought of eggs—fried, scrambled, boiled, or other-wise—held no appeal. But the bread and a swallow or two of milk?

Maybe . . .

The quick smack of a door closing against its frame stole her attention from the basket and its contents and led her back to the window in time to see Luke and a slightly shorter boy emerge from the main house. Luke led the way down the stairs and across the driveway to the gunmetal-gray buggy being hitched to a chestnut-brown mare by a man in a simple black coat and brimmed hat.

A second smack brought her attention back to the porch steps in time to see Lydia descending them with Nettie and another boy Dani guessed to be about five, maybe six. Like his brothers, the little boy was dressed nearly identical to their father, while Nettie's simple blue dress, white overlay, and white gauzy prayer kapp had her being Lydia's miniature clone.

Together, the trio walked to the buggy, parting ways as they reached it—Lydia onto the front seat, and the three boys in back with their little sister. Seconds later, Elijah climbed onto the seat beside his wife, gave the reins a gentle swish, and the buggy lurched forward in the very direction in which Dani, herself, had come less than eighteen hours earlier.

She strained to hear the clip-clop of the horse's hooves as her friend and the buggy disappeared from sight, but with the window closed, all she could really hear at that moment was the utter silence of the room save for the slow and unmistakable thud of her own heart. Here, in Amish country, so much was different. The homes were less elaborate, the furnishings were more simplistic, laundry dried on a clothesline, technology stayed outside the home, and horses did the transporting. But the people beneath all those differences? They weren't really all that different. Dads were dads; moms were moms; families were families. And just as she'd corralled Maggie, Spencer, and Ava into the van for church on Sunday mornings, Lydia clearly did the same with her crew.

It was hard not to wonder about their drive now that they were out of sight. Were they talking to one another or still shaking off the fog of sleep? Were the kids picking at one another in the back of the buggy or divvying up toys to make the drive go by faster? Were they—

Shaking her head, she backed away from the window only

to reclaim her spot as her gaze fell on the sun-dappled rocking chair on the other side of the glass pane. Positioned in such a way so as to not be seen from the street, the chair afforded a view of the barn, the main house, a pair of cats lolling around in the driveway, and even the same dozen or so sheep munching on the same stretch of grass from the previous day.

Unlike the long kitchen table with its bench seating and the full-sized bed with its two pillows, there was something about the singular rocking chair and being outside that beckoned. A glance at the clock and then Lydia's note made the decision easy. But first, Lydia's basket needed to be unloaded and its contents put away where they wouldn't spoil. A search of the cabinets yielded a bowl perfect for housing the pair of eggs in the refrigerator. The cinnamon butter, already in a bowl of its own, fit nicely alongside the eggs and the bottle of milk. And the bread, tucked inside its cloth covering, fit on the counter between the refrigerator and the sink.

Next, she returned to the bedroom, swapped out her pajamas for the jeans and long-sleeved paisley top, and then headed out to the front porch and its seating for one. Hiking her slipper-clad feet onto the rocking chair with her, she shrank against the wooden spools at her back and stared out over her friend's grounds. The windmill she'd spied from the car the previous day slowly turned with the same soft breeze that swayed the now-empty clothesline. The scooter Luke had abandoned in the side yard just inches from her parked car was now secured alongside four others in a bike rack one might see at a schoolyard. The size of two of the scooter bikes suggested adult usage, while the ones on the other side of Luke's were likely used by his younger brothers.

Sliding her gaze left, Dani took a moment to note the sheep and their obliviousness to her presence, and then moved on to the big red barn and the vaguely familiar tune that seemed to be coming from—

She dropped her feet back to the porch floor and rocketed up to a stand. Someone was in the barn . . . Someone who wasn't Lydia or her husband or one of the—

The whistling she was pretty sure she heard ceased in favor of a quick ping of metal followed by a distinctive thud. Seconds later, a laugh . . .

A *man's* laugh.

Slowly, quietly, she crept down the stairs and across the driveway toward the sound, any fear she'd felt at the onset bowing to anger at the intrusion on her friend's property and her own privacy. When she reached the barn, she peeked around the partially open door and surveyed the part of the interior she could see from her vantage point.

A handful of stray cats wandering the rafters . . .

Two roaming chickens stopping, now and again, to peck at the coating of hay that covered the ground . . .

A large mule idly watching her from his stall along the left wall . . .

Five cows moving their jaws in near perfect unison inside pens toward the back . . .

A man in a navy-blue Henley, with sleeves pushed up to his elbows, holding something big and white in his—

"You better turn around and get out of this barn right now or I will call the police!"

As he whipped around, the man's eyes skittered across the front end of the barn before landing square on Dani. "Whoa . . . Whoa . . . Slow down there, Sarge. It's just me—Caleb."

"I don't care what your name is or—Wait . . . Did you say *Caleb*? As in Lydia's *brother*?"

"You mean the one who showed you all the best places to hide on my dat's farm when we were kids? Yep, that's me." He started toward her only to stop as his left leg buckled forward. "Oh. Right, how could I forget," he said, shaking what she could now see was an oversized baby bottle as he turned his back to her and crouched down. "Someone doesn't quite have the patience for polite greetings yet, do you, Little Guy?"

Then, glancing over his broad shoulder at her, Caleb swayed to the side just enough to afford Dani a view of a small black calf jockeying for the bottle in earnest. "Come meet the newest member of the barn. He's persistent as all get-out when it comes to getting his bottle, but boy, is he ever cute."

"I—"

"C'mon. How can you resist this face?" Caleb said, directing her attention toward the calf with his chin.

She drank in the narrow black face, the dewy eyes, the cute stick-out ears, and the gangly legs, and finally inched forward through the narrow opening. "I don't want to scare him."

"There's a foolproof way to make sure that won't happen any time soon—watch." Angling the bottle slightly above nose level, Caleb waited for the calf to latch on and then flashed a warm, dimpled smile back at Dani. "I'm pretty sure a herd of African elephants running through the middle of the barn right now wouldn't scare this little guy off his bottle."

"What happened to his mother?" she asked. "Why isn't she feeding him?"

"She is—or *was*—a heifer."

She drew in a sharp breath that earned her barely more than a twitch of the calf's ear in return. "*Was?*"

"A heifer is a female that's never had a baby. But now that Molly has had *this* guy"—he made a face at the calf—"she's officially a cow. But I'm guessing her never having a baby before factored into why she didn't seem to know what to do with him, and why *I'm* playing mamma cow right now, instead of her."

"Will she come around?" Dani asked, stopping just behind the pair. "You know, once she realizes he's hers?"

Caleb's smile faded ever so slightly with his answering shrug. "No. Molly wanted nothing to do with him. That's why she's with the other cows," he said, motioning toward the back of the barn with his chin. "And why I'm standing here bottle-feeding him. Fortunately, though, this little guy doesn't know any better, so it's not like he's going to be needing years of therapy as a result."

She craned her head around Caleb and, again, took in the calf's wide eyes and stick-out ears as he nursed hungrily from the bottle. "I've never seen a newborn calf before."

"Which means you've never fed one, either . . ."

"No."

"Would you like to?"

"No, I-I don't need to," she said, taking a step back.

"I didn't ask if you *needed* to; I asked if you'd *like* to—two entirely different things. One is a chore, and one is something that makes you happy." Tipping the bottle downward, he gently pulled it from the calf's mouth and held it out to Dani. "Here. Give it a try."

"No, really, I shouldn't."

"Actually, you should." He cocked his head so he was looking directly at the calf. "Shouldn't she, Little Guy?"

Sighing, she took the bottle from Caleb's strong hand, crouched down beside him, and held her hand steady as the calf resumed eating. For a few moments, she lost herself in the sweet sucking sounds as the remaining milk disappeared. When there was nothing left, the calf gave a few persistent wide-eyed sucks and then pulled back to study Dani. "He's so cute," she whispered. "What's his name?"

"He doesn't have one yet." Caleb took the empty bottle from her hand but stayed crouched beside her. "The kids all had ideas, but as of last night when they left the barn and I hunkered down over there"—he pointed at a folded quilt in the corner—"nothing had been agreed on quite yet. So I've been calling him all sorts of stuff since then. Though *Little Guy* seems to have become my go-to."

She looked from Caleb to the calf and back again. "You stayed here overnight? In the barn?"

"Yep. Wanted to see if Molly would have a change of heart in those first few hours. Then, when that didn't happen, I stayed around because I felt bad for the little guy, you know?"

She rose up to a stand, brushed a few pieces of straw from her jeans, and gave Caleb a once-over as he, too, stood—quickly cataloging his strong jawline, his tall stature, his jeans, and . . .

"I didn't know you could wear clothes like that," she said, leading his amber-flecked eyes down to his shirt. "I thought, even in the barn, you had to wear the black pants and suspenders and all of that."

He carried the bottle over to a half wall and set it on top. "I would if I were Amish."

"If you were Amish?" she echoed. "But you are."

"I was being raised by Amish when Lydia and I met you, but unlike my sister, I chose not to be baptized. Which means I'm English just like you now."

"Oh. Wow. I-I didn't know."

He reached for a broom only to pull his hand away and tuck it, nervously, into the front pocket of his jeans. "Lydia told me about what happened to your family. I'm really sorry. I can't even imagine what you must be going through right now."

She dropped her gaze to the barn floor and tried to find her voice. But there was nothing. Just a throat-clogging lump and the promise of tears if she even opened her mouth. Instead, she shook her head, once—fast—and drew in the deepest breath her lungs would allow.

"Lydia told me she'd invited you to stay, but I didn't think you'd actually come."

"I didn't, either," she murmured, forcing herself to look up. "But it was the only place I could think of to go."

His answering nod was slow, thoughtful. "How long are you going to stick around?"

"I'll probably head back later today or early tomorrow."

Her words seemed to push him back a step. "But you just got here."

When she didn't respond, he walked over to one of the horse stalls, rooted around in his pocket, and pulled out a peppermint candy he promptly held in her direction. "Would you like to do the honors?"

"The honors?"

"Yeah, don't you remember feeding a peppermint candy to my dat's buggy horse when we were kids?"

She stared at him. "No . . ."

"You were afraid of the horses the first day. But by the end of the week, you were holding your hand out and feeding them peppermint candy just like Lydia and I did. Only you laughed the whole time." He unwrapped the candy, placed it in his palm, and held it up to the black mare eyeing him curiously from the other side of the stall door. Before Dani could even blink, it was gone. "Which made me and Lydia laugh, too."

His own laugh, sparked by the memory, echoed around the barn. "I still hear that sometimes when I'm handing out peppermints even now."

"Hear what?" she asked as the tightness in her throat began to recede.

"Your laugh. It was contagious."

Unsure of how to respond, she stayed silent as Caleb continued, his words, his very gaze, suggesting he was reliving another time. "Your laugh even got to my dat. Saw it myself." With a shake of his head, he was back in the barn—back in the present day. "Anyway, did you ever find a way to get one of your own?"

"You lost me."

"By the time you drove off that last day, you were determined you were going to get a horse of your own one day."

She had to laugh a little at that. "Uh . . . no. I'm pretty sure my dad squashed that idea before we'd hit the highway. Apparently, landlords in New York City don't allow horses in third-floor apartments."

"The nerve," he joked back.

"I know. I mean, did you foresee that little tidbit being an issue?"

"If it was a tidbit I'd truly grasped, yeah, I would've put two and two together." He reached into his pocket for another peppermint candy and, again, held it out toward Dani. "But considering I had no idea what *living in the city* meant, I had no reason to stamp on your dreams."

When she didn't move, he brought the candy to her while pointing his free hand toward a pair of field mules. "They like peppermint, too."

"I really shouldn't," she said, tucking her hand behind her back.

Caleb jerked his head toward the mules. "I'm pretty sure they disagree with that statement. Profusely."

"I'm not sure I remember how to do it, exactly."

"Sure you do. First, you unwrap it—which I'll do for you now." When the candy was free of its plastic wrapper, he guided her hand upward so her palm was parallel with the ceiling and then placed the candy in its center. "Now, hold it steady and—yep—there you go!"

She looked from her palm to the floor and back again. "Where did it go?"

"In Leo's stomach."

"Leo?"

Caleb pointed at the mule. "Meet Leo."

"But I didn't even feel it."

"He's fast."

"Clearly." She nudged her chin toward the second mule. "What about that one? Shouldn't he get one, too?"

"He thought you'd never ask." Caleb dug his hand into his pocket and retrieved yet another piece of peppermint candy. "You got this one?"

Nodding, she unwrapped the candy, stuffed the plastic wrap into her own front pocket, and lifted her candy-topped palm toward the second mule. One quick burst of air on her skin later, the candy was gone.

Caleb's rich and hearty laugh rang out around the barn. "Look at you, just as much of a pro as ever."

"Olympic level, no doubt." She wiped her hand down the side of her jeans and then wandered over to a barrel not far from where they stood. "I loved everything about your farm when I was a kid—playing hide-and-seek in the barn, jumping in the hay, chasing chickens, getting pulled in that little cart while your older brother learned to drive a horse . . . All of it. In fact, truth be told, the next time I got to blow out a birthday candle, I actually wished I could be Lydia."

"And Lydia and me? We'd seen English kids from the back of Dat's buggy a time or two. But we'd never actually gotten to play with them before. But you came around and you were just like us, only your dresses had flowers on them and you didn't wear a prayer kapp." Leaning against a nearby wall, he rubbed his thumb and index finger along his stubbled jaw. "You smiled and laughed all the time, and not just when you were feeding peppermints to the horses. Swinging on the front porch, finding another cat in the barn, and even eating a piece of my mother's bread made you happy."

"That bread was *good*," she quipped.

He held his finger to his lips, looked left and then right, and then modulated his deep voice down to an almost whisper. "You didn't hear it from me, but Lydia's might be even better. Especially with her cinnamon butter on top."

"She left me some of that this morning. In a basket."

"Then you know what I'm talking about, right?"

Shifting from foot to foot, she glanced down and shook her head. "I didn't try it."

"Why?"

"I wasn't hungry. I"—she swallowed—"haven't been very hungry lately."

When he didn't respond, she looked up to find him studying her closely, the lightheartedness of their banter no longer reflected in his expression. "Look, I know just being around each other is going to be good for you and for Lydia, but this whole not-eating thing isn't good."

This whole not-eating thing . . .

Like she had a choice.

Then, as if he sensed he'd overstepped some invisible line, he retrieved a large oval-shaped brush from a hook on the wall and began to groom the black mare with long, even strokes. "I remember your mom so clearly, even after all this time."

"You remember my mom?" she rasped.

"Sure do." He stopped, whispered something in the mare's ear in Pennsylvania Dutch, and then continued on with the brush. "Her laugh sounded very much like yours."

Had it? She'd never really noticed . . .

"How is she?" he asked, squatting down beside the horse. "Still pushing you to try new things?"

His question slapped her back so hard, she practically toppled over the barrel from the force of her answering gasp. In her haste to steady herself, she bumped against the stall on her left, startling the pair of mules inside as well as a pregnant cat traveling the rafters above.

"Danielle?" Caleb said, jumping up. "Are you okay? Did I say something wrong?"

She tried to wave him off, to excuse herself and run outside, but it was as if the walls of the barn were closing in on her so tightly she could barely breathe, let alone respond in any measurable way. Grabbing hold of a nearby hook, she held on for dear life while everything around her began to spin, faster, and faster, and—

"Danielle!"

Chapter 9

He was carrying her across the driveway when she came to, his hurried pace and the morning air filtering through the fog that hung heavy in her head. "Put . . . me . . . down," she murmured. "I-I . . . can walk."

"Just a few more feet and I'll have you inside. Hang on."

She willed her eyes to open, to focus, but it was difficult. "What happened? Did I fall?"

"Dropped like a brick is more like it. But I think I caught you before your head actually hit the ground. I'll know for sure when I get you inside and can take a closer look." Turning her slightly to the left, he ascended two steps. "You're staying in the grossdawdy house, yes?"

"I . . . yeah. Yes." Reaching up, she felt around her face, her forehead, and the crown of her head as he pushed open the front door and strode into the tiny kitchen. "I'm fine. Nothing hurts. You can put me down."

His eyes locked on hers before straying toward the bedroom and back. "I'd feel better putting you down on the bed. You did pass out, after all."

"I'm fine," she repeated, wiggling free. "Really. I just"—she swayed into the kitchen table—"whoa. Sorry about that. Maybe you're right. Maybe I should just sit for a little while."

In a flash, he was beside her, his hand on her back, guiding her onto the bench seat. "When was the last time you ate?"

"I'm not sure."

He pulled a face. "You're not sure?"

"Yeah . . . I tried to eat a little of the chicken Lydia brought over last night, but I wasn't hungry."

"So in addition to skipping dinner, you've had nothing yet today, either?"

"I . . . suppose," she said, shrugging. "But I'm not hungry."

"I think your body is trying to tell you otherwise." He crossed to the refrigerator and looked inside. "I could make you some eggs."

Just the word made her stomach flop. "No. Please."

He glanced back at her briefly, his left eyebrow rising. "Okay . . . Your plate from last night is still here and it doesn't look like you touched anything on it."

"I told you. I just wasn't hungry."

"You want some of that now? The chicken looks really good."

She covered her stomach with her hand and shook her head.

"Okay, moving on. Oh, here's Lydia's cinnamon butter," he said, holding up the small white bowl. "Where's the bread?"

"On the counter, next to the sink."

He pushed closed the refrigerator door, set the bowl of cinnamon butter on the counter, and peeled back the blue-and-white-checkered cloth. "Problem solved. For now, anyway."

"No, I can't. I'm just not—"

"You passed out, Danielle. That doesn't just happen." Grabbing a knife, he sliced a piece from the loaf and put it on a plate. "And it's like I said earlier, Lydia's bread—with this butter—is the best. You can't *not* eat it."

She wanted to argue, even opened her mouth to do just that, but the room was beginning to spin a little again. Leaning forward against the table, she forced herself to focus on the plate Caleb set at her spot along with a small glass of fresh cow's milk.

Breathe in . . .

Breathe out . . .

Breathe in . . .

Breathe out . . .

Slowly, the spinning began to subside. "Thanks," she whispered, motioning toward the waiting slice. "For this, and for catching me."

"Which reminds me." He came around behind her and slowly parted her hair at the crown. "This doesn't hurt?" he asked, pressing ever so gently.

"No. Really. You must have caught me before I hit."

"Okay, good." He pulled his hand back to claim a seat on the opposing bench. "Try a bite. Just one. With this"—he scooted the bowl of butter and a knife in her direction—"on it."

Reluctantly, she took the knife, dipped the tip in the butter, and spread a very thin coat across the slice of bread. When he prompted her yet again, she took a small bite.

"Good, right?"

The bread felt odd in her throat, but he was right. She took a second bite.

"I said something wrong, didn't I?" Fisting his hands in front of his bottom lip, he leaned forward, his gaze moving between the bread in her hands, and her face. "In the barn," he clarified. "Before you fell."

A third bite led to a fourth and a sip of milk.

"Danielle?"

She lowered her milk glass and looked at him across the top. "I don't know what you're talking about."

"You passed out because of the food," he said, lowering his hands to the table. "But your gasp? That was because of me, wasn't it?"

"My *gasp*?"

He nodded, his eyes trained on hers. "Yeah. In the barn. When I asked how your mom is doing."

Stopping, mid-chew, she pushed the rest of the bread and the plate into the center of the table and tried to rise up on legs that weren't ready to support her just yet. "I'm sorry," she mumbled. "I-I think it's time for you to leave."

Caleb's mouth went slack. "Wait . . . Why? I wasn't meaning to pry if you two had a falling-out or something. I just remember her as being really nice and always talking you into trying new things and—"

"My mom is *dead*, Caleb! She was in the car with my husband and my children instead of me! And why? Because I let her talk me into staying home and having"—Dani crashed her hands down onto the table—"*time for me*! But I didn't *ask* for time for me! I didn't *want* . . ."

This time, when she struggled to her feet, she was able to hold herself up, cross to the door, and smack it open against the wall. "I really need you to leave. *Now.*"

It was nearly five o'clock when she heard the clip-clop of the buggy as it made its way down the driveway. Gapping the edge of the shade, Dani peered out her bedroom window and watched as the horse stopped outside the barn door. Seconds later, Elijah, Lydia, and their four children exited onto the hard-packed dirt and scattered in different directions.

Elijah and the youngest boy headed inside the barn while Luke and the next tallest boy walked to the front of the buggy. With the ease of children who knew what was expected of them, they unhitched the mare, stroked her head, and then gently led her through the same door their father and brother had gone through.

Lydia and Nettie were halfway to the house when Luke popped his head out of the barn, clearly yelled out something to the pair, and then, after a little hopeful bouncing on Nettie's part, Lydia nodded. In the blink of an eye, the little girl was off and running toward her brother, and when she disappeared into the barn Dani felt her whole body sag in unison with . . . *Lydia's?*

No.

Lydia had everything . . .

Her husband, her—

Parting company with the glass, Dani released the shade from between her fingers and watched, through tear-filled eyes, as it drifted back into place. Part of her wanted to grab her suitcase and head for home right then and there. But another part of her—the part that doubled over in agony at the very thought of walking back into that empty house—wanted to hide away forever.

It wasn't that she didn't think about Jeff and the kids constantly in the grossdawdy house, because she did. They were there every time she closed her eyes, every time she opened them, every time she took a breath, every time she released it. Geography had nothing to do with any of that. But at home, when she looked out on the comings and goings of the neighborhood, it was as if Jeff and the kids had been photoshopped out of life, while here, in Amish country, tucked away behind the walls of what had once been Elijah's parents' home, the only one linked to Jeff and the kids was Dani. There was no one to continue on as if they'd never existed.

A soft knock broke through her thoughts, pulling her quietly toward the bedroom doorway and its view of the front door. On the other side, just beyond the door's single panel curtain, she could just make out the top of a white gauzy prayer kapp bent downward ever so slightly.

Lydia . . .

Wiping at her eyes, Dani used the time it took to retrieve the empty basket from the table to compose herself and then crossed to her friend. "Hi, Lydia," she said, cracking the door halfway open. "I heard you come back just now. Thanks for the breakfast food you left this morning."

"Yah." Lydia nodded, her eyes searching Dani's face like one might search a map after making a wrong turn. "Did you eat any of it?"

"Not much. But it wasn't anything about what you left." She looked up at the ceiling and then beyond Lydia to the barn. "It's just that . . . I don't know . . ."

"The sadness sits heavy, yah?" Lydia said, drawing her hand against her own aproned chest. "It leaves no room for food."

Surprise dropped Dani's gaze back to her friend. "That's it. Exactly. I know I should eat, but I just can't."

"Yah. But you must try. Even if it is just a nibble here, and a nibble there."

Nodding, she rested her head against the edge of the door. "I did that. With your bread. For a few bites, anyway."

"Something is better than nothing when it is difficult to eat." Lydia fidgeted her hands at her sides for a moment and then, after a quick glance at the barn, lowered her voice. "I am sorry Caleb did not know. But it is my mistake, not my brother's. If there is to be anger it should be at me, not Caleb. Please."

"I wasn't . . ." She felt the familiar lump working its way up her throat and tried hard to swallow it down. When it didn't budge, she played, instead, with the handle of the basket. "How did you know about that? I thought, when he left here, he left the farm altogether."

"He left a note on the table. He feels bad that he upset you so, and he does not understand why I did not tell him about your mamm."

A swell of unshed tears blurred the basket from view and she thrust it toward Lydia. "Here," she murmured. "This is yours."

"Danielle, I—"

"I am very tired. I think I should try to nap for a while."

Lydia's hand came down on Dani's. "I need you to know I

did not forget her when I spoke of what happened. It is only that I *meant* her when I said *your family*."

She tried to speak, but her throat was so full of emotion all she could do was close her eyes and try to breathe.

"I did not forget her," Lydia repeated.

Something about the thickness in Lydia's voice unleashed a pair of tears down Dani's cheeks. "I . . ." She stopped, took another breath, and waited a beat or two until she could complete an entire sentence. "I don't know how to do this without her, Lydia. My mother was the person I called to talk my way through tough times. It didn't matter how big or how small, Mom was my rock. *Always*.

"When this new girl came into Maggie's classroom and tried to come between Maggie and her friends back in the fall, I did everything to be calm and reassuring in front of Maggie, but the second she finished her homework that day and went out to play, I was on the phone with Mom, venting. The same was true when Spencer was sick with the flu shortly after he started kindergarten. I-I was worried because he wasn't getting better as quickly as he always had in the past and I was heartbroken at the thought he was missing out on the making-friends part of school. So I called Mom—not because I thought she could do anything different than I was already doing for him health-wise, but because I needed to get out my worry and my frustration. And she always listened. It didn't matter if it was early in the morning as I was running out the door with the kids, or while I was pulling dinner to-gether in the evenings—if I called, she always picked up, ready to listen.

"But now, there's so much I want to say. So much I *need* to say," she said between labored breaths. "That first day or so? After the troopers came and before the"—she squeezed her eyes closed—"wakes, I actually picked up the phone and called her. When she didn't pick up and I heard voicemail kick in, I actually hung up and tried again—imagined she heard

it ringing and just couldn't get to it in time. By the second ring
that time, I was sobbing and saying, '*Pick up, Mom . . . Please,
please pick up. There's been an accident and I need you.*' "

Pulling her arm from Lydia's grasp, she grabbed hold of
her head and doubled over at the waist. "It was like *I* forgot
she'd died—*my own mother*. What kind of daughter does
that? What kind of daughter forgets she lost her mother?"

"Do not say such things," Lydia said, guiding Dani over to
the bench. When Dani was settled with her head buried in
her hands, Lydia lowered herself onto the opposing bench.
"You were a good daughter, Danielle."

She lifted her head just long enough to meet Lydia's worried eyes. "Good daughters do not forget they have lost their
mother."

"You did not forget." The table creaked as Lydia leaned
toward Dani. "Miss Lottie says it is shock. That one can only
take in so much at a time."

"But I didn't remember that she was *dead*," she repeated.

"Your heart was protecting you. It was too heavy already,
too busy to take in all of God's will at one time."

She wrenched her head up so fast, Lydia actually drew
back, startled. "Why do you keep saying that, Lydia?"

"What do I keep saying?"

"That it was *God's will*. You can't really believe that,
can you?"

"Yah. It was God's will to take your family when he did,
just as it was God's will to—"

Scraping the bench backward, Dani stood, her entire being
shaking with anger as she paced her way back and forth
across the kitchen. "My *mother* is dead, Lydia! My *husband*
is dead! My *eight-year-old* is dead! My *five-year-old* is dead!
My"—her voice faltered and then broke—"*three-year-old* is
dead!"

Lydia fisted her hand against her mouth, her eyes pained.
"I did not mean to upset—"

"You say that is *God's will*?" Dani rasped. "Why? Why would He *want* to do that? They did *nothing wrong*! If . . . if it was God's will to do that to someone . . . why didn't He take me?" Sagging backward, she slid down the wall until she collapsed in a heap at the bottom. "He should have taken me!"

Chapter 10

Despite her nightly prayer to the contrary, her life marched on. Day became night, night became day, and soon she'd lived another week, another two weeks, another three weeks, another month without her family.

In the mornings, she was woken from the dream-filled version of her living nightmare by the crow of Elijah's rooster, the bird's timekeeping ability as good as any alarm clock she'd ever owned. She'd lie there, in the eventual and inevitable silence, staring at the ceiling, her eyes welling with tears at all of the things she should be doing . . .

Making a cup of coffee for Jeff.

Checking the morning temperature so everyone dressed in the proper clothes.

Going over her day's to-do list outlining what everyone needed to be doing and when/where.

Sometimes she could almost hear them in her head as they'd been in the early morning hours: Jeff's sleepy thank-you as she handed him his favorite blend, Maggie's pleas to read just a little before getting dressed, Spencer's need to talk through the day ahead, and Ava's sweet little *"good morning, friends"* ritual with her dolls and teddy bears wafting down the hallway. But that auditory track never lasted long. Instead, the snippets were quickly drowned out by the memory of a very different voice: *"Ma'am, there's been an accident."*

She knew she should be used to it by now. It was as much a part of her wake-up routine as the rooster. But try as she did to steel herself for its impact, the memory still reduced her to tears, first; nausea, second.

By the time she was done voiding her stomach of the limited food she'd eaten the previous evening, a peek out the front window would reveal a familiar basket filled with whatever breakfast foods Lydia had made for Elijah and their children. It was usually noon before her stomach was settled enough to take a bite or two of whatever Lydia had made, and even that could only be consumed while sitting in the chair Luke had set out for her beneath a nearby tree.

There, surrounded by the wide-open fields and the endless blue sky, she could detach from herself enough to breathe. Sometimes, she'd zone out so completely, she'd find that an hour, maybe two had gone by without her knowing. Other times, she'd catch a glimpse of one of the farm animals and then watch its every move until she finally grew bored and went inside.

The late afternoon and early evening hours took on a routine as well, with the basket she'd unpacked and left outside Lydia's front door reappearing on her own porch with items more reflective of dinner. And just as there was always a main dish, a side dish, and a slice of warm bread, there was also a note from Lydia.

The notes, themselves, were never long, just a quick word of encouragement or a reminder that Lydia was ready to listen if or when Dani was ready to talk. But she wasn't. Really, what was there to say? Her family was dead. No amount of talking could ever undo that fact.

That's why, after the contents of the dinner basket were added to the refrigerator, she took advantage of the fact that

Lydia and her family were eating in the main house to go for a long walk. The walks, themselves, had no rhyme or reason—no specific length or destination. Rather, they were simply a way to change her scenery and to try to work out some of the unfamiliar aches and pains that had begun to settle in her lower back and thighs.

By the time she returned to the grossdawdy house each evening, whatever energy she'd managed to harness to get herself down the road and back was gone, replaced by bone-reaching fatigue and a fresh round of guilt at the sight of her clothes, freshly laundered and folded, waiting for her atop the front porch when she returned.

All her life, she'd handled her own affairs, first as a latchkey kid, and then, later, as a wife and mother. Yet now, at thirty-five, something as seemingly simple as deciding whether to open the back door and step onto the deck or stay inside seemed too big, too daunting.

Pressing her head against the door's single glass pane, she peered out at the barley crop she'd watched Elijah walk through and tend over the past few weeks. If Lydia's husband thought Dani unfriendly or lazy for sitting on the back patio or beneath the tree, doing nothing but staring out at the land or sky most afternoons, he didn't let on, his daily nod of greeting no different after a month than it had been in the beginning.

Still, it was hard not to wonder if the hatted man with the easy pace and strong work ethic was growing tired of her presence on his farm. How could he not? Her car never moved, her laundry took up space on the clothesline, she avoided contact with him and his children, and her able body did nothing to earn its keep.

"*Elijah understands, Danielle,*" Lydia assured her, again and again. "*He really does.*"

"No. He doesn't. No one does," she whispered as she

pushed open the back door to the bright afternoon sun. Lifting her chin, she willed the warmth to stay with her as she crossed to the chair. There, as opposed to the rocking chair on the front porch, her very presence was obscured from the main house by the trunk of the pin oak tree, a saving grace when the guilt that invariably followed unleashed yet another round of cheek-soaking tears.

The sadness was always the same. She missed Jeff. She missed the kids. She missed Mom. And the thought of living the rest of her days without them pained her to her very core.

The guilt, though, that was always different, changing on a minute-to-minute basis. Guilt over staying home, guilt over having dreamed about time away from Jeff and the kids at a spa, guilt over losing herself in a book when her family needed her most, guilt over needing a stranger to tell her they were gone, guilt over being the one still alive and—

A quick squeal from the rear of the main house slanted her thoughts and her eyes to the left in time to see the heart-shaped back of Lydia's gauzy white prayer kapp through a small gap in the pin oak's budding branches. A second later, the kapp gave way to a peek at Lydia's high cheekbones pushed still higher by a growing smile.

"Do you want to sit on my lap, in the chair, or next to each other on the ground?" Lydia asked, her voice wafting across to Dani.

"I want to sit on your lap on the ground!"

Nettie . . .

Lydia's answering laugh distracted Dani's thoughts from their immediate jump to Ava. "I did not say those two together, silly girl."

"But I like them together very much," Nettie said.

Again, Lydia laughed. "Yah. I do, too. So"—her pitch shifted with a change in stance—"let us put them together now. Before the boys return from school."

A flurry of movement from behind the lowest part of the tree pulled Dani's gaze downward in time to see a rustle of blue fabric (Lydia's dress) and then, seconds later, the plop of light green fabric meeting blue. "I do not want to go to school," Nettie announced. "I want to stay here. Like you."

"I stay here *now*. But when I was five, as you will be next year, I went to school, too. That is how I learned how to count, how to read books, and how to know what the bishop is saying in church. It is these things that Luke and David and Mark are learning, too."

"I can count," Nettie countered. "One . . . two . . . three . . . six . . ."

"*Four*, Nettie. One, two, three, *four*."

Nettie's sweet voice filled the air again. "One . . . two . . . three . . . *four* . . . six."

"After four is *five*—four, *five*, six."

"One . . . two . . . three . . . four . . . five . . ." Nettie stopped, sucked in a breath, and then, cautiously, added, "six."

"Yah. That is it. In school you will learn to count to one hundred."

Nettie's answering gasp brought a small smile to Dani's lips. "I cannot count that high!"

"Not now you can't. But when you are in school you will, just as your brothers do."

A beat or two of silence gave way to Nettie's voice once again—a voice that was quieter, more hesitant than before. "But when I go to school I can only hug you in the morning and when I come back home."

"Yah."

"Hugs make you happy, Mamm."

"Do I get hugs from Luke?" Lydia asked.

"Yah. Many!"

"Do I get hugs from David?"

"Yah."

"Do I get hugs from Mark?"

Dani grinned at Lydia's tactic as Nettie's answering *yah* filtered its way through the branches.

"See?" Lydia said. "School does not stop hugs. It just teaches you things you must know *between* hugs."

"I know how to feed the baby cow with the bottle! I know how to put eggs in the basket without breaking them! I know how to pet all kinds of animals!"

"Yah. You do. But there are many more things you must learn. Like the boys. Like I did. And like Dat did, too."

"Dat went to school?" Nettie asked in the wake of a tiny gasp. "But Dat is big and I am little."

Lydia's laugh echoed in the crisp afternoon air. "Dat and I were both little once, too. Just like you." Then, "Don't you like when the boys read to you? Won't it be fun when you can read to . . ."

Dani cocked her ear in an attempt to hear the rest of Lydia's sentence, but there was only silence. Curious, she leaned forward only to duck back again as Nettie jumped up, the child's dress swooshing into place just above her tiny ankles.

"No! No! Don't go away, smile! I will be right back!" A few running steps led to silence, then to more running steps, and, finally, to a flash of yellow just before green fabric met blue fabric a second time. "See, Mamm? I picked you a flower—a yellow one! See? It is pretty! It should make you a smile!"

"I *am* smiling, silly girl," Lydia said, her voice thick with . . . *emotion*?

"No, a *big* smile! Like before! When you teached me to count, and spoke of Dat being little!"

Again, Dani leaned forward, her heart thudding softly in her ears.

Smile like she wants, Lydia . . . please.

"Like this?" Lydia finally asked.

"Yah! That is a good smile, Mamm! A very good smile!"

"I'm glad," Lydia said, her smile audible once again. "I love you, silly girl."

This time, the flash of skin Dani could just make out beyond the trunk of the tree belonged to Nettie as she wrapped her tiny arms around Lydia's neck with youthful, unadulterated joy. "I love you, too, Mamm."

Clamping a hand over her mouth, Dani dropped her head onto her knees and gave in to the answering sob she was powerless to stop.

She gave the piece of fried chicken one last push across the plate and then abandoned her fork once and for all, its answering clatter against the wooden tabletop muffled by the blows from the one-man boxing match inside her head. Round and round her thoughts went, her repeated attempts to feel good about herself as a parent undermined, again and again, by reality's one-two punch.

The memory of Ava saying, *I love you, Mommy,* became a race to actually remember a time when they'd sat outside on the back patio and just talked . . .

Answer: never.

The memory of Ava wrapping her arms around Dani's neck the way Nettie had done with Lydia led her on an internal search for times when she hadn't hurried through such a moment in favor of whatever was next on the schedule.

Answer: there were none.

The memory of Lydia's excitement as the boys arrived home from school on their scooter bikes yanked Dani's thoughts back to the afternoon schedule she was so often consulting when Maggie and Spencer first climbed into the car at the end of the day. She'd always looked up and smiled at them, hadn't she?

Answer: after I double- and triple-checked where we were supposed to go next . . .

The memory of watching Lydia and Nettie, hand in hand,

trailing behind the boys to the barn for the baby cow's after-school feeding had sent her own thoughts skittering about for those times when all three kids had enjoyed something so simple together.

Answer: last summer's vacation, maybe?

The memory of Elijah and Lydia standing near the barn, smiling and laughing together as they watched their children chase after a trio of chickens, left her trying to remember similar moments when she and Jeff had stood, side by side, simply enjoying their children's joy.

Answer: Christmas morning? Maybe the same beach vacation?

Each memory, each introspection, left her feeling more and more battered. Every night, when she was still Jeff's wife and the kids' mom, she'd gone to bed feeling satisfied, maybe even a little smug over the fact that every item on her day's to-do list had been crossed off. Even the things that hadn't been there in the morning yet had been added throughout the day.

Since the moment Maggie had been old enough to go to school, Dani had been the go-to parent for every teacher her daughter had. Books needed covering? No problem, Dani had lots of brown grocery bags at the ready . . . Parents needed to be called and cajoled onto various committees? No problem, Dani would call . . . A chaperone was needed for an upcoming field trip? No problem. Dani could go . . .

The same held true for every one of Maggie's and Spencer's activities. If there was a need, Dani filled it, plain and simple. And Ava? She was such an easygoing three-year-old. She went along for everything and never made a fuss. But during the day, when Maggie and Spencer were at school? That was the time for Ava's playgroup . . . Story time at the library . . . A stop at the grocery store . . . Running over to Jeff's office to plan a client meeting or drop off a baked treat for the staff . . . And for double- and triple-checking her to-do list.

"My good old to-do list," she murmured.

Pressing her fingers to her temples, she tried to will away the ache in her head that had grown progressively worse throughout the day. But like the pain in her lower back, it refused to comply. Some of it, she knew, was from all the crying. Another, equally large culprit was surely her inability to eat much of anything. But crying was her new norm, and the very thought of eating left her feeling sick to her stomach in much the same way she'd felt when—

She jerked upright on the kitchen bench.

Was it possible?

Could she actually be . . .

Noooo.

Jeff and the kids. They'd been gone seven weeks. If she was pregnant, she would know. She'd *always* known.

With Maggie, it had been the sudden aversion to eating. She'd think something looked good or smelled appetizing, only to change her mind at the last minute.

With Spencer, her appetite had lessened, as well, but it was the pervasive ache in her lower back that had alerted her to his presence.

With Ava, it had been all of the above, plus a kind of fitful sleep that left her feeling as if she'd run a full marathon before her feet had even hit the ground in the morning.

And while she was most definitely dealing with all of those same issues now, every single one of them—the loss in appetite, the body aches, the restless sleep—went hand in hand with grief and loss.

So, too, did her missed—

Dani's gasp filled the kitchen as her thoughts rewound to the days leading up to the accident. To standing with the kids at the airport, waiting for her mom to arrive . . . To calling the kids' favorite pizza place for their special night-in with Grandma . . . To the private dining room Jeff had reserved for the two of them so they could celebrate their anniversary alone . . . To the gleeful realization that her mom and the kids were all fast asleep when they got home later that night . . . To the candles Jeff had lit around their bedroom and the way his eyes had sparkled when he reached for her . . .

Swallowing hard, she struggled up onto shaky legs, crossed to the bedroom for her purse and car keys, and headed out into the dusk.

Chapter 11

In retrospect, it was really just a soft, almost apologetic sound, but against the deafening roar of silence that had been hers since about eight o'clock the previous evening, it startled her up and off the bench. Hurrying over to the door, she peeled back the curtain panel to find a nearly shoulder-high straw hat tipped back to reveal a pair of familiar eyes and an equally familiar smile.

Before she could truly process the ten-year-old's presence or her feelings about it, Luke lifted his mother's handwoven basket into view. "It is from Mamm," he said just loud enough for her to hear through the glass pane.

She drew in a breath, held it to a silent count of five, and then opened the door to the boy, hoping and praying her smile didn't look as forced as it felt. "Good morning, Luke. This is . . ." She stopped, took another breath, and tried for a softer tone. "This is a surprise. I didn't expect you to be at my door."

"I saw the basket sitting on the counter and I knew Mamm would want me to bring it to you." He peeled back the freshly washed cloth covering and pointed at the pair of brown eggs, piece of ham, and slice of bread inside. "David said I should put in more ham, but I heard Mamm tell Dat you do not eat very much."

She shrugged a nod.

"I do not know how to make Mamm's cinnamon butter, so I could not put any of that inside," Luke said, his smile drooping in tandem with his shoulders. "But I told Dat that Mamm's bread is good even without butter."

She glanced from Luke to the main house and back again. "You're right . . . it is."

"Dat ate only one piece this morning."

Unsure of what to say, she echoed his sentiment back to him.

"Yah. Dat *always* eats two pieces when he has Mamm's butter."

"I still have some. In the refrigerator. From yesterday," she hastily added.

And the day before that, and the day before that . . .

Luke's blue eyes widened ever so slightly.

"Perhaps, since I still have so much, you could take some back for your dat?" she suggested, sweeping her hand toward the refrigerator the boy couldn't see from his spot on the front porch.

Glancing over his shoulder toward the adjoining house, he tightened his grip on the basket handle. "If Mamm gave it to you, I should not take it away."

"You wouldn't be taking it, sweetie. I'd be giving it to you. Because I have more than I need."

His smile returned, albeit briefly. "If it is no trouble."

"It's no trouble at all." She stepped back and waved him inside. "I'll get that for you now."

The boy's bare feet made soft smacking sounds against the wood-planked floor as he followed her into the kitchen and stopped beside his late grandparents' kitchen table. With careful hands, he set the basket of breakfast items down as she yanked open the refrigerator and began shifting its contents around.

"I am good at adding things at school. Subtracting, too. Sometimes I must use my fingers and toes, but I usually get it right."

"That's . . . good." She reached past the bulk of last night's dinner and yesterday's breakfast for the bowl she'd been scraping butter into every day for nearly two weeks. "Math is an important skill."

"When I am fourteen, I will get to spend all day working in the field and looking after Dat's many animals." Luke drew in a breath. "Could I try this?"

"Try what?" She pulled out the bowl, closed the refrigerator, and froze—mid-turn—as her gaze followed Luke's to the center of the table and the cream-colored plastic stick that she'd been staring at all morning.

"I have not seen such an adding machine before," he said. "Dat's is square and gray and has all the numbers from zero to nine. *This*"—he picked up the pregnancy test, turned it over in his hands, and then held it up for her to see, his brow furrowed—"has only a plus sign."

Plunking the bowl onto the table, she grabbed the test from his hand and shoved it into her back pocket. "It is not an adding machine."

His eyes widened again. "What is it?"

"It's . . ." She cast about for something to say that would both answer his question and distract him onto something else. Something safer. "It is more of a yes or no machine."

He seemed to drink in her words. "A yes or no machine?"

"Yes. It . . . it tells you if something is to be or not."

Again his brow furrowed. "God will show you that."

God?

Nibbling back a response she knew wasn't appropriate to give, she pulled in a deep breath and released it, slowly. "So . . . The butter . . . That should be enough for your mom and dat and everyone else at dinner tonight, yes?"

His blue eyes dropped to the bowl. "Yah. If Mamm eats."

"Why wouldn't she eat?" Dani asked. "Is she not feeling well?"

He tilted his head as he seemed to consider her question. "I do not know, for sure. But Mamm is not always hungry when she comes back from a visit with Miss Lottie."

"Who is Miss Lottie?"

"She lives down the road." Luke pointed toward the window. "Mamm says she is a good listener and a good friend, and she makes very good cookies."

"Ahhh . . . cookies . . ." She felt the corners of her mouth twitch with a smile she quickly squelched. "Perhaps *that* is why your mother is not hungry after visiting with her friend."

Luke's cheeks flushed pink. "Mamm does not eat the cookies. She sits only in the rocking chair next to Miss Lottie's. The cookies are for me and David and Mark and Nettie. But when we are in school, it is just Nettie who will get cookies and blow bubbles with Digger. That is Miss Lottie's dog. He is very old, but Miss Lottie says chasing bubbles makes him think he is still a puppy."

"Luke?" They turned, as one, toward the partially open door and the slightly younger version of Luke peeking around its edge with a mixture of curiosity and . . . *hesitation*? "Dat says we are to go now or we will be late to school."

"But I did not feed Molly's baby," Luke protested. "It is morning and he is hungry."

The little boy slanted a shy glance in Dani's direction before shifting his slight frame across his trouser-clad legs. "Dat says we must go," the boy repeated. "Mark is not very fast on his bike."

"But Mamm is at Miss Lottie's, and Dat is to help Daniel Schrock with his buggy today."

"Yah. He has gone."

Worry sagged Luke back a step. "Who will feed the calf if I do not? It is morning. He is hungry. It will be too long until we are home."

Without really thinking about what she was saying, let alone doing, Dani rested her hand on Luke's shoulder and squeezed. "I will feed him, Luke. Don't worry."

Luke looked from Dani to his brother and back again, the worry in his eyes and stance only deepening. "But Mamm said we are not to ask things of you."

"Yah," the younger boy added. "That is what Mamm said."

"You didn't ask," she said, retrieving the bowl from the table and handing it to Luke. "I offered. Now, the two of you . . . Go put the butter in your refrigerator, get your lunch and your shoes and your little brother, and then head out so you won't be late for class."

Halfway to the door, Luke turned back, the hesitancy she'd first spied on David's face now alive and well on Luke's, too. "What if it upsets Mamm to see you feeding the calf?" Luke asked. "I do not want her to have more sadness."

"It won't upset her. I'll see to it that it doesn't. I promise."

She waited until the trio of hatted heads disappeared from her sight and then slipped into the barn through the wide-open door. Ahead, and to the right, the morning sun cast shafts of light into an empty stall. The missing horse, she suspected, was the one used to pull the buggy either Elijah or Lydia had taken. To the left of the empty stall was a series of full ones, each one boasting one of the larger, more powerful mules used in the fields.

Slowly, Dani inched her way into the largely unfamiliar surroundings, the occasional smack of a hoof against the hard-packed earth and the snorted exhalation from one or more of the barn's tenants reverberating off the walls of the otherwise quiet structure. She peeked into a few of the stalls she passed, but it was more out of curiosity than anything else. The not-so-occasional moo of a clearly unhappy calf was all the directional guidance she needed.

"Shhhh, little one, I'm here." She sidled up to the half wall that separated the baby cow from the rest of the animals and peeked over the edge at the large brown eyes that instantly locked on to hers. "You thought you'd been forgotten, didn't you?"

His answering moo tugged a fleeting smile to her lips.

"Luke had to go off to school, so you get me this morning. Me, and"—she lifted the milk bottle into his sight line—"*this*."

Instantly, the calf stretched his head toward the bottle, latching on to the nipple so hard and so fast, she nearly lost her grip. "Whoa, whoa, whoa, slow down there. If you spill this, you're going to *really* be hungry."

Shifting her weight forward against the wall, she held the bottle steady against the strong tug of the calf's every suck, his dark eyes still locked on hers. "You really were starving, weren't you, you poor thing—"

"I see he's got you wrapped around his little hoof, too, eh?"

Startled, she stepped back so fast she pulled the bottle from the calf's mouth. The calf, in turn, lurched forward, but her gaze, her attention, was now on the lone figure standing just inside the open doorway. The sunlight wafting in from outside made it difficult to make out specifics of the person's face, but she could see enough to know it was a man—a tall one, with broad shoulders, a cowboy hat, and—

Moooooooo . . .

"I didn't mean to interrupt breakfast," the man said, stepping out of the shadowed entryway to reveal a royal-blue and black plaid shirt . . . faded blue jeans . . . the scuffed toes of brown leather boots . . . defined cheekbones . . . and the same friendly amber-flecked eyes she'd run from her first full day on the farm. "I just stopped in to make sure he'd eaten and, well, here you are, doing my nephew's job."

Diving her gaze back to the bottle and then the calf, she threw up a quick shrug and returned to the task at hand, her gaze, if not her words, focused on the clearly grateful animal. "Luke ran out of time before school. So I offered to feed this little guy."

"That's not like Luke to fall behind on his chores." Caleb rested his elbows on the top of the wall, nodded at the calf, and then turned his chin toward Dani. "Was there some sort of problem?"

With two last tugs, the calf drained the milk from the bottle, leaving her with nothing to focus on besides the man standing less than two feet away, waiting for her answer. Setting the empty bottle on the wall beside her own elbow, Dani used a second, longer shrug to gather her thoughts. "He saw the basket Lydia usually uses for my breakfast sitting on the table. So he filled it and brought it over to me. I guess we got to"—she closed her eyes against the memory of the pregnancy stick in his little hands—"*talking* and the time he would have had to feed this guy slipped away. As it was, I have to wonder if Luke was able to pack a proper lunch for himself and his brothers before they were scootering down the driveway and onto the road."

"Where was Lydia?"

Something about the sudden thickness to his voice had her abandoning her view of the now-satisfied calf in favor of the sudden tension in Caleb's clean-shaven jawline. "Oh . . . no. It's not like she's sick or anything. She just went off on a visit. With Nettie."

"Before the boys left for school?"

"Yes. Apparently."

Straightening up, he strode over to a metal rake propped against a nearby upright and, after a moment's hesitation, grabbed it and carried it over to the buggy horse's empty stall. Two steps shy of his destination, he turned back to Dani.

"I'm sorry about what I said that first day here in the barn. I really am. And while I know it's not a good excuse, I didn't know. I thought it was just . . ." He inhaled his eyes up toward the ceiling and shook his head. "I didn't mean *just*. There's nothing *just* about any of that. I . . . I just didn't know your mom was in the car, too."

The on-again, off-again lump inside her throat was back, making it impossible to answer with anything more than a quick nod.

"I know we haven't seen each other in more than twenty-five years, and that back then we were just kids who played together a few times over the course of a week, but if you need anything—someone to scream at, someone to vent to, someone to hold you when you cry, someone to help you feel a little less alone with the pain—I'm here. And I'm a good listener . . . Then again, maybe I'm just kidding myself considering my own sister keeps going to . . ." Waving off the rest of his sentence, he reached into his front pocket, pulled out a small cream-colored card, and crossed back to her with it, his hand extended. "Anyway, I'm willing to listen. Any time. Day or night. Just call my cell."

She knew she should say something. An *okay*, an *I'll keep that in mind*, a basic *thank you*—something, anything, to acknowledge his apology, his kind offer, and the card she'd yet to take. But she couldn't. Not when the walls of the barn seemed to be closing in on her, stealing the oxygen from the air and the strength she needed to remain standing there any longer. Instead, she turned and ran from the barn.

Chapter 12

She didn't need the wall calendar she'd failed to turn to know another Saturday had dawned. The sounds emanating through the open kitchen window told her that all on their own. Instead of the occasional giggles or squeals or sweet conversations between Lydia and Nettie that marked the prelunchtime hour for Dani most days, the audible joy that both intrigued and pained her was magnified by the presence of Luke and his two brothers.

There were chores to be done still, of course—a chicken to corral, mules to help hitch, tools to fetch from the barn—but yet, amid all of that, the Schlabach family still managed to have fun, to thoroughly enjoy one another's company. Even the spring rain, beating a steady pattern on the front porch, seemed unable to dampen the lighthearted fun happening from the vicinity of the driveway, maybe the stretch of grass in front of the main house.

Pushing back from the table and the breakfast she'd been trying but failing to eat for nearly two hours, Dani stood and wandered over to the window and the shade she'd yet to open on another day. She slid two fingers between the side of the dark green fabric and the window's edge and gaped a hole just big enough to see out without being seen. Sure enough, as the sounds had indicated, she spied three straw hats and one heart-shaped kapp bobbing up and down as the children who sported them hopped back and forth across a water-filled rut in the center of the driveway.

One by one they took their turn. First Luke, then David, then the youngest boy she knew only by name, and, finally, Nettie, her inability to jump as far as her brothers landing her inside the puddle and showering water onto the bottom edges of her pale blue dress and the pants of all three boys. Instead of chorusing *watch out* or some other equally gritted reprimand, Luke and the other boys laughed and squealed. Again and again they did the same thing with the same outcome, and each time the resulting laughter was as heartfelt and genuine as ever.

"Jump bigger, Nettie," Luke advised each time the little girl stepped to the edge of the rut for her turn.

"Yah! Bigger! Bigger!" chimed the younger boys in near perfect unison.

Nettie's kapped head would nod . . .

Her little bare feet would run in place for a moment . . .

She'd emulate the crouch Luke demonstrated each and every time . . .

And then she'd jump straight into the puddle, her answering squeal just barely audible over the belly laughs of her brothers.

Movement over by the barn stole Dani's attention just long enough for her to realize Elijah was watching the whole encounter, a smile stretched across his bearded face. Seconds later, Lydia emerged from the barn, stood beside her husband for a few moments, and then, after a quick gesture toward the house, strode side by side with him toward the children.

Dani braced herself for the disappointed reactions she expected when the puddle jumping was brought to an end, but they never came. Nor did the puddle jumping stop. Instead, first Lydia, and then Elijah, joined in on the fun, their own clothes growing wetter and wetter with Nettie's repeated attempts to perfect her jump.

Elijah demonstrated . . .

Luke demonstrated . . .

David demonstrated . . .

Mark demonstrated . . .

And when it appeared as if the child was simply too little to clear the puddle-filled rut, Lydia took her hand, waited for Nettie to bend her knees just so, and then, on the count of three, they jumped—and cleared—the puddle together, the feat drawing claps and smiles from Nettie's father and brothers.

"I did it!" Nettie shouted, looking up at Lydia. "I did it, Mamm!"

"Yah! You did it!"

"Can I try again? By myself?"

Lydia and Elijah exchanged amused looks, with Elijah's answer coming via a single nod of his hatted head.

Nettie ran around to the side of the rut she clearly saw as the starting line. She bent her knees . . . She fisted her little hands . . . And she pushed off the wet ground as her brothers stepped forward in the hope of getting wet once again. But, lo and behold, the little girl who now believed she could do it thanks to her mother cleared the puddle with nary a slip or a splash.

"I did it again! I did it again!"

Elijah and the boys gathered around the little girl while Lydia stayed just outside the group, her hands clasped together in quiet joy.

"I liked getting splashed," Mark said.

"It is to rain for many hours," Lydia said, glancing up at the sky and then back at her four children. "But now it is time to go inside and have lunch before the afternoon work is to be done."

Luke looked up at his father. "Can I still help you and Uncle Caleb fix the fence?"

"Yah."

"Me, too?" David asked. "I want to help, too!"

"Yah. There is much work to be done."

"Can I feed the calf this time?" Mark looked from Elijah

to Lydia and back. "I will not let him pull the bottle from my hand again."

Elijah looked down at his youngest son. "You must hold it strong, Mark."

"Yah. I will."

"Then you may try again." Bending down, Elijah tapped Nettie on the nose. "And what will *you* help *Mamm* with, wee one?"

"We can't hang clothes in the rain . . ."

"No."

"We can't plant flowers in the rain . . ."

"Not really, no."

"I could . . . I know!" Nettie rocked back on her heels. "I could sweep!"

"That would be good."

"And . . ." She looked up at Lydia, clasped her little hands under her chin, and rose up on the tips of her muddy feet. "I could help punch the dough."

"Dough for what?"

"For Mamm's bread!"

"I like bread," Elijah said, his tone playfully serious.

"And I could shake the butter, like *this*!" Nettie said, her earnest demonstration kicking off another series of giggles from her brothers.

Elijah's eyebrow lifted in mock seriousness. "*Cinnamon* butter?"

"Yah!"

"That is a very good thing for you to do with Mamm." Elijah straightened to his full height and herded his children onto the porch. "Let us go inside and eat. All that jumping has made me hungry."

Shifting forward so her forehead rested against the window's edge, Dani watched Lydia and her family head inside, their cohesiveness stirring an ache-filled smile to her lips. Oh how she longed for a chance to jump across puddles in the rain with Jeff and Maggie and Spencer and Ava the way Lydia and her crew had just done . . . Yet standing there, looking out at the now-deserted puddle that had been the center of so much fun for the Amish family, she knew it was something she, her-self, would have walked right by, her thoughts, her focus, on getting lunch on the table or checking off another item on her list. And if Maggie, Spencer, and Ava had been unable to re-sist the pull, she'd have shooed them away from such a messy activity. After all, dirtying clothes meant having to get dressed and maybe even bathed again, something that didn't work when there was a schedule to uphold.

But Lydia didn't have to worry about that. There were no soccer or baseball games to rush off to. No scouts or music lessons to squeeze into her day. Just school, chores, and jumping puddles.

Dani's view of the puddle grew blurry as her thoughts re-wound through the weeks leading up to the accident. For Maggie, there had been Favorite Character Day at school, a flurry of birthday parties to attend for various classmates, and a recital. For Spencer, there were swim lessons, play-dates, and a smattering of party invites, too.

Had it been busy? Sure. When wasn't it? But there had been smiles and—

She shook herself back to the present and stared out at the puddle. Maggie and Spencer and Ava laughed. In fact, Ava was known around the neighborhood and the kids' school as Little Miss Smiley.

But when had Dani's kids laughed the way Lydia's just had? When did they just get to lose themselves in being kids without her urging them onward to the next thing, the next place, the next have-to?

They didn't . . .

"Because I didn't let them," she whispered against the screen. Then, through clenched teeth, she said it again, each successive word more anger filled than the one before. "I. Didn't. Let. Them."

It wasn't that Lydia didn't *have* to fill her kids' every moment. She chose not to. She chose, instead, to leave the gaps open for exploration, for conversation, for bonding, and, yes, for laughter.

Drawing her hand to her abdomen, Dani imagined the puddle-jumping scene as it had been. Only this time, instead of the Schlabach six, it was the Parker five—soon to be six.

Movement just beyond the puddle lifted her misty gaze to the now-familiar man lumbering on foot toward the main house. As seemed to be the norm, Caleb was dressed in a long-sleeved flannel shirt, blue jeans, and work boots. In his left hand was a decent-sized toolbox, and in his right was what appeared to be keys to his truck. The same cowboy hat he'd worn the previous day was perched forward on his head, the generous brim helping to keep the now-driving rain off his face.

As he came up on the puddle, he stopped, surveyed the myriad of muddy footprints covering the surrounding area, and, cracking a grin, continued on toward the front porch. Midway to the steps, he stopped and turned his sights in her direction. Slowly, deliberately, he cocked his head just enough to afford himself an uninhibited view of the grossdawdy house before narrowing his attention on the very window from which she was peeking back at him. Like a finger on the receiving end of an unexpected electrical charge, Dani jumped back so hard and so fast she was powerless to stop the edge of the shade from smacking back into place against the glass.

Her breath held, she prayed for him to keep walking, to go up the steps into Lydia's house, to bypass his obvious need to try to fix something that could never be fixed, never be talked through, never truly understood. She remained, frozen in place, listening for anything resembling footfalls outside her window, a knock on her front door, a—

Sure enough, the distinct sound of approaching footfalls on the other side of the window wafted around the closed shade, stopped, and then retreated into silence once again. Closing her eyes, she made a silent count to twenty and then, when the next sound she heard was the creak of Lydia's screen door opening and closing, she reclaimed her spot at the window, her gaze falling on the cream-colored business card tucked into a minuscule gap between the screen and the wall. Printed across the front, in an attractive black font:

Finely Crafted Birdhouses
Elijah Schlabach
Blue Ball, PA

Underneath the preprinted lines, in rain-soaked ink, were Caleb's name and phone number. Beneath that, but still hand-written, was a four-word sentence that looked as if it had been added in haste:

I'm a good listener.

Chapter 13

The next few days passed in a blur of should-haves and could-haves, each fresh new round of recriminations sparked by a moment spied between Lydia and one or more of her children. It didn't matter where Dani was—in the house, on the front porch, on the back patio, sitting under the tree, or getting ready for a dinnertime walk as she was at that moment—examples of Lydia's prowess as a mother were everywhere.

They were there in Luke's careful watch over his brothers and sister . . .

They were there in David's genuine affection and consideration for all God's creatures, from the animals on the farm he conversed with daily to the butterflies that flew around his mother's flowers . . .

They were there in Mark's ability to be content doing whatever his older brothers wanted or needed him to do . . .

They were there in Nettie's sweet laugh and curious questions as she helped Lydia hang clothes or sweep the porch . . .

They were there when the little girl cuddled in Lydia's lap while they ate cookies together on the front porch . . .

And they were there in the abundance of joy-filled sounds that seemed to pepper the air from sunup to sundown, every day.

Looking back, Maggie had been a lot like Luke, always looking out for Spencer and Ava. With Spencer, that concern had taken the form of making sure he had all of the right gear for whatever practice or game they were running off to. With Ava, it was making sure her food was cut if Dani's attention was needed elsewhere, or holding the three-year-old's hand as they navigated their way up the bleachers at the soccer field or baseball diamond.

And Spencer . . . How many times had he crouched down in a parking lot or a field to inspect a bug she'd invariably say didn't matter? Too many. Now she'd never know if his fascination with every creepy-crawly he found was because of his age or if, like David, he felt an internal pull toward God's various creatures.

Ava's smile had been ever present like Nettie's. People commented about it all the time. But how often had Dani really just sat back and soaked it up the way Lydia did? Not often enough, that's for sure.

Yet there she'd been, always thinking of herself as this superstar mom—someone who threw intricately themed birthday parties, showered her kids with the kinds of opportunities and experiences she'd missed as a latchkey kid, and could go from leading a troop of twenty girls to helping her husband woo a potential client over dinner and drinks at a five-star restaurant with barely a blink of her eye.

What a lie she'd been living.

What a lie she, herself, had been . . .

Stepping onto the front porch, Dani quietly made her way past the main house where Lydia and her family were sitting down together for the evening meal. She knew it was Lydia's hope that one day soon Dani would join them inside rather than eat alone from a basket an hour or so later. But she simply wasn't ready. Not yet. If ever.

On the one hand she knew it was probably time to return home. She knew from the once-daily, now more like once-weekly, post-accident texts from Emily that her houseplants were *doing fine*, her mail was *piling up*, and the Liberty Street barbecue she and Jeff had started shortly before Maggie was born was *scheduled for the first weekend in June with Libby and Dale Rothman at the helm.*

Knowing Emily, the chatty nature of the weekly messages was designed to be upbeat and friendly. It wasn't in the woman's nature to be anything else. But sometimes—no, *most* times—upbeat and friendly only served to deepen Dani's pain.

It wasn't that she wanted Emily to tell her the plants were dead, or that Dani was no longer on anyone's radars, or that something she and Jeff had put so much time into each year really never mattered to anyone, anyway. Because she didn't want that, either. But in Emily's attempt to be lighthearted came the painful realization that life was moving on without Dani and without the five people who meant most to her in the entire world.

Blinking hard against a new spate of tears, Dani slipped past her car and headed toward the road, the day's fading sun taking with it the daytime sounds of Amish country—the clip-clop of a passing buggy, the snap of a clothesline, the call of a father to his son from the back of a mule-pulled tractor, the staccato tap of a hammer against wood, and even the clang of a bucket as it filled an animal's trough. Soon, the stark quiet of the supper hour would segue into a quick flurry of last-minute chores inside the barn before the busyness of the day gave way to quiet conversations on porches and in sitting rooms up and down the street.

Two sheep, one large and one medium sized, eyed her curiously as she strode by, the peace and tranquility of her surroundings negated by the voice inside her head that never stopped, never took a breath.

Go home . . .

Stay here . . .

Find a local obstetrician . . .

Make an appointment with Dr. May back home . . .

Each thought, each worry, rushed in like a crashing wave, receded, and then, before she could pick up her head long enough to catch her breath, knocked her down again.

"I don't know what I'm supposed to do," she said, her teeth gritted. "I'm drowning."

"Then get out of the water, Danielle."

She stopped dead.

"You need a break."

"Mom?" she whispered, looking left and right, ahead and behind.

"You can brave the waves better when you're rested, Danielle. Trust me."

Swallowing against the growing knot in the base of her throat, she willed herself to focus, to see the sheep to her left, the lowering sun to her right, her car and the main house at her back, the road in front. Mom was gone. The voice, the words, were a memory just as they'd been back in New York when she hadn't eaten so much as a nibble of food in those first few days following the accident.

She'd *needed* to eat then. And while she knew she still wasn't eating enough now, especially with a baby on the way, at least she was trying. A nibble here, a nibble there . . .

The timing of *that* memory, of Mom's voice, made sense.

But this one?

She was landlocked in Amish country with the closest beach a good hour and a half away . . .

Still, she was tired. Not sleepy tired, necessarily, but definitely brain tired. There were simply too many things to remember, to grieve, to work through, to beat herself up over, to—

"Trust me."

Again, she swung her gaze onto the sheep only to find the larger of the two staring back at her. "You're not hearing that, right?" The sheep blinked at her. "Yeah, I didn't think so."

Abandoning her view of her wooly but silent audience, Dani stepped out onto the road, the warmth of the western sun on her face making the decision as to which direction to go an easy one. She took a moment to pull in a deep breath and to let it go, her senses slowly but surely beginning to take over.

Step by step she made her way past a farm with a wind-mill . . . a farm with a barn that looked as if it had been recently built . . . a narrow, winding creek that appeared on her left, disappeared from view beneath her, and then meandered out to her right . . . Up ahead, a charcoal-gray buggy emerged from a dirt lane and turned in the opposite direction, the horse's purposeful cadence leaving her to wonder, briefly, where the occupants were going.

At the end of the road where it teed with another, she went right, the still-lowering sun diffusing the sky in varying shades of yellow, orange, and red. A brown and white dog with a red collar and big pink tongue fell in step beside her as she rounded a bend in the road and then disappeared, enthusiastically, at the sound of a woman's voice in the distance.

She slowed outside a white single-story building set back about ten yards from the road. Even from where she stood, Dani could just make out a series of construction paper flowers arranged across the glass portion of the front door. Above that, in large block letters and also cut from construction paper, was a single word: **Welcome**. To the right of the building, she spied a simple swing set with two swings suspended by chains from a metal pole. Silent now, she could almost hear the sounds of Amish children at recess, some swinging, others playing tag, and still others running around the bases of their non-regulation-sized baseball diamond.

For a few, fleeting moments, she considered walking up to the front window and peering inside, curious as to whether the happy, whimsical nature of the front door carried into the interior, but she didn't. Instead, she continued down the road, the gentle spring breeze and welcomed exercise working wonders on the dull throb in her head and the persistent stiffness in her joints.

Just beyond a second, slightly longer bend in the road, a fenced enclosure surrounded by farm fields drew her gaze toward a series of headstones protruding from the grass in neat rows. Unlike its more elaborate and showy English counterparts, the clearly Amish cemetery held no flowerpots, no American flags, no long dead miniature Christmas trees. The budding branches of a single tree planted just outside the enclosure stretched across the gravesites and provided a protective canopy of sorts. The grass itself looked sparse but tended, and the graves themselves ranged from weathered to new. A small grassless mound near the back fence, as well as a freshly shoveled pile of dirt on the eastern side of the cemetery, pointed to two recent additions.

Part of her wanted to turn and run from the pain she felt bubbling back to life inside her heart. But another part of her wanted to answer the inexplicable pull to slip inside the gate and feel whatever she wanted to feel in a place where others had felt some of the same things.

Step by step, hand twist by hand twist, the longing for connection won and quietly deposited her just inside the open gate, steps away from someone's beloved. She inched forward toward the back row, her mind's eye quietly cataloging the information noted on the first gravestone she found.

Eli Esch
September 7, 1951
October 2012

"Sixty-one." A bird, sitting atop a nearby branch, flew off, clearly startled by her voice. "Were you a father? A husband? A grandfather? Were your parents still alive when you were buried?"

She paused as if waiting for someone to provide those answers—for someone to step forward and give voice to the kind of man Eli Esch had been in life. But there was nothing. Just a curved stone marking what had once been someone's loved one.

Wiping her hands against the sides of her jeans, Dani moved on to the next name, the next lost soul.

Mary Weaver
January 18, 1987
November 4, 2002

"Nineteen eighty-seven to two thousand and two..."
Dani whispered as her mental calculator spewed out the un-
thinkable answer. "Fifteen? How—"

Her gaze leapt ahead to the next several stones, her shoulders sagging in momentary relief when the names and date of
death they reflected didn't match. She glanced back at the
name and the young girl's age and then scanned the farms
bordering the property. Somewhere, in one of those homes,
or perhaps as far as a few roads over, a mother ached for her
daughter, the hopes and dreams she'd had for her offspring
gone. Did she wake up crying each morning? Did she sit on
the front porch, staring out at nothing while her insides
turned to stone? Did she, too, wish she'd died with her child,
or, at the very least, instead of her child?

Summoning up the courage to keep walking, Dani took in
the name etched into each gravestone she passed, the bulk of
the deceased having lived a full life. A few, like Mary Weaver,
never made it through childhood, their age and the unfair-
ness that was their death calling to Dani, again and again.
Twice, she came across children—one boy, one girl—who
never made it to ten. The girl, Fannie King, slipping away at
six, and the boy, Daniel Miller, a newly turned eight-year-old.

She forced herself to keep moving, to keep reading, to keep
acknowledging the lives lost. Row by row, she made her way
from the front to the back as the sun slipped still farther toward the horizon.

Abram Bontrager, thirty-four ...

Miriam Dienner, eighty-two ...

Naomi Stoltzfus, seventy-six ...

Jonah Troyer, ninety-one ...

Rose Schlabach—

Pressing her hand hard against her ensuing gasp, she shifted her eyes to the small grassless mound jutting up from the ground and then back to the flat white rectangular marker.

October 15, 2019
November 30, 2019

Slowly, Dani lowered herself to her knees as her focus returned to the six-week-old's name.

No . . .

It wasn't possible.

If it were, she would have known.

After all, December may have been busy with the usual holiday trappings and parties that came with having a family, but there was no way Dani would have missed something so tragically awful in Lydia's annual—

The punch of truth pushed her back onto her haunches with a strangled sob.

There had been no letter from Lydia this past Christmas. No update on the children, or Elijah, or even Lydia, herself.

No, for the first time in twenty-seven years she hadn't heard from the woman who'd gone on to open her heart and her home to Dani, and Dani hadn't even noticed . . .

Sinking down beside the tiny mound, she buried her head in her hands and began to cry. "Oh, Lydia . . . I'm so sorry, my sweet friend. I-I didn't know . . ."

Chapter 14

Even without a clear vantage point of the driveway's intersection with the road, Dani knew the buggy carrying Lydia and her family had made the turn toward whatever farm was hosting church that week. The man standing beside the barn with his hand now back in his front pocket told her that.

On any other day, the epic battle of goodbye waves between the uncle and his niece might have coaxed something resembling a smile to her lips, but at that moment, all she felt was relief that it was finally over.

Slipping into the jacket she'd draped over the kitchen bench, Dani stepped onto the front porch, drew in a fortifying breath, and then made her way toward the barn and the insistent moos reaching through the open door.

"Every day you act as if you're being starved, don't you, Little Guy?" The ping of metal, followed by a muted thud, told her Caleb had liberated a bucket from its hook and turned it upside down on the ground within arm's reach of the rapidly growing calf. A quick peek before she stepped inside showed she was right. "Yet I know you already had your first bottle of the day little more than three hours ago."

As he held the bottle steady while the calf latched on, Caleb's low, quick laugh echoed across the barn. "That's right, Little Guy, I know what you're up to. You may be snowing other people with your act, but you're not snowing me . . . I'm on to you and your ways. *Big-time.*"

"He really is a bit of a drama queen, isn't he?"

Caleb's head whipped around until she, rather than the calf, was the recipient of his slow, even smile. "Greeaat. Now you've gone and taught him just how far-reaching his cries can go." He glanced back at the calf, mid–eye roll. "No place—not even the grossdawdy house—is immune from your theatrics, eh?"

When the only answer came via a hard tug on the bottle, Caleb muttered something about gratitude and humility and then brought his complete focus back on Dani, his brow furrowing as he did. "You don't look like you got much sleep last night."

"I need to ask you something," she said, crossing to the pen and the view it afforded of both the calf and Lydia's brother. "Something important."

His gaze traveled back to the calf for as long as it took to gauge the bottle's rapidly decreasing contents. "Absolutely. I'm all ears."

She cut to the chase. "Did Lydia lose a child in the fall—a little girl named Rose?"

The second the words were out and she saw the way Caleb pulled back on the bucket, she rushed to smooth away the crassness of her delivery. "I'm sorry. I shouldn't have blurted that out the way I just did. It's just that . . ." Tilting her head back, she searched for the right words, the right tone. "I went for a walk yesterday. While everyone else was eating dinner. I-I needed to clear my head. Needed to distract myself with something other than my life for a little while."

"Okay . . ."

"I walked that way"—she pointed in the direction she'd gone—"and I saw a few farms, a creek, and the one-room schoolhouse I imagine the boys attend."

A strong tug from the calf, followed by a satiated moo,

prompted Caleb to withdraw the now-empty bottle and rest it atop his knee. "Construction paper flowers in the window?"

She nodded.

"Then, yeah, you found their school." He turned the bottle round and round inside his calloused hand and then rose onto his feet. "Same place Lydia and I went to when we were kids, too."

She heard his answer, even processed it on some level, but the one-room schoolhouse was already in her mind's rearview mirror. "I still had enough daylight to keep walking after that, so I went a little further."

"You went to the cemetery." It was a statement, not a question.

Again, she made herself nod, her throat tightening.

"And you saw Rose's grave."

Squeezing her eyes closed against the image of the tiny dirt mound, she nodded a third time.

"I see."

"Tell me," she whispered.

Caleb tipped the brim of his cowboy hat lower on his forehead and turned his face from Dani's direct view. "I can still hear the slam of the front door when Lydia came running out with the baby in her arms that day. I was standing right there"—he nudged his chin toward the area to the left of the main door—"helping Elijah fix a wheel on the buggy. I heard the door, I heard the sound of feet running across the front porch and down the steps, and when I looked outside, and saw the way she was looking down at Rose, I knew it wasn't good."

"What happened?"

"It was SIDS."

"Sudden Infant Death Syndrome," she said, processing.

He spread his arms wide, the bewilderment he still felt even now, months later, plain to see. "She wasn't wrapped too tight, she wasn't in a room that was too cold, and she'd been on her back, not her stomach. But none of that stuff matters with SIDS. It just happens. No rhyme or reason."

Pushing back from the pen, Dani wandered over to the stall where Elijah's buggy horse had started her day. Inside, waiting for the animal's eventual return from a day of worship and visiting, was a bale of hay, a bucket of water, and the remnants of an oat breakfast. Dani tried to focus on her surroundings, to let them quiet her growing restlessness, but she couldn't.

"It's only been what?" she asked, moving on to the mules and the pigs before circling back to Caleb. "Six months?"

"Five as of last week."

Five months . . .

"I thought maybe it was a different Schlabach at first. Maybe a niece or a cousin of Elijah's . . ."

Returning to the calf's pen, Caleb scooped up the bucket on which he'd been sitting, and carried it back to its hook. "You should have seen Nettie and the boys with her. They were always trying to outdo each other in the hopes they'd be the first one to make her laugh. And they were close. Her little smiles were getting bigger and coming faster every day. It wasn't gonna be long before she was doing that funny little *heh* sound babies make when they laugh at that age."

She remembered it well.

"I . . ." She cast about for the right words, the right something, but came up empty. "I don't know what to say."

Even after the bucket was safely back in place, Caleb still kept his hand on the hook as if he needed it to remain standing. She realized he did when he leaned his head against the wall and released a breath so labored and so troubled it stole her own. "I tried to bring her back. To do CPR until the crew got here, but she was gone. At six weeks old."

"Where were the other kids?" she asked when she could think of nothing else to say.

"The boys were still at school, and Nettie was inside with my sister."

"So Nettie was there? When Lydia found—" She stopped, unable to finish the sentence.

"Yes."

It was too much to take in, too much to absorb.

"I took them home to my house that night. The four of them. I wanted Lydia and Elijah to have some time alone before the buggies started arriving, in droves, for the viewing and then the funeral." He pushed back from the wall and wandered his way back to the calf's pen. "The Amish believe death is God's will. Always. But even the most devout have to struggle when it's someone so young. I know I did. Still do, as a matter of fact."

She thought about Maggie and Spencer and Ava and how she could barely move, let alone function, without them. She thought about Jeff and how she felt his loss most at night, when his arms should be around her, holding her close. She thought about her mom and the sensation of being rudderless in her absence. She thought about how the passage of time only made everything harder.

"I don't understand," she said, shaking her thoughts back into the moment. "How . . . How can Lydia be so cheerful all the time? How can she go on the way she does—playing with the children, making sure I have food, keeping up with all the chores around the farm? How does she go on at all?"

He reached across the top of the pen, rubbed the calf between the ears, and then turned back to Dani, his expression pensive. "She has to," he said, his voice not unkind. "The Lord called Rose to be with Him, not Lydia."

"But that was *her baby*," Dani rasped, wrapping her arms around herself. "She carried that child inside her for nine months for . . . what? So He could snatch her back six weeks later?"

"It is not the Amish way to question God's will."

The weight of his words pressed down on her chest. "God's will?" she echoed. "God's *will*? Have you *seen* the kind of mother Lydia is? The life she's giving those children? They smile all the time! She lets them be kids who play with kittens, and feed baby bottles to cows, and"—her voice faltered and broke—"get soaking wet jumping in puddles in the rain. And she does it *with* them."

Caleb nodded, his gaze never leaving her face.

"*Lydia* isn't the type to dream about time away from her kids," she continued. "No, that was—" Clamping her lips together, she waited for her breath to slow, her budding anger to abate.

"Finish your sentence, Danielle."

She held up her hand, palm out. "I just don't know how she can go on the way she does. How she can move through her days so unaffected."

Caleb jerked back as if her words were a slap. "I didn't say she was unaffected, Danielle. Quite the contrary, in fact. I said she goes on because the Lord called Rose home, not Lydia. That doesn't mean she doesn't hurt, doesn't mourn, doesn't struggle with all the whys and hows you'd expect in the wake of something so awful."

"But she smiles, and she *laughs*," Dani said by way of explanation. "I can't imagine ever being there again. I'm in too much pain. And"—she lifted her gaze to his—"I'm *angry*."

"At whom?"

"Myself, mostly. For not going with them, for not nixing the outing completely, for not insisting they come home sooner, for losing track of time, for—" She stopped, closed her eyes, and then opened them to find Caleb watching her, waiting.

"Who else?"

"Who else what?"

"You said you're mad at yourself, *mostly*. That means there's someone else, too."

"I'm mad at God."

"For taking them?" he asked.

"For not taking me, instead." Dani started toward the

door but thought better of it and returned to her spot beside the calf's pen. "The way Lydia still smiles and laughs? That won't ever happen for me again."

"Lydia smiles and laughs on occasion, sure. But she has hard days, Danielle. Really hard. There are days when she has difficulty getting up in the morning, and other days when she barely has enough energy to get through a conversation or a routine chore. There are days when the smile that has always come so easily for her is just not there. And sometimes there are days when I can tell, just by looking at her, that she's somewhere else completely. Somewhere dark and sad and lonely, somewhere I just can't reach no matter how hard I try."

Something about his words rewound her back to the last time they'd been in the barn together. So much of what he'd said at the time seemed inconsequential. Yet now, in light of the news about Lydia's profound loss, it all took on new meaning.

"On days when she goes all blank like that," Caleb continued, "I try to draw her out, to get her talking in the hope that'll help her somehow, but I can't seem to get it right. I prod when she doesn't want to talk, and I miss the boat when it seems like she does." He looked past her to something she knew wasn't in the barn. "But even with all that, Miss Lottie was the one thing I've done right. For Lydia and for me."

The name rang a faint bell of recognition. "Who is this Miss Lottie person, again?"

"An English friend to many."

"Including you?"

"Including me." He removed his hat and slowly turned it between his hands. "In terms of Lydia and losing little Rose, Miss Lottie helped me to see that there are other ways I can help my sister that go beyond trying to get her to talk. I can play with the kids so Lydia can take a moment for herself here and there, I can stop by to help with some of the more odds-and-ends kind of chores she might otherwise have to do, and I can even pop over for dinner from time to time so the kids can pelt *me* with all their stories from the day."

Stilling the hat, he released a weighted sigh. "That said, though, I still wish she would *talk* to me about what she's thinking and what she's feeling. Keeping all that sadness bottled up inside isn't making it better."

"Nothing *can* make it better, Caleb." She traveled her gaze to the open barn door and the Sunday morning sky beyond. "Nothing short of a total do-over of that day, that is."

Chapter 15

Double-checking the address on the car's display screen with the address on the front of the single-story office building, Dani pulled into a parking spot not far from the front door and cut the engine. If it weren't for the fact that her fingers smelled like gasoline from her brief stop at the station a mile or so back, she might actually consider the possibility she was having a nightmare.

But unlike those nightly occurrences, this one didn't have her walking along the side of a highway searching for her family, or reaching toward their outstretched arms only to wake up alone, drenched in sweat and feverishly wiping a trail of tears from her cheeks.

No, this one had her sitting outside a nondescript brown brick building, with an equally nondescript matching sign, and marveling at a reality that was both cruel in its timing and ironic in its delivery.

Movement to her left had her glancing over in time to see a woman, about her own age, opening the door of a white SUV and carefully placing an infant seat onto its base atop the back seat. Once the carrier was secure enough to the woman's liking, she took a moment to whisper a kiss across the snippet of baby skin Dani could see from her vantage point and then pushed the door closed. Feeling her body begin to tremble, Dani deliberately turned away, her watery gaze falling on the front door just as another woman was escorted through it by a man wearing a smile as big as the woman's protruding belly.

Dani skirted her eyes to the ignition key and gave some thought to the notion of restarting the engine and making haste back to the Amish countryside, but she couldn't. Because if she didn't make herself do this now, Lydia would soon enough.

Lydia . . .

How many times had she stood at the window and quietly observed her friend with a fresh pair of eyes since the conversation with Caleb in the barn? A dozen, maybe more . . . And now that she knew about Rose, she could see something lurking beneath the surface whenever Lydia was alone. The slump of her shoulders . . . The slow, almost directionless steps . . . The rush to don a smile when Nettie or one of the boys came galloping around a corner or across the front porch . . .

Lydia, who saw with her eyes.

Lydia, who knew that simple didn't have to mean boring.

Lydia, who encouraged her loved ones.

Lydia, who truly drank in her children, her husband.

Lydia, who'd masked her own soul-crushing grief to be a safe harbor for Dani.

"God's will," Dani mumbled, tossing the keys into her purse. "If taking a baby from someone like Lydia is Your will, then . . . yeah . . . no thank You."

She tilted her head back against the headrest, breathed her way through the anger now holding her jaw and her fists hostage, and then stepped from the car onto the pavement. Once she was inside, a check of the building's directory had her entering the first door on the right.

"Good afternoon, do you have an appointment?"

Dani turned toward the voice and the sixty-something woman seated behind a desk with a welcoming smile on her face and a headset atop her thick gray hair. "I-I do. I'm Danielle

Parker. I called yesterday afternoon and you squeezed me in on a cancel—"

The woman's eyes glanced up from the computer she was already consulting and the clipboard she was already sliding across the desk in Dani's direction. "Please fill out this packet of information as completely as possible. The first page goes over your rights as a patient, the next is about your insurance, and the last two concern your medical history. When everything is filled out, just bring it back to me here at the counter, and the nurse will be out shortly thereafter to get you. If you have any questions, don't hesitate to ask."

"I—Okay. Thanks." Pulling the clipboard to her chest, Dani made her way toward the waiting area and the row of empty seats bookended along the back wall by two large potted plants.

The first page was easy enough. She read the standard disclaimer, signed and dated on the appropriate lines, and moved on, her fingers tightening around the pen as she stared down at the second page.

Returning to her feet, she picked her way around the couple she'd seen entering the building, a woman reading a magazine while repeatedly checking her phone, and a nervous-looking teenager seated next to her equally nervous-looking mother. At Dani's approach, the receptionist looked up. "Yes? Do you have a question?"

"I'm not sure if—" She stopped, cleared her throat of its audible tremor, and dug into her purse for her wallet. "Does insurance stop if the person who carried it through their job is . . ."

Unable to continue, Dani looked up at the ceiling.

"Mrs. Parker?"

Blinking hard against the tears she wanted nothing more than to keep at bay, she modulated her voice down to a rasped whisper. "My husband . . . He . . . He's . . . He . . ." She squeezed her eyes closed. "He died. Two months ago."

The woman's chair groaned with the sudden shift of her

weight as she jumped up. "I'm so sorry, dear. Come. Come with me."

Warm hands shepherded her through a door next to the receptionist's desk and into a long hallway flanked by a series of doors—some open, others closed. At the first open one they came to, the woman, who introduced herself as Martha, guided her inside and over to an exam table, her thick glasses unable to mask the empathy in her warm brown eyes. "Here," she said, handing Dani a tissue. "You poor thing. I'm so sorry."

She wiped her eyes and nodded.

"So you had insurance before, yes?" Martha asked.

Again, she nodded.

"Did you get notification from the company about continuing?"

"I don't know." She played with the tissue a moment, wiped her eyes again, and then crumpled it inside her palm. "I've been staying here. In Lancaster—Blue Ball, actually. I haven't been home to deal with mail in almost five weeks."

Martha cringed. "Five weeks, huh?" Then, wrapping her hand around Dani's, she offered a gentle if not entirely reassuring squeeze. "I'll see what I can find out on my end while you wait in here for the doctor."

"Will he see me if I don't have insurance?"

"Let's hold off worrying about that until I know more, okay?" Martha turned toward the door, glancing back at Dani before she slipped into the hallway. "What a beautiful gift your husband gave you."

She listened to the receptionist's receding footfalls and, when they were gone, took in the walls of the examination room as she struggled to slow her breath. A poster next to the door showed a growing fetus inside a womb. A check of the two-month mark showed the embryo to be roughly the size of a kidney bean.

The wall to her left boasted the doctor's medical school credentials as well as a number of awards he'd won for his work in obstetrics. To her right, a series of cabinets lined the wall above a narrow countertop with a small sink on one side and a trio of silver-lidded glass jars filled with cotton balls, gauze, and swab-topped sticks. A calendar sat beside a calculator and a stack of notepaper edged in a rainbow of whimsical colors.

On the only remaining wall, a smattering of framed photographs were arranged in rectangular fashion—black and white for some, color for others. All were stunning in their own right, but it was the one in the center that seemed to reach out to Dani with a calming hand.

A quick knock pulled her attention off the picture in favor of the slowly opening door and, seconds later, Martha's wide smile. "You have insurance, Mrs. Parker."

"I-I do?"

"You do. And it's quite good." Martha retreated, said something to someone farther down the hall, and then popped her head in once again. "Becky will be right in to take your vitals and go over your medical history with you. When that's done, Dr. Braden will be in to see you."

Swallowing against the growing tightness in her throat, she tried for something as close to a smile as she could muster. "Thank you."

"Oh, honey, you are most welcome."

Then Martha was gone, replaced, within seconds, by a dark-haired woman of about forty. "Mrs. Parker? I'm Becky, Dr. Braden's nurse."

"Hello."

"If it's okay, I need to go over your medical history with you real quick."

The forms . . .

"Oh. I-I didn't finish those papers the receptionist gave me."

Becky held up her hand. "It's nothing we can't do together here." The nurse rolled out a stool from beneath the counter and stopped it in front of a small laptop. "You've taken a home pregnancy test?"

The tightness was back. "Yes."

"When was that?"

"Last week."

"First day of your last period?"

She said the date aloud as her mind's eye skipped back two weeks further—to her last and oft-revisited night with Jeff.

"Is this your first pregnancy?" Becky asked, her own eyes fixed on the laptop screen.

"No."

"First live birth?"

"No."

Becky glanced over her shoulder at Dani, waiting.

"It's my fourth."

"Any problems with those births?"

In a flash, she was back in the delivery room with first Maggie, then Spencer, and, finally, Ava, her arms aching with a longing so powerful she could hardly breathe.

"Mrs. Parker?"

"No," she finally answered. "No problems."

"C-sections?"

"No."

"Morning sickness with those?"

"Nothing too bad. A little queasiness now and again. Some body aches, that sort of thing. But nothing major."

"And now?"

"I don't know. I don't know what's from the pregnancy and what's from . . ." She straightened her back, the motion stirring a crinkling sound from the paper beneath her. "Anything else?"

Becky looked at her for a moment and then returned to the computer screen. "How about your parents? Still alive?"

Swinging her focus back to the wall of photographs, Dani willed the one of the Amish farmhouse at sunrise to work its earlier magic, but whatever calming properties it had once held were gone. "No. My father died when I was a teenager. Heart attack."

"And your mom?"

She closed her eyes.

"Mrs. Parker?"

"Car accident."

"I'm so—"

"With my husband."

She heard the gasp, but, still, she couldn't open her eyes.

"Oh, Mrs. Parker, I'm—"

"And my three children."

The answering squeak of the stool's wheels was quickly followed by a whiff of lilac-scented perfume and the press of a tissue against the palm of her hand. "Can I get you anything?" Becky whispered.

She shook her head. Swallowed.

"Are you sure?"

Nodding, she turned away from the voice.

"Okay. But I'll be right outside if that changes. In the meantime, once you're ready, here's a cup. Use the bathroom right behind that door to collect a sample and set it behind the small metal door in the wall next to the sink. When that's done, get yourself undressed and put on the gown I've left on the counter here for you. Put it on—open to the front—and give a knock at the door so I know you're ready to see Dr. Braden."

"I will. Thank you."

"Of course." The woman's footsteps receded against the click of the door as it was opened and closed, leaving Dani alone, once again.

Breathe in . . .

Breathe out . . .

Breathe in . . .

Like a programmed robot, she stepped down off the exam table, left a urine sample inside the adjacent bathroom's two-sided wall cabinet as instructed, and then returned to the exam room and the folded gown waiting atop the counter. Outside, just beyond her closed door, she could hear the nurse's muffled voice interspersed by a soft clucking sound she attributed to Martha, and then, seconds later, the rumble of a man's voice.

She didn't need to hear what they were saying to know they were talking about her—the woman in Room Three. The one who'd lost her husband, her children, her mother in a single car accident and was two months pregnant with her fourth child. The words were impossible to pick up, but the pity with which they were spoken was as palpable as the slamming of her heart inside her chest.

Slipping her bare arms and body into the coarse cotton gown, she crossed to the door, gave the requested knock, and climbed back onto the exam table seconds before a portly man in his late fifties strode into the room with a warm smile and solemn eyes. "Mrs. Parker, I'm Dr. Braden. Welcome."

She released the edge of her lip from between her teeth just long enough to issue a quick greeting in return.

"My nurse ran your sample. I'm happy to confirm that you are, indeed, pregnant. And based on the date of your last cycle, I'm putting you at about ten weeks."

"Yes."

"How are you feeling? Physically? Emotionally? My nurse filled me in on what happened and I'm terribly sorry about the loss of your family."

She managed a quick thank-you and a half nod.

"Were you in the accident?" he asked, lowering himself to the stool and wheeling himself over to the exam table.

"No."

"Thank God."

She stared at him as he continued. "So the biggest hurdle we have in regards to this baby at the moment is managing your stress. Have you been eating?"

"A nibble here, a nibble there."

"No appetite?"

"No appetite," she repeated.

"You need to eat, Mrs. Parker. If you can't handle a big meal, then eat smaller amounts more often. Fruits and vegetables are important, sure, but calories are, too. So get yourself a milk shake from time to time. That'll help."

He looked down at the tablet in his hand, typed something in, and then looked back up at Dani. "How about sleep? You getting any?"

"Some," she said, shrugging. "Here and there."

"You'll need more of that, as well, although I'm sure that's easier said than done in light of everything you're going through." At her slight nod, he slipped the tablet into the pocket of his white coat and stood. "Exercise can help in that regard, as well as with the kind of body aches you mentioned to Becky."

"I try to walk in the evenings."

"Good. Good. Any cramping in your legs when you're walking?"

"No. Not really. Maybe once in a while."

"Eating better will help with that. But, just in case, don't walk too far by yourself." He crossed to the sink, washed his hands, and then moved toward the door to summon Becky in for the exam.

"You have family here in Lancaster, Mrs. Parker?"

She shook her head and looked down at her hands. "I'm staying with a friend. She . . . she's Amish."

"Friends are important. Especially now." He opened the door, poked his head into the hall, and then returned with Becky and her laptop in tow. "We'll need to call in a prescription for prenatal vitamins to Mrs. Parker's preferred pharmacy before she leaves, and I'd like you to send her home with some pamphlets on appropriate support groups in the area. I think they might be helpful."

At Becky's nod, he turned back to Dani. "Before we get to the exam, do you have any questions or concerns for me at this point?"

Lifting her attention to the center photograph once again, she drank in the simple farmhouse, the quiet dirt lane, the rocking chairs on the front porch, and the sun rising above it all. "Yes, I have one."

Lowering himself to the wheeled stool, he scooted closer, waiting.

"Have any of your patients ever placed their child up for adoption?" she asked.

"On occasion, yes."

"Is it difficult to do?"

"Emotionally, yes. Of course. But if both parental parties are in agreement, the legal aspect tends to go quite smoothly." He paused, considering her words. "Do you know someone who is considering placing their child up for adoption?"

Dropping her gaze to his and her hand to her abdomen, she nodded. "Yes. Me."

Chapter 16

She spotted the stack of mail the second she let herself into the grossdawdy house. Secured with a rubber band and standing roughly six inches tall, the pile sat atop the kitchen table with one of Lydia's flowery sticky notes affixed to the top.

Releasing the sigh she hadn't realized she'd drawn in at the sight, Dani crossed to the table, dropped the adoption pamphlets onto the otherwise empty surface and took in her friend's careful penmanship:

> *This came for you today.*
> *I hope it brings you a smile.*
> *Your friend,*
> *Lydia*

"I doubt it," she mumbled, flicking the edge of her index finger down the upper right corner of the stack.

Even without removing the rubber band, she knew the bulk of the envelopes were of the personal greeting card variety. Sympathy cards, no doubt. A few others appeared to be the more standard bill fare, while one—a cream-colored one with the logo of Jeff's company emblazoned in the return address field—caught and held her breath for a beat, maybe two.

Lowering herself onto the closest bench, she slipped the envelope from the stack and fingered the logo she'd helped Jeff create over a pair of lattes and a double chocolate brownie at a local coffee shop some eleven years earlier. Together, they'd played with fonts and graphics on his laptop for hours, his enthusiasm more than a little contagious. When the one they'd come up with won the go-ahead from the board he and Tom had painstakingly assembled, she'd helped Jeff celebrate by putting it onto cupcakes and cookies she'd made from scratch and delivered to the simple, storefront style office that had housed Parker & Gavigan in those early days. Two weeks later, Jeff had gotten down on bended knee during a Saturday afternoon picnic and asked for her hand in marriage—her *"selfless spirit," "sweet genuineness,"* and *"crazy beautiful smile"* three of the qualities he'd professed to loving as he slipped the half-carat ring he could afford at the time onto the fourth finger of her left hand.

Seven years later, when they were driving home from the hospital with their third baby in five years, they'd marveled at just how far they'd come. The fancy five-bedroom home, so different from the studio apartment they could barely afford their first year of marriage . . . The brand-new car he was driving and the minivan he'd bought her when, in the beginning, they'd shared a two-door hatchback with more rust than actual paint . . . The could-barely-afford lease on the ten-thousand-square-foot office building on the outskirts of town that had been replaced with an almost paid-off mortgage on a two-story brick building in a more sought-after and visible location . . . And, of course, the twosome they'd once been had grown into a family of five.

As they'd pulled into the driveway and Mom had come running out to greet them with a then five-year-old Maggie and an almost three-year-old Spencer, Jeff had reached for her hand across the center console and interlaced her fingers with his own.

"We've come a long way, babe. A long, long way. What do you say we keep it just like this for the rest of forever?"

She closed her eyes against the memory of her response. Her misty-eyed *"yes"* had prompted him to lift her hand to his lips and linger a kiss against her skin even as Maggie and Spencer were jumping up and down near the back window, anxious to welcome their new sibling home.

"I said yes," she whispered fiercely. *"I. Said. Yes."*

Flipping the envelope over, she slid her finger beneath the seal, ripped the flap back, and yanked out the matching cream-colored linen paper she, herself, had selected for company correspondence. Like the envelope, the logo was prominently displayed, its rust-and-gold color scheme popping across the top of the now-unfolded piece of paper.

> *Dear Dani,*
>
> *I know, from your neighbor Emily, that you are visiting with a friend out of state and that is why you haven't reached out or returned any of the dozen or so voicemails I've left you since the memorial service. I know you need your space. I get that. I really do. But, in light of the company and our clients, we could not wait any longer to deal with certain matters.*
>
> *First, your insurance. Jeff made arrangements for your medical insurance to continue as necessary in the event of his death. I had Kelly submit all the necessary paperwork changing over subscribership to you, and everything is all set there. A new card will be sent to you in the next seven to ten days. The number is the same, but it will now list only your name. It is Kelly's hope, and mine as well, that this change will*

eliminate any unnecessary pain every time you go to use it.

Her laugh held no shred of humor as she continued reading.

Jeff's last check was direct deposited into his account, as always, and we took the initiative of sending a copy of the death certificate to the life insurance company listed in Jeff's file in order to get that ball rolling for you, as well. From what I gather, that money will be direct deposited into your account by the end of the month, if it hasn't been already. If any issues arise with that, let me know.

If you need anything, no matter how big or small, I am here. Day or night. We'll get you through this, Dani. I promise. We're not going anywhere—also a promise.

Everyone here is praying for you, Dani. We loved Jeff, we loved Maggie, we loved Spencer, we loved Ava, we loved your mom, and we love you, too. Parker & Gavigan was never just a company; you know that. We were—we are—a family. Forever and always. You were a big part in helping to create that for all of us these past eleven-plus years. Please, let us be that same family for you now.

We love you, Dani.

With love,

Tom (and everyone at your Parker & Gavigan family)

The words, while kind and generous, pinged off her like gravel against tires. *Family . . . love . . . Forever and always . . .* those words, those concepts, didn't go with her anymore. Mom, Jeff, and the kids were gone. *They* were her family; *they* were who she loved. And forever and always? Without them, she didn't want *tomorrow*, let alone a forever.

Lurching forward against the table, Dani refolded the letter, shoved it into the envelope, and returned it to the pile. A quick glance through the rest of the mail yielded nothing else she wanted to open, let alone read. Instead, she stood, dumped it all into her empty suitcase in the corner of the bedroom, and then returned to the kitchen and the contents of the evening's dinner basket waiting to be unpacked.

With hands that knew the drill, she transferred the still-warm meat and side dish onto the last of the plates inside her cabinet and carried it to the refrigerator. Inside, she hunted for an open space among the scads of untouched food and found one toward the back of the first shelf—in between yesterday's soup and the previous day's chicken.

She'd tried to convince Lydia to stop sending so much food, but every day, like clockwork, more showed up.

Days' and days' worth of dinners had gone from Lydia's basket to the refrigerator with little more than a quick sniff and a very occasional nibble. Three months earlier, the smells alone would have overtaken any desire Dani might have had to watch her caloric intake. But now, after everything, even the most tantalizing aromas held no real power.

"You need to eat, Mrs. Parker. If you can't handle a big meal, then eat smaller amounts more often. Fruits and vegetables are important, sure, but calories are, too. So get yourself a milk shake from time to time. That'll help."

Pushing the refrigerator closed, she stepped over to the cloth-wrapped mound that had been part of her breakfast basket that morning and fished out the piece of cold yet still-soft bread. She considered returning to the refrigerator for a smear of butter but opted, instead, to take the plain slice outside on the front porch, where she could watch the sheep and the chickens in private while Lydia and her family sat around the dinner table sharing tales of their day over the same turkey and dressing supper currently residing on the top shelf of her refrigerator.

"You should try the swing."

Startled, she looked up from the rocking chair she was inches from claiming and spotted Caleb striding toward her with his cowboy hat atop his head and a shy smile inching its way across his generous mouth. "Oh. Hi. I didn't know you were here," she said, sliding her gaze beyond his to the empty spot where he tended to park his truck.

"My truck is over at my folks' house up the road." He motioned her attention back to the farthermost corner of the porch and the wooden swing suspended from its ceiling by a single chain on each end. "That's always been my favorite spot. The view is a little different from what you get sitting on the rocking chair, but there's something mighty nice about losing yourself in it while your big toe does all the work."

"It's okay; the rocking chair is fine."

"You're right; it is. But the swing is better. Trust me," he said, stopping just shy of the porch's two-step staircase. "Try it."

Too tired to protest, she carried her bread over to the swing and slowly lowered herself onto the bench-like seat, its answering sway leaving her to make a mad grab for the armrest with her free hand. "Whoa . . ."

His laugh spilled onto the porch. "Give yourself a second to get used to it and then just look out," he said, spreading his thick and calloused hands outward. "It doesn't get a whole lot prettier than that."

She waited for the swaying to lessen and then followed his gaze past the tree she favored for shade to the gently rolling pitch of the countryside. There, from the swing, the lush green of the growing spring crops seemed to stretch all the way to the ends of the earth only to merge seamlessly with the brilliant blue sky above. "Oh. Wow."

"I know." Lowering himself onto the top step, he rested his forearm across the top of his knee and pointed a lazy finger at her lap. "Is that an appetizer or dessert?"

She followed his gaze down to the slice of bread balanced atop her thigh and quietly sank against the wooden slats at her back. "It's dinner."

His left eyebrow rose nearly to the brim of his cowboy hat. "Now don't get me wrong. I love my sister's homemade bread as much as the next guy. I, personally, like it best plain, the way you've got it there, but it ain't bad with butter, either. That said, I'm pretty sure she didn't mean it to be your only dinner."

"She didn't." Dani lifted the bread to her mouth, only to return it to her lap, untouched. "I'm just not hungry."

"Today? Or still?"

She traveled her gaze back to the sky and the colorful sunset beginning to tease from behind a few white, puffy clouds. "Still, I guess. But it's . . . hard."

"You'll get there. Maybe you just need something different than that," he said, pointing again at the bread.

Turning her back flush with the armrest, she rested her arm against the back of the swing and cushioned her face against her sleeve. "I *have* different. Three refrigerator shelves' worth of different, in fact."

"That's a lot of different." He tilted his head against the railing at his back and then, after a beat or two of silence, lowered his gaze back to hers. "From what I remember, Lydia's eating always slowed down in the early part of her pregnancies, too. Although she never turned down ice cream."

She sat up so tall, so fast, the still-uneaten bread fell to the floor and sent her chasing after it, the denial she desperately wanted to give lodging itself inside her throat.

"I was driving through town with a coworker shortly after lunch when I saw you," he continued. "When I pointed you out to him, he told me the office you were coming out of was a baby doctor, and that the pack you were carrying was one the front desk gives you when you're expecting."

He pointed at the recovered slice of bread in her hand. "You can just toss that out onto the driveway if you want."

At his amused nod, she wiped a little of the dirt onto the side of her jeans and threw it, piece by piece, over the railing, the activity a welcome distraction from a conversation better left in the rearview mirror.

Halfway through the throwing process, he broke out in a grin. "You can just toss it in one piece, you know. Chickens aren't picky."

"Oh . . . Right . . ." she mumbled, flinging the remaining piece into the driveway. "I guess I wasn't thinking."

"So? Was he right?"

"H-he?"

"My coworker." Dropping his hand onto the step, Caleb leveraged his weight against the wood and stood. "You know, about you being pregnant?"

Oh how she wanted to deny it—to Caleb and to herself. But she couldn't. Instead, she drew in a breath, held it to a silent count of five, and then released it along with her truth. "I guess you could say I missed a lot of the usual signs these past few weeks," she said, looking back at the reds and oranges beginning to intensify along the horizon.

The quick clap of his hands stole her gaze back to his. "Oh, Dani, this is *wonderful* news! Wow! Congratulations, Mommy—"

"Please. Don't." Pressing her feet flush against the floor, she waited for the swing to slow enough she could stand. "It's not wonderful news. Not for me, anyway."

"Excuse me?"

"I'm not fit to be a parent—not a good one, anyway."

"What are you talking about?" he asked, the smile he'd boasted just seconds earlier gone.

She leaned forward against the railing, her tone wooden. "This baby. It's a second chance I don't deserve."

"Don't deserve?" he echoed. "Why are you saying that?"

"Because it's true. Look at what's happened—look *at me.*"

With slow, almost tentative steps, he came to stand beside her at the railing, the setting sun unnoticed by eyes that sought only hers. "What happened to your family, Dani, was an accident. Lydia said you weren't even in the car."

"Exhibit A."

"Exhibit A? What are you talking about?"

"I should have been with them," she said, her voice ping-ponging between hushed and shrill. "I was the mom. I should have been at the park that day, too!"

"Were you sick?" he asked.

"No."

"Then why didn't you go?"

"Because my mom insisted I needed time for myself. She was always after me for going, going, going all the time."

Hiking the tip of his left boot onto the railing's bottom rung, he shrugged. "Everyone needs to slow down now and again. It's normal."

"Maybe so. But . . ." She pushed at the sudden weight pressing down on her shoulders. "I can't. It's just so . . . so awful."

He turned to face her. "Try me."

"I put up a fight that morning. About not going. And my arguments sounded sincere enough that I actually believed them myself. But the truth is, underneath all my protests to the contrary, I'd been fantasizing about time away from the kids for a while."

"Okay . . ."

"As in, I sent away for information on an adults-only retreat in upstate New York—a place with walking trails, and spa services, and fancy food, and wine-tasting tours, and luxurious beds, and quaint balconies, and twenty-four-hour room service."

"I'm not seeing a problem here, Dani. The place sounds incredible."

"And it should—to a single guy like yourself, or even a couple without children. But I wasn't part of a couple without children. I was a mom." She pressed a hand to her lips, but alas, it was too late to completely silence her quick yet tortured sob. "I was Maggie and Spencer and Ava's *mom*. And they were great kids. Good kids. Smart kids. Thoughtful kids."

Like a genie unleashed from a bottle, the words began to pour out, slowed only by her own shallow and raspy breaths. "But instead of being grateful, instead of soaking up the three beautiful gifts I was given the first go-round, I was constantly sneaking peeks at the pamphlet I got back from the retreat place in the mail. A big . . . colorful . . . glossy thing that left me yearning for time without them—with or without Jeff. Oh, I talked a good game . . . I-I could barely hide my disdain every time my next-door neighbor, Roberta, went off to play cards with her friends, or took a girls-only getaway with a certain group of moms at the school or in the neighborhood. But despite all my eye rolling and talk to the contrary, I was *looking*, Caleb. I was *wishing*. And you know what?"

Reaching forward, he brought the pad of his thumb within wiping range of her tears only to let it fall to his side as she reared back. "What?"

"God saw me looking at that pamphlet. He knew what I was longing for. He heard me call that place a few days before the accident to inquire whether *adults-only* really meant no one under eighteen. And he gave me exactly what I wanted. I'd looked a gift horse in the mouth and my family paid the price for that with their lives."

This time, when he reached toward her, it was to grab hold of her upper arms and wait until she was looking at him, rather than the ground. "Dani, please. Tell me you don't really believe what you're saying. Tell me you're just having a bad day here."

"Do you know what I did that day instead of being with

my family?" she rasped, the words flowing from her mouth now with no rhyme or reason. "I wrote thank-you notes to everyone who came to my daughter's birthday party the day before. And when those were done, I-I just can't. I can't say it."

"There's nothing wrong with taking advantage of some quiet time to get a needed task done, Dani."

She stared at him. "Do you know what I was doing when the state troopers came to my door to tell me my family was dead? I was reading! I was so wrapped up in some fictional world I had absolutely no idea what was happening—what *had* happened—to them. There's no excuse for that. *None.*" Yanking free of his grasp, she paced her way back and forth between the swing behind her, the staircase to their right, and the railing where he stood staring at her, his mouth agape. "You've seen Lydia. She's an incredible mother. She lets her kids play in the rain, not caring one iota about the extra work all that mud will ultimately mean for her in the end. Because seeing them so happy matters to her far more than the inconvenience of having a few extra pants and dresses in the laundry basket. And she gets such a kick out of watching them, she decides to get in on the fun *with* them, muddying up her own clothes in the process."

Caleb smiled, no doubt at the image borne on her words— an image he'd missed out on witnessing by little more than ten minutes.

"A few days before the puddle jumping?" she said, moving on. "I was hiding from life, and everyone associated with it, on the back patio when Lydia and Nettie came outside after lunch. Next thing I knew, Lydia was sitting on the ground with that sweet little girl in her lap. Nettie started chattering away about a million different things and Lydia actually *listened*. I mean, really listened. To. Every. Single. Word. And Nettie? You could just hear the happiness dripping out of her knowing that she had her mamm all to herself."

"Dani, I'm sure you gave your full attention to your kids. I don't believe otherwise."

She spun around, her teeth clenched in a sudden burst of anger. "Then you're wrong. Because I didn't."

"Dani, I—"

"Do you know what Maggie—my eight-year-old—asked me almost every single night?"

His answering shrug was labored, sad.

"Maggie has—*had*—this window seat in her room. I included it in the building plans because, in my head, I envisioned her sitting there one day, brushing her dolls' hair with the sunlight raining down on her. And that happened, sure." Dani flicked her hand toward the kitchen window at her back. "I could probably pull up a half dozen pictures of her doing exactly that in my phone right now. But the reality was that Maggie liked that window seat for entirely different things, like getting lost in one of the dozens of chapter books she read every month. She'd sit there every chance she had and read, read, read—either alone, or with her brother and sister snuggled up alongside her, listening."

"I'm missing the issue here," he said, spreading his hands wide.

"Maggie loved the stars. She loved looking up at them and making wishes, and imagining what kind of wishes kids her own age—kids in faraway places—might be making on the same exact stars at the same exact times. She asked me every night for years to sit with her on the window seat so we could make wishes together, until, one day, she just quit asking."

She walked to the stairs, turned, and headed back toward the swing, her path both purposeful and aimless. "Side note: I didn't even realize she'd quit asking until after . . ." Spinning back toward the stairs again, she continued, her returning anger propelling her forward. "And do you know why she quit asking? Because only once—maybe twice—in all that time, I actually sat with her and looked up at the stars. *Maybe twice.* That's it. The rest of the time, I had to hurry downstairs to make up snack bags or decorate cupcakes for the next day's soccer game or scout meeting. Or there was a cabinet I'd planned to organize that day and, Lord knows, I couldn't just carry it over to the next day's to-do list."

This time, when she reached the stairs, she just stopped. "Seeing checkmarks on every line of my daily to-do list was of utmost importance to me."

"Dani, I think you're being awfully hard on your—"

Her back still turned to him, she pulled in a slow, steadying breath. "Now juxtapose that story of my stellar mothering against the one I just shared about your sister and Nettie on the ground."

"Dani, don't."

"Don't what?" she asked, glancing back at him over her shoulder. "Don't tell it like it is? Sorry. I think I lived with my head in the clouds long enough. Your sister is *Amish*, Caleb. That alone means she has all sorts of tasks and chores that must be done every day both inside and outside the farmhouse. Yet there she was, sitting outside on the ground, soaking up her child. And Nettie? Her smile could have lit the sky for miles all on its own."

The opening creak of a door sent their collective attention toward the main house. A chorus of laughter, just seconds later, let them know the Schlabach children were done with dinner and looking for a little fun in the backyard. For a moment, maybe two, she drank in their joyful sounds before crossing the porch to her own door.

"I get why God took my family," she said, stilling her fingers on the door handle. "I didn't appreciate them enough; I didn't treasure them for the gifts they were. But to take a child from someone like your sister? Someone who lets her kids be kids? Someone who takes the time to listen to their ideas, their thoughts, and their fears? Someone who knows that being a mother isn't about how many activities your kids are in or what's next on some color-coded calendar? Someone who most surely would have sat on a window seat next to her

daughter every night, making wishes on stars?" Squeezing her
eyes closed against the memory of everything she hadn't been,
Dani continued, the tremble in her voice slowly giving way to
the kind of calm borne on conviction. "I don't get why He did
that, and I never will. But getting it and fixing it don't have to
go hand in hand. Not for me, anyway."

Chapter 17

Dani studied the picture of the towheaded man smiling down at the pretty dark-haired woman and the tiny baby sleeping contentedly in her arms. The man, listed only as Tim, was thirty-eight, his wife, Sheila, thirty-six. The couple, according to the write-up beneath the thumbnail-sized picture, were unable to have children due to an unnamed medical condition. But because of the courage and selflessness of an unwed mother on the other side of the state, they—

" 'Are now Mom and Dad to their sweet son, Ryan,' " she read aloud.

Flipping the brochure over, she searched for a date and, when she found none, she resorted to guessing how old Ryan might be today. Two? Three? Maybe four or even older? Then, was he happy? Were Tim and Sheila good parents? Had they brought another baby home by now, making Ryan a big brother?

And what about the unwed mother? Did Sheila and Tim send her reports on Ryan's progress? Did they have plans to tell their son about his birth mother one day or would they keep the details of his birth from him?

Slowly, she opened the brochure Martha had quietly handed to her across the counter on her way out of Dr. Braden's office and willed herself to breathe, to focus. *Knowledge was power*; it was a favorite expression of Jeff's and one he used quite often around the house with the kids, and at work with Tom and the rest of the team. Ava, of course, was too young to understand the meaning behind the words, but Maggie—and sometimes even Spencer—seemed to grasp its gist most days.

A soft tap at the front door pulled her attention off the list of the top five most frequently asked questions and fixed it, instead, on the snippet of cowboy hat she could see above the simple cloth panel blocking everything else from view. Quickly, she closed the brochure, slid it underneath the empty breakfast basket she'd yet to set back out on the porch, and stood, her frustration over the interruption powering her not-so-quiet sigh.

As she neared the door, the cowboy hat swiveled around to reveal the top of a forehead and the uppermost creases of anticipation.

"Hey," she said, cracking the door open to the full-body view of her host's brother. "What's up?"

Hooking his thumb over his shoulder at the now-familiar black pickup truck parked in front of her porch rather than the barn, his mouth inched upward in a smile. "I'd like to take you somewhere if you have a little time?"

She looked from Caleb to the truck and back again. "I don't think so. I really should just stay here."

"Did you eat breakfast?"

"Not really. I-I wasn't hungry."

"Lunch?"

She thought about the apple she'd tried to eat, but after the first two bites she'd shoved it in the refrigerator on reflex. Not wanting to lie, she followed her shrug of indifference with a whispered "some."

"Come with us," he said, taking a step backward. "We won't keep you out for long. I promise."

"Us?"

This time, when he pointed toward the truck and she actually gave it more than a cursory glance, she saw the same basic view she'd had of Caleb from the table. But instead of the top edge of a cowboy hat above a curtain panel, she saw the top edge of a small, white kapp above the passenger side windowsill.

"I passed Elijah out on the road this morning and he told me Lydia was feeling low. Since the boys are at school, anyway, I offered to take Nettie out for a treat so Lydia could have a little time to herself."

"Is she okay?" Dani asked, abandoning her limited view of the little girl in favor of the main house and, finally, Caleb again.

"Lydia? She"—he closed his palm over his mouth only to let it slip slowly down his chin to his side—"has her good days and her bad days. Today, for whatever reason, is the latter. But hopefully, with a little time to breathe or cry or do whatever she needs to do, she'll swing back the other way sooner rather than later."

The sound of a steady knock against glass led their eyes back to the truck and the happy little face now peeking out at them.

"At first, when I told Nettie I was going to take her out for a little while, she wasn't all that excited at the news. When she sees that Lydia is struggling, she wants to be with her, doing everything she can think of to make things better. But at times like this, Lydia just needs a break, much to Nettie's despair."

"She looks pretty happy now," Dani mused as she returned the little girl's wave.

"That's because she wants you to come with us."

Dani drew back. "Me? Why? I haven't spoken two words to her since I showed up in her driveway five weeks ago."

"Apparently that first encounter was enough for her to know what Lydia and I knew twenty-seven years ago."

"And that is . . ."

"That you're a nice person, plain and simple."

Releasing her hand from the edge of the door, she waved at his words as if they were a swarm of pesky bugs. "Really, I'm fine here. I've got something I need to look into and . . ." She readied the door for closing. "Thank you. I appreciate the invite and everything but—"

"Come on, Dani; do this for Lydia. It'll only take thirty minutes—an hour, tops. I promise."

Again, she let her gaze drift toward the truck and the little girl whose smile seemed a little less certain, a little less all-encompassing, than it had just moments earlier when Dani had been returning her sweet wave.

"Caleb, I can't. I really need to—"

"Consider this your version of what she's done for you." He swept his hand toward the house and the fields. "You know, by letting you stay here and making sure you're not bothered."

Caleb was right.

She owed Lydia.

Squaring her shoulders, she pushed open the door the rest of the way and stepped onto the porch. "An hour, tops."

She'd barely stepped more than three feet from the pickup truck when Nettie's small hand, warm and soft, found its way inside her own. "Do you like ice cream, Mamm's friend?"

Slipping her gaze left toward Caleb and then forward toward the powder-blue and white awning on the roadside ice-cream stand, she managed a quick nod.

"I do, too, Mamm's friend!"

Caleb skirted the hood of the truck and quickly scooped the little girl off her feet, her answering squeal piercing the still afternoon air. "Mamm's friend has a name, you know."

"She does?" Nettie peered at Dani across her uncle's shoulder, her brownish-blond eyebrows rising. "What is it?"

"You could ask her and find out," he said, reaching for Nettie's belly and giving it a giggle-inducing tickle.

When the tickling was over, Nettie poked her head across Caleb's shoulder a second time. "What is your name, Mamm's friend?"

"Dani."

Tapping her index finger to her chin, the little girl considered Dani's answer as she wiggled her way back onto the ground. The second her feet hit the pavement, she hop-skipped her way back to Dani's side. "My name is Nettie."

She felt the faintest twitch of a smile. "I know your name, sweetie."

"But I did not know yours . . ." Nettie scrunched up her face. "Mamm said I am not to knock on your door when you are inside, and I am not to run outside and talk to you when you sit in the chair behind the house where Grossdawdy and Grossmudder lived until they went to be with God."

Then, dropping her cornflower-blue eyes to the ground, she released a dramatic sigh. "Do you not like us, Mamm's friend?"

"No . . . It's nothing like that," Dani said, squatting down to Nettie's eye level. "It's just that, well, I need to be alone right now. To think."

"Mamm goes into her room sometimes. When I go like this"—Nettie tilted her head to indicate her ear—"at her door, I hear Mamm and she is crying."

Caleb doubled back to squat down beside Dani. "Big people get sad sometimes, too, kiddo."

"Yah." Nettie tightened her grasp on Dani's hand and swung their arms together, stopping after a few seconds, her voice so quiet Dani and Caleb nearly bumped heads when they leaned closer. "Mamm did not want God to take Rose. Mamm wants Rose to still be here. I do, too. She made big smiles when I was silly. But she did not make any smiles when Mamm runned with her to the barn. She did not even open her eyes. I wish she did so Mamm would not cry. I wish I made her smile that day."

Releasing Nettie's hand from her own, she pulled the child close. "What happened to your baby sister wasn't your fault, sweetie. She just . . ." Dani cast about for just the right words and, when she couldn't find them, used her eyes to send Caleb a silent plea for help—a plea he answered after a hard swallow of his own.

"Remember the litter of kittens we found in the barn last fall?" Caleb asked. At Nettie's slow nod, he continued, his gaze meeting Dani's briefly over the top of his niece's kapped head. "Do you remember how many there were at first?"

Nettie turned so her body was still up close to Dani's, but her eyes, her focus, were on her uncle. "Six."

"That's right. There were six. But do you remember what we found the next day when we went out to the barn to check on them after the boys got home from school?"

With a quick nod, she looked back at Dani. "We founded only five."

"That's right. One did not live through the night. Do you remember what your dat told you about the kitten that did not live?"

Nettie looked from Dani to Caleb and finally at the ground, her little head nodding her assent. "Dat said God wanted to keep that kitten."

"That's right, kiddo. And that's the same thing Dat told you about Rose, right?"

"Why didn't God want *me*?" Nettie asked. "Did I do something bad?"

Dani's answering gasp drew the eyes of both Nettie and Caleb. "No, of course not," she said in a raspy burst. "He . . . he *does* want you, sweetie. Just not yet. Not now."

"Dani is right, kiddo. God wants you here, with all of us." He tapped the tip of her nose and then followed it with a kiss on her forehead. "Now, how about we get us some ice cream?"

And just like that, the little girl's sadness was swept to the side by the promise of ice cream, and for that Dani was glad.

Standing upright, she took a moment to steady her breath, and then fell into step beside Caleb while Nettie ran ahead to the ordering window.

"You okay?" he asked, glancing over at her, his hazel eyes dulled by worry. "Because I didn't see that coming when I asked you to come along. I figured she'd just be her usual happy self."

"She's worried about Lydia," Dani said, swallowing.

"And I know that—or, at least, I thought I did. But yeah . . . I didn't see that coming."

Nettie came running back, her cheeks pink with excitement. "I want the yellow kind!" She reached for Dani's hand again and tugged. "Come on; you will like the yellow kind, too! It is very, *very* yummy!"

Yellow kind? she mouthed back at Caleb while quickening her pace in time with Nettie's.

Caleb's laugh rumbled to life from deep inside his chest. "Oh, I could have fun with this . . ."

"Please don't."

Lurching forward, he scooped his niece back off the ground, tickled the spot just below her neck with the top of his cowboy hat, and then carried her the rest of the way to the window. "How about we let Dani choose what sounds best to *her* tummy, okay?"

"But what will *her* tummy like?"

"That's a good question," Dani mumbled as she stopped in view of the flavor board, waiting for her stomach to roil at the very thought of food.

When Nettie's order for yellow ice cream was placed, translated to the Amish teen behind the counter as vanilla with butterscotch sauce by Caleb, he motioned Dani close. "So? Is anything calling out to you?"

She scanned the flavors, shrugging as she did. "Nothing is jumping out, but nothing is telling me no necessarily, either."

"That's progress if nothing else, yes?" His eyes flitted down toward her stomach before returning to the flavor board and then Dani, herself. "I could pick out something for both of us if you'd like. Something that's not yellow . . ."

She waited for her stomach to protest the very notion of food, but, when the protest didn't come, she found herself nodding. "Sure, why not?"

"My sentiments, exactly." He set Nettie on the ground and smiled down at her. "Show Dani where your favorite table is and I'll bring the ice cream as soon as it's ready, okay?"

"Yah." Nettie's hand slipped into Dani's a third time, the subsequent tug taking them away from the counter and toward a slew of picnic tables on the far side of the parking lot. "I hope Upside-Down Ducky is here," Nettie said, bouncing along on the toes of her black slip-on shoes. "He's funny."

They wound around one table, then another, and still one more before Nettie retrieved her hand to leverage herself onto the attached bench and then to pat the empty spot on her right side. "You can sit here! Next to me!"

Dani glanced back at the ice-cream stand, saw Caleb reaching through the window, and turned back to the little girl. "Maybe we should let your uncle sit there since it was his treat to bring you here."

"He sits there," Nettie said, pointing at the spot opposite her own. "So he can see me."

"He can still see you if he sits *next* to you."

"He wants to see me *there*."

Dani let the tiny finger guide her attention toward a man-made pond with a fountain in the middle, a few lazy ducks floating around the edges, and a glass-fronted metal box filled with pellets atop a pole. "I told him I am almost big like Mark, but he says I cannot go to the water if he is not looking."

"He's right, you know." She swung her leg across the bench and slowly lowered herself next to Nettie. "Even big girls like me can lose their footing sometimes."

"I've told her that very same thing, haven't I, kiddo?" Caleb sidled up to the table, a dark blue tray in one hand, a stack of napkins in the other. "That's why there's no looking for Upside-Down Ducky without me, right?"

Nettie shifted up and onto her knees to peek over the edge of the tray, her answering squeal of delight spawning an excited clap. "Look at all that yellow! There is lots and lots!"

"Tell me about it. *I* ask for butterscotch—I get a single pump's worth. *Nettie* asks for butterscotch and, well"— winking at Dani, he lowered the tray onto the table and brandished his hand toward the kid-sized cup in the center— "they completely hook her up."

Pulling a face, he took a spot on the opposing bench and threw his hands up in mock confusion. "I don't get it. I really don't."

Nettie's giggle lasted about as long as it took for her to reach onto the tray for her ice cream. "Did you say please?"

"I did."

"Did you say thank you?" Nettie asked, digging her spoon into the sauce.

"I did that, too." His eyes crackled with amusement as he tried to maintain his confusion for Dani. "See? I don't know what I'm doing wrong. Do you, Dani?"

"You don't look like that," she said, nudging her head toward Nettie.

Like an actor playing a multi-faceted part, Caleb drew back, covered his mouth and then his chest with his hand, and, finally, collapsed his head onto the table, narrowly missing the tray and its remaining contents. "I'm . . . crushed— crushed, I tell you."

The giggling was back. "I see you peeking at us," Nettie said, pointing at the part of her uncle she could see between his arm and his cowboy hat. "Your great big eye is looking at me!"

Caleb straightened up, his love for his niece evident in the smile that reached far beyond his mouth. "You caught me, kiddo." He slanted a look at Dani. "I can't get away with anything when this one is around . . ."

Nettie set her spoon on the table, licked a trail of melting ice cream off her wrist, and then pointed her recovered spoon at the one treat void of butterscotch sauce. "What kind did you get, Dani?"

"I figured we'd start her off easy this first time." Caleb transferred the single-scoop cup from the tray to Dani's spot. "Basic vanilla. No sauce, no toppings, no fanfare."

Her stomach's answering gurgle was short and quick, but there was no denying its existence based on the way Nettie's eyes widened just before yet another fit of giggles.

"Looks like I made a good call, eh?" Grabbing one of the two remaining spoons on the tray, he handed it—along with a napkin—to Dani. "There's a chance I'm biased about this place on account of the fact I've been coming here since I was Nettie's age, but this is some of the best ice cream around."

Dani looked from the ice cream to the spoon and back again, waiting for the warning bells her stomach tended to throw up as a matter of course these days, but they never came. Instead, all she heard was an encore of its earlier gurgle.

"It's something," Caleb said, modulating his voice to a level intended just for Dani. "And something is better than nothing right now."

He was right and she knew it. Somehow, someway, she needed to start eating again. For the baby . . . For—

"It's Upside-Down Ducky! Look!" Nettie set her spoon beside her remaining ice cream and climbed down off the bench, her blue eyes ricocheting between the pond and her uncle. "Can I go say hello?"

"You haven't finished your ice cream yet, kiddo."

"I just want to say hello," Nettie said, turning to look at a small brown and green duck floating in their direction. "I will not be long."

He opened his mouth in what, to Dani, looked to be a protest, but, in the end, he took a bite of his own ice cream, nodding as he did.

Nettie started to run toward the water but slowed to a walk at her uncle's stern direction. When she reached the water's edge, the child crouched down and began to move her hand in a part wave/part beckoning gesture that, to Dani's surprise, seemed to attract the duck in question.

"He looks like he's actually listening," she mumbled in awe while simultaneously scooping up a little ice cream and depositing it into her mouth.

"Because he is." Caleb, too, took a bite of ice cream, his eyes never leaving his niece or the duck actively floating into the little girl's reach. "I can't explain it, especially with how busy this place normally is at this time of year, but he remembers her every bit as much as she remembers him."

Sure enough, the duck responded to the child's sweet hello with a single, muted quack. When she informed him about the ice cream Caleb had gotten her, he quacked again.

"See? It's like that with the two of them every single time we come, and we're not here all that often."

She pivoted on the bench so she could both eat and watch at the same time. "How did he get the name Upside-Down Ducky?"

Caleb's laugh drew a quick over-the-shoulder glance from Nettie—a glance he waved back toward the duck. "First time we saw him, he was dunking himself the way ducks do. Only this guy stayed that way almost the whole time we were eating our ice cream. Nettie, of course, thought it was hilarious. When I took her over to get a closer look when we were all done, he swam over to see if we were going to give him something to eat. Nettie bent herself over, headfirst, and begged him to dunk his head again. And he did it . . . And then, when she flipped herself again, he did it, too! Next thing I knew, there were four other kids around Nettie's age standing next to us trying to get this guy to follow their commands, too. But he didn't. When they flipped over, he just looked at them. When Nettie flipped over and then righted herself, he quacked and dunked his head. Every. Single. Time. Watch . . ."

Pausing his spoon a few inches shy of his next mouthful of ice cream, he nudged her attention back to his niece. "Hey, kiddo, can you make him go upside down so Dani can see?"

"Yah." Nettie bounced up to a full stand, flipped herself over at the waist, and then, when she righted herself once again, the duck quacked and dove his head into the water, his little yellow webbed feet breaking the surface.

"Whoa," Dani managed around her spoon.

"I know. Crazy, isn't it?" Setting his now-empty ice-cream cup onto the tray, he stretched his arms high above his head. "I get such a kick out of watching that, I'm not sure who wants to come here more these days, Nettie or me."

"Have *you* tried?" she asked, alternating her attention between Nettie and the man seated on the other side of the table. "Will he do it for you?"

Caleb laughed. "Oh, I've tried. More than a few times, I'm embarrassed to say. But all I get for my efforts is dizziness."

"And the duck?"

"He just sits there."

"What about Luke and the other boys? Have they tried?"

"They have. And same thing—nothing. Nettie does it and, *quack*, he flips." Resting his forearms atop the table, Caleb leaned forward, shaking his head in disbelief. "I'm telling you, Dani, he *remembers* her."

"There's a cat like that out by one of the soccer fields," she said, going in for yet another bite. "We're pretty sure he's a stray on account of the fact he doesn't have a collar and he's pretty skittish whenever anyone gets too close. But Spencer? It's like he's this cat whisperer or something, because every time he's around, that cat comes bounding over to see him like a dog might—"

The sound of her own laughter stopped her cold, forcing her gaze down to the empty cup in her hand.

"Keep going," Caleb prodded as Nettie's return to the table freed his gaze back onto Dani. "Did he give the cat a name?"

Did he . . .

"I can name a cat!" Nettie plunked herself back onto the bench and pointed Dani's eyes back to the now-empty cup in her hand. "You ate it all up!"

I can . . .

She stared down at the milky residue inside her cup, her throat closing so tightly she was forced to breathe through her nose.

Two words, two children. One present, one . . . *not.*

Breathe in.

Breathe out.

Breathe in.

"Dani?"

She could feel Caleb's questioning eyes, could see Nettie's sticky hands moving in time with whatever the little girl was saying. But in that moment, all she could hear, all she *knew,* was the voice of disgust inside her head.

You laughed . . .

Chapter 18

She heard the soft thud of his approaching footsteps as he came around the back of the grossdawdy house, but she didn't look up. If she were lucky, he was looking for Elijah or a wandering cow and would simply keep on walking, oblivious to her presence. But the sound of her name, hushed and uncertain on his tongue, squashed that hope in record time.

"Hey . . ." Caleb crossed the patio and squatted down beside Dani's Adirondack-style chair, the lines above his brow pinched together with worry. "I'm really sorry, Dani. I wanted to look in on you sooner, but Lydia wasn't back from Miss Lottie's when we pulled up. I didn't think I should bring Nettie here, so I let her help me feed the calf."

"I wasn't expecting you to look in on me."

If the wooden tone of her answer surprised him, he didn't let on. Instead, he cocked the front brim of his hat upward with his finger and shifted his weight across his bent legs. "But I wanted to. It's clear that something upset you there at the end and if it's something I did, or something I said, I'd like to know. So I can apologize."

"You did nothing."

"Are you sure? I've been told I talk a little too much, sometimes."

"I'm sure."

The lines around his eyes softened a smidge. "I thought it

was a good sign that you ate all of your ice cream. Made me wish I'd gotten you the next size up, instead. Next time, though . . ."

"There won't *be* a next time." She fixed her gaze on a windmill spinning in the distance and tried to tamp down the anger she felt building inside. "Not with me, anyway."

Surprise swayed him back. "I thought you said I didn't do anything wrong . . ."

"I did. Because you didn't."

"Then why—"

Stopping his question with her hand, she abandoned her view of the windmill and dropped her feet back onto the patio. "Look, you have nothing to apologize for, but I don't need you looking in on me, now or ever. I came here, to Lancaster, because your sister said I could have my own space. If that's changed, or if I've overstayed my welcome, just say that and I'll leave."

"Whoa." He sprang upward, his tall frame blocking her path to the back door. "Slow down. No one said anything about you overstaying your welcome or wanting you to leave. I just know something happened at the ice-cream place today because one minute you were actually laughing and—"

Feeling the heat of shame on her cheeks, she pushed past him, desperate to make it inside before the tears began. Two steps from the door, however, he rushed forward, stopping her with his hand. "Dani, wait! Is *that* what this is about? That you *laughed*?"

She tried to wiggle free of his hand, to reach out for the door handle and pull, but she couldn't see through the rush of tears ignited by his words. "Please," she managed as the threat of full-on sobbing marched its way up her throat. "I want to go inside."

Instead of loosening his grip, he turned her so they were face-to-face, the worry he'd worn on his face just moments earlier replaced by . . . *understanding*?

"Dani, you weren't doing anything wrong. You were sharing a story that made you *happy*—a story about *your son.* That's nothing to feel bad or guilty about. Ever."

She stared at him through the watery haze, grief rapidly giving way to anger. "I can't be happy! My husband, my three children, and my mother are gone, killed in a car accident that shouldn't have happened—that *wouldn't* have happened if I'd been a better mother, a better wife, a better daughter!"

His grip softened. "Dani, you *looked* at a brochure, that's it. That doesn't make you an awful person and it certainly doesn't make you responsible for what happened to your family. That's on the driver of the other car, not you."

"I stayed behind," she countered, her voice rising. "I stayed behind to-to *read.*"

Slowly, he released his hold on her arm. "Didn't you say your mother insisted you stay home?"

Had she? She couldn't remember . . .

"That she didn't like how little time you took for yourself?" he continued.

She looked past him, the windmill swimming in her vision while his questions landed like grenades.

"That even after they left for the park, you spent your time writing thank-you notes for your daughter's birthday gifts?" Hooking his finger beneath her chin, he guided her eyes back to his. "That's not the description of a selfish woman, Dani. Not even close."

"My job was to soak them up the way Lydia does! To play with them! To laugh with them! To be present in the moment with them! Not running around trying to be some award-winning mother or wife in the eyes of-of . . . other parents, or clients, or whoever else I was always trying to impress!" She paused, trying to collect herself, but she couldn't. Now that the words were flowing from her mouth, she couldn't stop them. Not yet. "I shouldn't have been writing thank-you notes, or planning class parties, or reading some book my mother left behind on the coffee table! I should have been *with* them that day! I-I should have been *with* them in that car!"

"Why? So you could be dead, too?"

"Yes! Yes!" she sobbed. "Yes! A million times, *yes!*"

Bookending her shoulders with his hands, he squeezed her full attention back to his face, the look of horror she found there ratcheting up the volume on her sobs. "Don't say that, Dani! Don't *think* it, don't *say* it, and don't *believe* it—ever!"

She tried again to break free of his grip, but he held fast. "I can't listen to this," she wailed.

"Sorry, Dani, but you have to. You're in a bad place right now. A horrible place. I *get* it, I really do . . . or"—he glanced up at the sky as if searching for something—"or at least I can *imagine* what this must be like for you. And every time I do, I don't know how you're still standing; I really don't."

"That's just it: I don't *want* to be standing. I want to be *with them*. Like I should be!"

"You *are* where you should be, Dani."

"How-how can you say that?" she stammered.

"Because you *weren't* in that car."

She yanked free of his hands, anger blooming again. "Are you saying you think my family *should be dead*?" she hissed.

"No . . . Not *should*. But for whatever reason, God wanted you to stay here. For now."

"God?" she half yelled, half shrieked. "*God?* What *God* wants to take a wonderfully brilliant husband and father in the prime of his life? What *God* wants a kind, sweet, empathetic *eight-year-old,* or a *five-year-old* who just lost his first tooth and was loved by everyone? What *God* wants a *three-year-old* who grew happy-face flowers for her mommy and never even got to try out all of her birthday presents? What *God* takes a mother who supported her only child through everything the way my mother did?"

"You're angry. That makes sense."

"It does? I'm so glad you think so . . ."

He palmed his mouth, only to let his hand slip down his

chin to his side. "I'm not trying to patronize you, Dani. I'm really not. What I just said about anger—it's normal after a loss like this. Miss Lottie said there are five stages of grief and anger is definitely one of them. Not everyone goes through all five stages, and the order may be different from one person to the next, but anger is a big one. I read about it after I left her house."

"Is laughter one of them?"

Oblivious to her sarcasm, he paused, considering her question. "No. I don't think it is. I'm pretty sure it's denial, anger, depression . . . bargaining, and acceptance."

Acceptance.

As if that could ever happen . . .

To Caleb, though, she shrugged, the gesture labored as the fight began to drain from her body. "I laughed today, Caleb. *Laughed.* And in that moment, anyone looking at me would never know I lost my entire family eight weeks ago. What kind of person—what kind of *mother*—does that?"

"A wonderful mom who loved her children, who took joy in the memory of a moment with one of her kids, who—"

She threw up her hand, stopping him mid-sentence. "A *wonderful* mom?"

"That's what I said."

"You didn't know me as a mother," she argued. "You didn't know my husband, my kids. You can't make an assumption like that."

He squared his jaw, pulling himself up to his full six foot two. "It's not an assumption, Dani. I know *you.* A title like wife and mother doesn't change that."

"Please. You met me, what? A few times over a course of a single week when I was eight and you were ten? That was a lifetime ago."

"In years, maybe. But I don't think the core of who you are has changed. Not even a little," he said.

"The core?"

Crossing his arms in front of his chest, he met her eyes, the irritation she knew they held showing no effect on him. "You were kind, gentle, and generous in nature."

"Twenty-seven years changes people, Caleb."

"Some, maybe. But not you."

"You can't know that," she said, flustered.

"I can, and I do. Which is why I stand by my earlier assessment about your laugh. You were recalling a special memory—the way a wonderful mom would."

This time her laugh held no sign of humor, lightness, or anything resembling joy. "*Wonderful* moms don't long for time away from their kids! *Wonderful* moms aren't surprised when they look out their window and see something their child told them about six months earlier yet didn't truly absorb in the moment because they were too preoccupied with I don't even know what!"

Her voice broke, but she forced herself to go on, her throat growing rawer and rawer by the second. "*Wonderful* moms get down on the floor with their sons and happily play cars and trucks for hours! *Wonderful* moms go to the park with their children and their husband and their mother instead of staying home by themselves! *Wonderful* moms are *with* their children when they need her most!"

"Enjoying a book and a little time for yourself doesn't mean you weren't a wonderful mom," Caleb countered. "It means you needed a recharge. That's it. *Everyone* does at some point. As for what happened to them? You didn't cause it . . . It didn't happen as some sort of punishment for you . . . It just happened. And it's horrible, and it's heartbreaking, and you've got a long road ahead of you, but you'll get there. In time."

"There's nowhere to get," she rasped. "Nowhere I want to be other than *with* them."

"One day, when the time is right, you will be. But for now, you're here."

She sagged back against the door, twisting her hands at her

sides. "I miss them so much," she whispered. "It's like there's this hole inside of me that just keeps getting bigger and bigger."

"And it will, for a while. Until you start filling it back in with your happiest memories and all of the new moments and joys still to come."

"New joys?" she echoed. "There won't *ever* be new joys!"

He led her gaze down to her abdomen, held it there a moment, and then brought it back to his own with a dramatic cough and a follow-up smile. "I'm pretty sure that's not true."

Turning, she grabbed the handle and gave it a fast tug, the answering whoosh of the door cut short by his hand.

"Okay . . . Okay . . . I won't push. But you're still here, on this earth. Remember that." He let go of the door's edge. "Joy is *everywhere*, Dani. Sometimes it finds you just like news of that baby coming did. And sometimes you go out and find it all on your own, just like you did today at the ice-cream place when—"

"I didn't do that," she argued. "I didn't find anything even close to joy."

Returning his cowboy hat to its forward position, he held her gaze for several long beats and then turned and walked away.

Chapter 19

It was just shy of eleven o'clock the next morning when she heard the shout, the fear, if not the reason for it, reaching through the screen and yanking her to her feet. Dropping her pen onto the lone paragraph she'd written thus far, Dani ran across the kitchen, through the front door, and down the steps, her ears straining for anything that could pinpoint the direction she should go.

A second, louder shout sent her racing across the driveway into the barn. Her pounding footsteps and minor stumble against the open door brought the sound of running feet in her direction.

"Tell me you found her . . ." Caleb said, bending at the waist, his hands on his thighs as he worked to catch his breath.

"Found who?"

"Nettie!"

Dani clapped her hands to her mouth as the sheer terror she saw resurrecting itself in Caleb's eyes became hers. "She's missing?"

"She was right here"—he jammed his finger toward the empty baby bottle standing upright on the hay-strewn floor—"five minutes ago! And now she's gone!"

"Maybe she just went inside. With Lydia."

"Lydia is at a doctor's appointment," he said, glancing inside one stall and then another, his mouth growing tighter each time.

Spreading her hands wide, Dani closed the gap between them with four . . . five . . . six steps. "Hold still a second. Think. Maybe she walked into the field to see Elijah."

"Elijah is with Lydia." Caleb fast-stepped his way past the remaining few stalls and then whirled back to Dani, his eyes wide, his hands linked behind his cowboy hat. "I was supposed to be watching her, and I was! I let her give the calf his last few slurps from the bottle while I mucked out one of the stalls. That's it!"

She took a moment to think, to process, a strange yet familiar calm settling in around her. "Okay. How long has it been?"

"Since I last saw her? Five minutes," he said again, his eyes darting around the barn as if seeing it for the first time. "Tops! And I've been looking for her for four of those five!"

"Was anyone else in here with the two of you?"

Dropping his arms back to his sides, he made a mad dash to the opposite side of the barn, where various implements hung from hooks mounted into the walls. "No. It was just us. The boys are at school, Elijah and Lydia aren't due back for another hour, at the very least, and there's no way anyone else came into this barn without me knowing."

"Okay, so let's think this through."

"Where did she go?" he yelled. "*Where?* I mean, one minute we're feeding the calf and she's telling me all about Wooly and how she thinks maybe he's getting better and . . . Where. Is. She?"

She held up her hand. "Who's Wooly?"

"One of the sheep. He's a little slow, borderline blind, and maybe even a wee bit hard of hearing, too, but the kids love him and have managed to talk Elijah into not—"

"Is he with the rest of them?"

"He, who? You mean Wooly?" At her nod, he gestured in the general direction of the driveway. "Yeah, he's with the others."

Beckoning for Caleb to follow, Dani led the way around the satiated calf, through the open barn door, onto the dirt driveway, and . . . "Voilà! Your niece."

Caleb staggered back a step, cupping his hand over his mouth.

"She's four," Dani said by way of explanation. "That makes her pretty easy to figure out as long as you're paying attention to all the clues."

His eyes drifted from Nettie to Dani and back again before he took off in a sprint much to the wide-eyed surprise of his target. "Nettie!" He dropped down to the little girl's eye level and gathered her hands inside his own. "I've been looking all over for you! Why didn't you come when I called you?"

"Hi, Dani!" The little girl flashed a huge smile at Dani and then pointed at the slow-moving sheep on the other side of the split-rail fence. "I pretended I couldn't hear like Wooly."

"Nettie, you can't do that! You scared me; I thought—" At Dani's hand on his arm, he stopped, caught the subtle yet rapid shake of her head, and drew in a long, slow breath instead. "Next time you want to come out here to check on Wooly, just tell me, okay? That way I can come see him, too, instead of running around the barn looking for you."

"Yah." Then, pointing into the sheep pen, Nettie looked up at Dani. "That's Wooly. He's my friend."

She squatted down beside the little girl and looked through the opening between the fence rails. "He looks like a nice friend."

"He is!"

"I'm glad." For a few more moments, she watched the animal move across the pen, one blade of grass at a time, and then turned the little girl so they faced each other. "It's important to let your uncle know where you're going, okay? Because when your mamm and dat are not here, he needs to know."

The kapped head bobbed in a nod that lasted all of about a second before the cornflower-blue eyes that had dropped to the ground in shame were back on Dani's. "I holded Little Guy's bottle and he drank it all up!"

"That's very good."

Nettie's answering smile dimmed almost the second it appeared on her round face. "But I didn't say goodbye!" With a fast wave to Wooly, the little girl took a step or two toward the barn, stopped, and turned back to her uncle. "Can we go see Little Guy?"

"Yes. We can." When she resumed her trek to the barn, Caleb held out his hand and helped Dani back onto her feet. "Thank you. For coming when you heard my shouts, for having the presence of mind to stop and think, and for keeping me from losing my mind completely. I know it couldn't have been a pretty sight in there."

Her eyes followed Nettie back to the barn. "You're fine. Really. It's par for the course with that age group. They wander."

"But you were so calm, so cool headed, and I was"—he snorted a laugh—"*not.*"

"Practice, I guess," she mumbled as she branched off toward the grossdawdy house. "Anyway, I'm going to head back inside and—"

He stepped forward, back into her eyesight, and swept his hand toward the barn. "Could I ask you a favor? It'll only take a few minutes—ten, fifteen, tops."

Wary, she stopped. "What kind of favor?"

"I . . ." He looked from the barn, to the house, to his truck, his subsequent swallow slow and . . . *nervous? Un-*

sure? "Yeah, I left something at my dat's farm that I really need. Something I want to show the boys when they get home from school. So I was wondering, if you don't mind, maybe you could look after Nettie while I run over there?"

She glanced down at her watch and then back up at Caleb. "The boys aren't due home for almost three hours. Won't Lydia be home before then?"

Again, his eyes drifted past hers, his Adam's apple bobbing with yet another swallow. "I think so, but I can't say for sure. They hired a driver to take them."

"Okay, so why don't you just take Nettie with you? I'm sure she'd love to see her grandparents."

He looked toward the barn again. "I could. But you saw her just now—she's in her animal zone. Pulling her away from that for what will be a seconds-long stop seems kind of unfair, you know?"

She took a step backward, her thoughts narrowing in on the letter she still had to write. The single paragraph she'd managed to pen so far needed a few tweaks, if not a complete redo.

"It would be a huge help," he continued, pulling her back to the present. "And I'm quite sure it would make Nettie's day."

"Why? She barely knows me. It seems like she'd much rather tag along with you than—"

"She wouldn't. Watch." Lifting his chin, he called out so his voice would be heard inside the barn, "Nettie? Can you come out here a minute?"

Dani stepped forward. "What are you—"

He silenced the rest of her question with his index finger. "Nettie?"

Seconds later, the Amish child came running out to her uncle. "I am here," she said, hopping from bare foot to bare foot.

"I see that. Thank you." Dropping down to Nettie's eye

level, he nudged his chin at Dani. "I have to run down the street real quick to get something I forgot. Would you rather get stuck in the car or would you rather stay here with Little Guy, and Wooly, and Dani?"

"Caleb, if you word it that way she's—"

Nettie ran to Dani, took her hand, and tugged her toward the barn. "Come see Little Guy. He is a very nice calf."

"I've met your calf," she said, glaring at Caleb. "If you go with your uncle you can see—"

"Oh. Hey. Did you check on Sunshine and her babies yet today?" Caleb motioned first toward the barn and then at Dani. "One of the barn cats had a litter of kittens sometime over the past few days. Luke and I found them last night as we were closing things up for the night."

Nettie's eyes widened with her smile. "Yah! She had six kittens." Releasing her hold on Dani's hand, she held up two fingers. "This many kittens have black spots on their tummies! And *this many*"—she bent one finger back down and then pointed at her nose—"have a spot *here*. And three have stripes!"

"They're really cute," Caleb chimed in. "They're so little you can't really tell where their ears and eyes are. But that'll change soon, right, kiddo?"

"Yah!" Nettie returned her counting hand to Dani's and tugged again. "Come see, Dani! Come see!"

Caleb rocked back on the heels of his boots and grinned. "So then it's settled. You two go look in on the kittens and I'll be back in a few minutes. You won't even notice I'm gone."

"Come, Dani! Maybe their eyes will be open!"

"Probably not yet, kiddo, but you never know. And remember, you and the boys only named four of the kittens. That means two don't have names yet. Maybe Dani will have a good idea for one, or both."

She tried to meet his gaze, to let him know—albeit silently—she wasn't pleased with the latest turn of events, but to no avail. Instead, he smiled at Nettie, gestured them toward the barn with a swoop of his thick hand, and then strode toward his truck with nary so much as a glance back at Dani.

Seconds later, as his engine purred to a start, he tapped his hand against the exterior panel of the driver's side door and grinned. "Be back in a couple of seconds."

Lifting her wristwatch into the swath of sunlight coming in from the barn door behind them, she bit down on her lower lip in an attempt to stifle her groan. Somehow *a couple of seconds* had become five minutes . . . Ten minutes . . . And now fifteen minutes. But still, there was no sign of Caleb or his truck.

"Do you want to name *that* one"—Nettie pointed from a white and black fist-sized mound of fur to an even smaller mound of tiger-striped fur—"or *that* one?"

She glanced back at the still-empty driveway and listened closely. No gravel against tires, no slam of a car door, no tune being whistled, no *I'm here* filtering its way toward the hay-strewn corner of the Schlabachs' barn now doing double duty as a temporary feline maternity ward.

"Dani?"

"I'm here, sweetie." Giving in to the frustrated sigh that was no more Nettie's fault than her own, Dani lowered herself onto the ground beside her friend's daughter and really took a moment to soak up the mamma cat and her six sleeping newborns. "They sure are little, aren't they?"

"Yah! They are *this* big." Nettie cupped her little hand in the space between them. "Luke says they are only a little bigger than the size of Little Guy's hoof."

"So that's the calf's official name? Little Guy?"

"Yah!"

Nodding, Dani shifted to the left to afford a more unobstructed view of the barn's newest additions. "Which kitten did you get to name?" she asked.

Nettie scooted up onto her knees and inserted her finger between the railing's first and second slats to indicate the little mound closest to the mother cat. Like one of the two she'd offered to Dani to name, this one was white with a few large, almost cow-like black spots visible on his exposed side. "I call him Spots. Because he has spots."

"I see that."

"And that one, he is Silly Nose. Mark named him that." Nettie's face grew serious. "I don't think he has a silly nose. It is just hard to see because it is little."

Not wanting to disparage the six-year-old's choice in names, she verbally nudged the little girl's attention onto the next kitten. "And who is this one?" she asked.

Nettie scooted forward until her chin was resting on the wooden rail. "That one is Mr. Paws. Luke picked that name."

"That's a cute name."

"Yah. And that"—Nettie pointed to the next kitten—"is Bender. David named that kitten."

"So we have Spots, Silly Nose, Mr. Paws, and Bender. Very nice," she mused. "Good solid names for"—she stopped, looked over at Nettie—"what is the mamma cat's name again?"

"Sunshine!"

"That's a pretty name."

"She likes to sit in the sunshine," Nettie said. "When I want to play with her and I cannot find her, I look for the sunshine and there she is!"

Dani looked back at the feline now busily licking her babies, the fingers of sunlight through the open barn door stopping well shy of their makeshift bed. If the animal noticed, though, she showed no indication, her focus, her every ounce of energy, directed toward her young.

"Which one, Dani?"

Shaking away her gathering gloom, she turned back to Nettie. "Which one, what?" she echoed.

"Which kitten do you want to name?"

She looked again at the two nameless babies and, after careful consideration, pointed to the tiger-striped member of the crew. "How about we call that one Smokey? Or maybe Shadow? Or Fluffy? Or—Wait! I know; we could call it Button!"

"Button?"

"Because it's cute as a button cuddled up to its mamma like that."

Nettie tilted her head left, then right, clearly considering the name. Then, poking her head through the slat, she looked down at the kitten in question, his tiny striped head now the focus of his mamma's tongue. "Do you want to be Button?"

After a second, maybe two, Nettie began to nod. Hard. "I think that kitten would like to be called Button."

"Do you think maybe we should check with Sunshine first? Since it is her kitten?" Dani asked.

"Yah! I will ask!" Nettie poked her head through the opening again. "Sunshine? That kitty you are licking"— Sunshine paused in her licking to look up at the little girl and blink—"is Button, okay?"

Sunshine blinked again and went right back to licking the kitten in question, much to Nettie's clap of delight. "Sunshine likes it, Dani! She really, really does!"

Dani answered Nettie's near face-splitting smile with a tiny one of her own and then pointed the little girl's focus back to the last unnamed kitten, its position next to Button making it a veritable shoo-in for the next lick bath. "Now what about that little one there? The one that looks a lot like Spots? That one needs to have a name, too, right?"

"But Rose went to be with God." The little girl's smile dis-

appeared as she deflated back down to the floor, her seemingly boundless energy gone in an instant. "She cannot name
her kitten."

"Oh, sweetie, I'm sorry. I . . ." Recovering her gaze from
its immediate nose dive, Dani looked up to find Nettie closing the gap between them with one big scoot. Less than a second later, the child's head was nestling against Dani's arm.

"I miss Rose. She meeted Wooly, but she did not meet Sunshine or Poppa Pig." Nettie slanted her chin to see the kittens
again. "I think she would like Sunshine and Poppa Pig. I
think she would like Spots, and Silly Nose, and Mr. Paws,
and Bender, and Button, too. They are very nice. They are my
friends. They would like to be friends with Rose, too."

Then, her tiny voice trembling, the child abandoned her
view of the kittens in favor of Dani. "I like to make Rose
smile and laugh with my jumps. I like to wave my hand at
Rose when she eats. I like to walk on my toes very quiet
when Mamm says she is sleeping. I like to sit with Rose right
here"—she pointed at her dress-draped lap—"when Mamm
sits next to me. I like to take walks with Mamm and Rose.
They make Mamm happy. Now Mamm does not smile when
we walk. She makes"—Nettie lifted her finger to Dani's
cheek—"wet like that, too."

Oh how she wanted to run, to put as much distance between herself and the woebegone face peering up at her as if
she could provide some sort of answer, some sort of fix for
that which had neither. Instead, she swiped the tears from her
cheeks and quietly pulled the four-year-old onto her lap.

"I want Rose to come back," Nettie said, her bottom lip
puckering with ready tears of her own. "But Luke says she
cannot. Not ever."

Dani glanced back at the door, her heart pounding.

*Please, Caleb, please . . . Please come back . . . It's been
too long . . . I can't do this . . . I—*

A flutter of activity in her lap became a hug as Nettie buried her face against Dani and began to cry—a sound so raw, so all-encompassing, it took a moment to find any words, let alone the right words.

"Once you give someone your heart in love, they will never be far away."

Squeezing her eyes closed, she let the words, and the voice that delivered them in her thoughts, travel her back to a moment she hadn't visited in years. There, she could feel her mother's hand rubbing circles against her back. There, she could hear the soft, gentle sounds of reassurance and love. And there, the emptiness inside her chest felt a little less empty.

It was a nice place to be if even for a little while—a place she needed, a place Nettie needed, too.

Dani looked down at the little girl through parted lashes and began to rub her back, around and around and around. "Shhh . . . Shhh . . . It's okay, Nettie," she said against the little girl's ear. "I'm here. I'm here."

Seconds turned to minutes as she held the child close, letting her know, again and again, that she was there, and that it was okay to cry just as Dani's mother had done for Dani so long ago.

When the little girl's tears finally subsided, Dani loosened their embrace just enough to afford a view of Nettie's face. "Do you know what *my* mamm told me when my grandma—*my grossmudder*—died?" she asked, lacing her fingers behind Nettie. "When I wasn't much older than you are now?"

Nettie's red-rimmed eyes widened. "Were you sad? Like me?"

"Very much."

Shame dove the child's gaze down to Dani's lap. "Did you cry and cry like me?"

"I sure did," she said. "Because I loved my grossmudder very much. But when I stopped crying, my mom—*my mamm*—told me something very special."

"What?"

"She told me that once you give someone a piece of your heart, it is theirs forever—even when you cannot see them. Like . . ." She trailed off, searching for the best way to help a four-year-old understand something so big. But just as she was fearing she couldn't, the words just seemed to appear on her tongue. "Like right now. Your mamm is not here in the barn with us, right?"

Nettie shook her head.

"Okay . . . But you still love her and she still loves you, right?"

"Yah!"

"Tell me about her."

"About Mamm?"

"Yes."

"Mamm bakes yummy bread that I can eat!"

"What else?"

"She plants pretty flowers!"

"What else?"

"She cleans my clothes!"

"Hmmm . . ." She weighed the direction the answers had taken and then subtly reclaimed the wheel. "Tell me something she does that makes you feel all happy inside."

"She kisses me right here"—Nettie pointed at her forehead, a smile stretching her cupid bow mouth wide—"before I go to sleep."

Bingo . . .

"Is that why you smiled just now? Because it made you happy *to think* about her doing that to you?"

"Yah!"

Halfway there . . .

Tipping forward, she rested her forehead against Nettie's. "Now tell me some things about Rose that made you happy inside."

"The way she kicked and kicked her feet when I would make her smile!"

"That's a good one. Anything else?"

"When I would hold her on my lap, she would open her eyes real big at me!"

"Anything else?"

"When she sleeped, she'd do this"—Nettie closed her eyes and puckered her lips—"lots of times. Sometimes I would sit on the floor next to her cradle and try to make the same face. *See?*" Again, she puckered and released her lips. "It was very cute."

"It makes you happy inside to remember those things about her, doesn't it?" she asked, sitting back.

"Yah!"

"Then *that's* what you do when you miss her, sweetie . . . You remember those moments, those things about her that made you feel happy inside. Because then she'll still be with you right *here*"—she moved the tip of her finger from the little girl's forehead to her chest—"and right *here*. Always."

Rocketing up onto her knees, Nettie wrapped her arms around Dani, her earlier tears replaced by the kind of smile that reached far beyond just the confines of her small mouth. "Can you help me name Rose's kitty before you go?"

"Before I go?" she echoed. "I'm not going anywhere. Not until your uncle gets back, anyway."

Nettie clapped a hand over her mouth in a failed attempt to hide a giggle. When she nodded at something beyond Dani's shoulder, Dani turned to find Caleb standing to the left of the stable's main aisle. "I didn't hear your truck." She scooted Nettie off her lap and then pushed herself up off the ground, her gaze flitting between the driveway and the man looking everywhere but back at Dani. "Caleb? Is something wrong?"

"Nope. Truck's in the same place it usually is."

"Did something come up at your parents' place?"

"Nope. All good."

She bent her wrist up to indicate her wristwatch. "You were gone for almost a half hour."

"Was it that long?" he asked. "Wow. Sorry. I got a call from a coworker just as I was pulling up to my parents' farm and"—he slid his palm down his face—"I don't know, I . . . I guess I lost track of time."

Crossing to the stall at Dani's back, he reached down, scooped his niece off the ground, and swept his hand in the direction of Sunshine and her babies. "So, how are the wee ones doing today?"

"Dani named one!" Nettie declared, her tone one of triumph. "*That one*," she added, pointing down at the gray-and-black-striped mound rising and falling with each slumbered breath. "The one with stripes!"

"Did she name it *Sleepy*?" he asked.

"No . . ."

"Did she name it *Kitten*?"

Nettie's nose scrunched tight. "No . . ."

"*Cat?*"

"No . . ."

"Then, if she didn't use any of those names, what is its name?" he asked, peeking back at Dani with a ready grin and a wink. "Because those are pretty solid names if you ask me."

"She named it *Button*!"

"Button, eh?" He took in the kitten for a moment, slanting his head from left to right as he did. "Button . . . I like it."

"Sunshine likes it, too!"

Caleb's laughter echoed around the large barn. "Well, if Sunshine likes it, that's good enough for me!" He planted a kiss on Nettie's cheek and then looked back down at the cat and her kittens again. "And Rose's kitten? Does it have a name yet?"

Nettie shook her head.

"Can I name it then?"

Nettie looked from Caleb to Dani and, finally, back to the nameless mound of white and black fur. "What do you want to name that kitten?"

"Always."

Dani's quiet gasp stole Nettie's attention from the task at hand, but only for as long as it took Caleb to continue, his gaze focused on the cat. "Because, like Dani just said, that's how long Rose will be with us in our hearts."

Chapter 20

She waited until she was sure the tiny white kapp and the head it was covering were out of hearing range and then whirled around, hands on hips. "You had no right," Dani hissed. "No right at all."

"What are you talking about?"

"Don't play dumb. You were in that barn long before Nettie or I knew you were there. Which means you were listening to our conversation—our *private* conversation."

His cheeks flamed crimson. "Dani, I didn't—"

She shot up her hand. "Please. Save it. I'm not an idiot." Propelled by her growing anger, she took a few steps toward the sheep pen, stopped, and then stalked back to Caleb. "I was talking to Nettie, not you."

"I know that. And I'm sorry." Craning his head to her left, he found and held a smile for as long as it took to placate his curious niece, and then lowered his voice to a level only Dani could hear. "I didn't set out to listen; I really didn't. I just got out of my truck, looked for you guys outside, and then stuck my head in the barn to see if you were still inside. I was just about to call out when I heard Nettie crying. When I walked all the way in, you were rocking her in your lap and talking her through what was clearly a difficult moment. I didn't want to ruin it by taking a chance she'd hear me leaving or something."

"I see. So you just stood there and listened, instead?" she said, her voice rising.

"Yes, I just stood there. But I didn't *listen*. I *heard*. Big difference if you think about it." He abandoned eye contact just long enough to check on his niece again. "But if it upset you, I'm sorry. It wasn't my intention. I was just so grateful you were able to connect with Nettie like that—to give her something so good, *so true*, to hang on to."

Again, he looked toward the sheep pen and the little girl happily talking away to the partially blind and deaf sheep on the other side. "You forget sometimes that kids that age feel grief, too. I mean, yeah, you know they're thrown in the moment, but then you see them doing stuff *like that*"—he nudged his chin forward—"and you think they're doing okay. So you turn your attention elsewhere . . . But clearly, Nettie isn't okay."

"I wouldn't say she's *not* okay." Her anger decreasing, Dani began to walk, Caleb's footsteps quickly falling in line with her own. "I'd say it creeps up on her sometimes, and she doesn't want to upset Lydia by talking about it, or asking about it, or—in today's case—crying about it. Even at just four years old, she's empathetic enough not to want to upset her mother any further."

He slowed their pace in an obvious effort to buy them more time to talk. "I ask Nettie, every time I see her, how she's doing and if there's anything she wants to talk about, but I don't like to get too specific as to what I'm asking about in the event my questions *put* the pain there."

"The pain is already there," Dani said. "In this case, it just bubbled up to a point where she couldn't keep it inside anymore."

"I'm glad you were there when it happened."

Shrugging, she toed at a random pebble, watched it roll back and forward, back and forward . . . "I won't always be."

"Why?" he asked, shifting his weight across his boot-clad feet. "You're not thinking about leaving, are you?"

"Lydia invited me for a few days, Caleb. I've been here almost six weeks now."

"Lydia doesn't care."

"Says you."

"Says the fact she's not pushing you toward your car." He looked again at Nettie, his feet remaining planted in place. "I like what you said to her today. About memories keeping Rose close. It's like you gave her a little bit of control over a situation where she had none."

"If that makes her *feel* as if she has some control, I'm glad."

"Wait a minute. Are you saying you don't believe what you just told her in the barn?"

"I think it made her feel better. In that singular moment. That's the beauty of being a child. They're easily distractible, easy to influence."

"Influence?"

"Into viewing something in a way they wouldn't have otherwise. And in that moment, that's what she needed from me so she could find her way out of a hole that had gotten far too big for someone so small."

"Moments can add up, Dani. If you let them."

She stared at him, her mouth running dry. "What are you talking about?"

"At the ice-cream place," he said by way of explanation. "Your smile. When you were telling me that story about your son and the stray cat. Your whole face lit up. It's why I said what I said about—"

The sound of a car door closing somewhere just beyond the sheep pen stole their collective attention and sent it skittering toward the road in time to see a silver minivan drive off in the direction of town. Seconds later, Elijah and Lydia came into view, sending Nettie in a run to greet them.

The joy in the little girl's squeals as she spread her arms wide for her parents was unmistakable. So, too, was the love Elijah had for his daughter as he crouched down to collect her sweet hug. But Lydia, Dani noticed, lagged behind, her milky skin nearly ashen, her gait one of . . . *dread?*

"Oh no," Caleb said beneath his breath.

"What?"

"I don't think it went well."

Confused, she looked from Caleb to Lydia and back again. "You don't think *what* went well?"

"The doctor's appointment." Caleb cupped his mouth for a second, maybe two, and then let his hand drift back down to his side. "Lydia was hoping that what he said when Rose was born wasn't set in stone. But that look on her face right now"—he shook his head—"says otherwise."

Again, she let her eyes drift toward the Amish couple and their daughter, Elijah's smile present but muted while Lydia's struggled to appear at all. "What did he say?"

Caleb started to speak, stopped, and then stepped forward, tipping his cowboy hat forward on his brow. "I think I should probably let Lydia fill you in on that. Besides, I think it's safe to say—looking at her—that she could probably use a friend right about now."

"What about Nettie?" she asked as the child wrapped her arms around her mother's legs. "She's had enough sadness for one day."

"Agreed. That's why I'm going to see what I can do about rustling up some outdoor chores the two of us can help Elijah with before the boys get home from school. That'll give you and Lydia a little privacy."

Nettie held on for what seemed like forever and then, after a slew of uncertain glances up at her mamm, stepped back, her smile wilting.

"I don't know, Caleb. Your sister might just want some time alone . . ." she mumbled.

And just like that, Lydia swung her attention off the barn, the ground, the sky—basically everything and anything she could find to throw Nettie off the scent—and fixed it, instead, on Dani, her answering sag of relief impossible to miss.

"No," Caleb said, swallowing. "She needs a friend, Dani—she needs you." Powered by an audible inhale, he strode over to Elijah and Nettie, said something to both of them she was too far away to hear, squeezed his sister's shoulder, and then, with a pointed nod in Dani's direction, disappeared into the barn.

Dani, in turn, pulled in her own deep breath, steadied the sudden tremble in her hands, and inched her way toward the woman now inching her way toward Dani. Even from their rapidly decreasing proximity to each other, it was easy to see Lydia was troubled. It was there in her weighted gait. It was there in the absence of her warm smile. It was there in the repeated wiping of her slender hands down the sides of her dress. It was there in the dodging of eye contact.

"Good afternoon, Danielle," Lydia said, the upbeat note to her voice forced at best. "It is good to see you outside enjoying the sunshine."

Dani tilted her chin toward the sky, the answering warmth on her face doing little to chase the pervasive chill from her being. "Nettie introduced me to the new kittens in the barn."

Lydia's fingers whitened against the soft pink of her lips. "Oh, Danielle. I am sorry she was a bother. I have told the children you are to have your time alone."

"No . . . Please . . ." She decreased the gap between them to a single arm's length and rested what she hoped was a reassuring hand atop her friend's. "Nettie did not seek me out. I-I . . . sought her out."

It wasn't the truth, exactly, but it was clear, even without verbal confirmation, that something was weighing heavily on Lydia's heart. Hearing that Nettie had frightened Caleb by disappearing out to the sheep's pen without his knowledge was an added weight she didn't need.

"That is good to hear," Lydia said, sagging.

It was on the tip of Dani's tongue to say something about the sweet names the children had come up with for the newborn kittens, but when Lydia's sag became a wobble she lurched forward with a steadying arm, instead. "Whoa there . . . Let's get you inside where you can sit. Then, when you are settled, I will go out to the barn and get Elijah."

"Please do not get Elijah," Lydia said, waving at Dani's words. "I have taken enough of his time from his chores."

Slowly, Dani guided her friend toward the main house, the woman clearly fighting back tears with each and every step. "I'm sure Elijah's chores can wait. And if they can't, Caleb is here. He'll do them."

"There is nothing for Elijah to do or say that he has not already done or said. The doctor's words are God's will. I must learn to accept them."

"Are . . . Are you okay?" she asked, on the heels of a hard swallow. "Are you sick?"

"No, I am not sick in the way that you mean." At the base of the porch steps, Lydia glanced up at the sky and then over her shoulder toward the road. "The boys will return from school soon. Perhaps they will stop in the barn to see the calf before they come into the house. That will give me time to be Mamm again."

"To be Mamm?" she echoed.

"Yah. One who listens when they speak. One who does not wipe tears she does not want them"—Lydia's voice faltered with a stifled sob—"to see."

Tightening her hold on Lydia's waist, Dani changed direction toward the grossdawdy house. "Why don't we sit inside here for a little while, instead?"

"I do not want to be a bother."

"*A bother?* After everything you've done for me since I came? Please." She led the way inside and over to the first of the two tableside benches in the kitchen. With Lydia settled, Dani crossed to the cabinet for a glass, filled it with ice water, and carried it back to the table. "Here. Drink this."

Lydia took one sip, then another, her gaze meeting and then abandoning Dani's in favor of the window and a view Dani doubted she saw.

Lowering herself onto the bench opposite Lydia's, Dani leaned forward against the edge of the table, her breath shallow. "Lydia, I-I'm so sorry about your baby. I . . . I didn't know."

Lydia's answering nod was labored. "Caleb told you?"

"I saw the grave the other night when I was out walking. Caleb simply confirmed what I feared."

"I am sorry I did not send a Christmas letter this year." Lydia pulled the glass against her chest and closed her eyes for just a moment, her voice shaking along with her hand. "I could not quiet my heart enough to write one."

She reached across the table for Lydia's free hand. "Oh, Lydia . . ."

"I miss her so much it is hard to breathe."

"I know."

"I want to think it didn't happen, that it is all just a bad dream. But it isn't—it's . . . real."

"I know that, too."

"I know that it was God's will and I must accept that but—"

"Rose was your daughter, Lydia. Your baby. There is no accepting a loss like that."

Lydia's eyes widened. "But I must. *You* must. It is God's will for me—*for you*—to be here."

"I get why *you're* still here. That's clear," she murmured, retrieving her hand. "You are a wonderful mother. Luke, and David, and Mark, and Nettie, and any others you and Elijah have in the future need you. But—"

Lydia peered down into her cup, her shoulders, her lips, her very being, sagging. "There will be no others."

"I'm not saying *now*, Lydia. I just mean later, when you're ready." She traced her finger along a knot in the table's surface, her throat growing tight. "I've seen you with them these past few weeks. You are everything I should have been and wasn't."

Curiosity lifted Lydia's gaze to Dani's. "I don't understand. What have you not been?"

"An incredible mother."

"I do not believe that, Danielle. You have written me so many beautiful Christmas letters over the years and—"

Her answering laugh held no shred of humor. "Ahhhh, yes . . . My prowess with pen and paper . . . I looked to that as proof of my mothering ability, as well. But I was wrong. One only has to spend a day watching you to know that."

"Watching me?" Lydia echoed, her brow furrowed. "I don't understand."

She held up her hands. "And you don't need to. Especially not today. Let's just keep this about you and why you're upset, okay?"

Lydia looked as if she was about to protest but let it go. Instead, she traveled her gaze back to the window, her voice growing faint, almost far away. "I cannot bear Elijah any more children."

Gasping, Dani drew back so fast the bench wobbled beneath her. "What? Why? Are you sure?"

"Yah. The doctor said it is so. There were complications with Rose's birth."

"Did you *want* to have more children?" she asked.

"Yah."

Again, she reached across the table for Lydia's hand and held it tight. "Oh, Lydia. I'm so sorry."

"It is God's will."

"You say that without any shred of anger . . ."

"To anger is to question. It is not for me to question God's wisdom."

She bit down on the answer she couldn't give, not to Lydia, not now. Instead, she pulled in a breath, held it, and then released it, slowly. "Rose was your child, Lydia. You're

entitled to feel everything you want to feel right now—
sadness *and* anger. It's . . . *normal.*"

Lydia's head bobbed with her answering nod—a nod that
seemed far more rote than it did sincere. "That is what Miss
Lottie says."

"The Englisher you speak to?"

"Yah. Caleb has told you about Miss Lottie?"

"Only that she lives somewhere near here and . . ." Trailing off, Dani searched for a way to frame the rest of her answer without leading Lydia to believe Caleb had betrayed
some sort of confidence. Before she could, though, Lydia
spoke.

"Miss Lottie lives down the road. Just beyond the second
bend. In the winter, when it is cold, there is a fire in the fire-
place. When it is warm and sunny, there is lemonade and
cookies on her front porch. But always, there is one who will
listen and offer wisdom. That is why the walk *to* Miss Lottie's home is always long and the walk *from* her home is always much shorter."

"You take different ways?" Dani prodded.

"No, I take the same way. But it is how I feel inside that
makes it different."

"Meaning?"

"When Caleb first brought me to Miss Lottie, I could not
stop picturing that day. I could not stop being angry with myself."

"Angry with yourself?" she echoed. "For what?"

Setting her glass on the table, Lydia rubbed at her face, her
every movement heavy, taxing. "Perhaps, if I had looked in
Rose's cradle sooner, if I noticed something was not right before I put her down to nap, if I—"

"What happened to your baby had nothing to do with
you." She squeezed Lydia's hand until she had her friend's
eyes and attention. "Nothing."

"Yah. That is what the doctor said. But how can he be so sure? How can you be so sure? How can Miss Lottie be so sure?"

"Because crib death just happens. They don't know why, but it just does."

"But—"

"There are no buts, Lydia. There was nothing you could've done. Nothing."

Lydia's answering nod was so labored, so pained, it took every ounce of restraint Dani could muster not to scream at the injustice of it all.

"You, Lydia Schlabach, are the most wonderful parent I have ever seen," she said, resting her forehead against her friend's. "The kind of parent every kid should be allowed to have in their corner."

"I miss her so deeply, Danielle."

"I know you do, Lydia."

"Sometimes," she whispered, "when I am sitting in the rocking chair, I can still feel her in my arms. But when I look, she is not there."

Releasing Lydia's hand, she pushed back against the table, the legs of the bench scraping against the simple wooden floor. "Would you like something to eat? A cookie? A piece of bread? A—"

"That is why I have stopped looking. Have you?"

"I have leftover chicken from last night," Dani said, throwing her leg over the bench and rising. "And some turkey from the night before."

"I give you those things so you will eat them, not save them."

"I eat what I—"

"In the mornings when I would wake, I would peek over the edge of Rose's cradle and she would stop wiggling to look back at me." A slow smile made its way from one side of

Lydia's mouth to the other. "When I would greet her to a new day, she would start to wiggle again. That last morning, when I peeked in, she smiled at me."

Dani crossed to the refrigerator and looked inside, the plates of food and pitchers of barely drunk milk blurring in front of her as Lydia continued. "It was a cold morning. But when she smiled at me like she did, it was not cold any longer."

Something about the upward lilt of Lydia's voice had Dani glancing back at the table, the sadness that had weighed her friend down just moments earlier suddenly absent. "When I think of her smile instead of her loss it is easier to wake to a new day."

"That makes it easier for you?" she said, letting the door close on the food she had no appetite to eat.

"Yah." Lydia turned her head back toward the window. "I am grateful to Miss Lottie for that."

"I don't understand . . ."

Lydia's eyes returned to Dani's. "In the beginning, when I thought of Rose, I could remember only that day. The way she looked. The way I scooped her from her cradle. The sound of my own screams as I carried her out to Elijah and Caleb. The way Caleb tried to help. I would see and hear those things every night when I would lay my head on the pillow. I would see and hear those things each morning when I would open my eyes to a new day. And I would see and hear those things every time one of the children would mention Rose. I could not stop it from happening.

"That is when Caleb took me to see Miss Lottie. At first, I did not want to go. I did not want to share my sorrow with anyone. But now, I am glad. Because now when I think of Rose most days, it is of Rose—her sweet sounds, her sweet smell, her wiggles, and the smile she gave me that last morning instead of just my screams."

Dani pulled a face. "Weren't you just there? The other day? The day Caleb and I took Nettie for ice cream?"

"Yah." Shame lowered Lydia's gaze to her lap but only for a moment. "That was a day I did not let Rose in as I should."

"Missing your child doesn't mean you didn't let her in," Dani argued.

"No, but it means I did not let her in as she would want to be let in."

Chapter 21

Dani rounded the second bend and slowed to a stop, the crunch of fine gravel beneath her shoes growing silent. At first glance, the house wasn't much different than the one before it or, looking ahead, the one after it, either. Simple at its core, the house was little more than a freshly painted white square with a few windows in front, a few windows on the side, and a chimney rising from the roof.

Not far from the side windows was a small garden boasting an array of spring flowers in yellows, pinks, and blues. Nestled among them was a small eastward-facing wooden bench and a birdbath complete with what appeared to be a bird—maybe two—splashing away in the early afternoon sun.

Returning her attention to the house itself, she noted the screen door, the wide front porch, the pair of cushion-topped rocking chairs arranged to invite conversation, and the small side table perfect for housing the pitcher of lemonade and plate of cookies Lydia had mentioned. Just beyond the house, a small white sedan, parked where a barn might otherwise be, served as proof she'd found the right place.

"I should've known there was a reason I got to making cookies a little while ago."

Startled, Dani's gaze flew back to the house and landed on an elderly woman standing on the other side of the screen.

"I reckon you're the one staying out at Lydia's place." The door creaked as it deposited the woman onto the porch.

"Yes, that's right." Dani drew in a breath and released it slowly. "How did you know?"

"You're English. And you look just like Lydia described."

She fidgeted her fingers along her jeans' outermost seams, only to still them with a fortifying breath. "I'm sorry. I really shouldn't have come."

"Clearly the Lord feels differently or He wouldn't have led you here." Miss Lottie beckoned Dani onto the porch with a small nod and a welcoming smile. "And clearly you're the reason why I practically tore my cupboard apart looking for a bag of chocolate chips to go into the cookies I had a sudden calling to make about thirty minutes ago."

She brushed the offer aside. "Please. I don't want to be any trouble."

"Meeting new friends the Lord has chosen to put in my path is never any trouble." Again, she motioned Dani onto the porch. "Come. Sit. It's a beautiful day to be outside."

"Are you sure?" Dani asked, lifting her fingers as a shield against the sun. "I don't want to take your time from whatever you were doing."

"I was wondering who was going to help me eat those cookies. Now I know."

She waited a beat and then crossed to the stairs, extending her right hand as she did. "I'm Dani—Dani Parker."

The woman took Dani's hand inside her soft, wrinkly one and shook it warmly. "I'm Lottie—Lottie Jenkins."

"It's nice to meet you, Ms. Jenkins."

"You can call me Miss Lottie. That's what folks have been calling me since I moved back here more than twenty years ago." Lottie pointed at the first of the two rocking chairs with her cane. "Why don't you make yourself comfortable in that chair right there, and I'll be along in a few minutes with some cookies. Do you drink lemonade?"

"I do. But I don't want you to go to any trouble. Really."

"It's no trouble."

"Can I at least help you carry everything?"

"I wish I was still spry enough to decline, but"—Lottie led Dani's eyes down to her cane—"denial only works for so long before you have to face facts."

She liked this woman. Liked her directness, her warmth. "I suspect you're spryer than you realize."

Miss Lottie's laugh surrounded Dani. "In my mind, I agree. Wholeheartedly. Unfortunately, my body is talking a whole lot louder than my mind these days."

Turning, the woman caned her way toward the door, glancing back at Dani every few steps. "So I understand you met Lydia when you were both children?"

"Yes. We were both eight. We met when I was visiting the area with my folks. We became fast friends that week."

"And you kept in touch all these years?" Miss Lottie tugged open the door and motioned for Dani to follow her inside.

"We were rabid pen pals all through my elementary and high school years. It slowed down when I went off to college and, eventually, got married, but we've managed to keep in contact on at least a once-yearly basis since then. Mostly at Christmastime."

"I see." At the kitchen doorway, Miss Lottie again pointed with her cane. "If you can get the pitcher of lemonade out of the refrigerator and grab us two glasses from the cabinet next to the sink, I can manage the cookie plate."

Nodding, Dani collected the pitcher and glasses, waited for Miss Lottie to ready the plate with two cookies each, and then led her back out to the porch and over to the rocking chairs. When they were each settled with a cookie on their laps and a glass of freshly poured lemonade on the floor at their feet, Miss Lottie began to rock, her gaze drifting out over her front yard.

"How did Lydia's appointment go yesterday?"

"Not well."

Miss Lottie tsked softly beneath her breath. "God's will is a tricky thing to understand at times."

"In Lydia's case it sure is."

Folding her hands atop her lap, the woman brought her focus back on Dani. "Lydia told me about what happened to your family, dear, and I'm so very sorry for your loss. How are you holding up?"

She paused her glass just shy of her first sip and slowly lowered it back down to her lap. "I'm angry."

"About the accident?"

"About the accident . . . About decisions I made that day . . . About what I've come to realize was my atrocious mothering . . . All of it." The lemonade sloshed inside her glass as she lifted it to her lips a second time. While it was tasty, it was difficult to get the lemonade past the lump of emotion inching its way up her throat. "But I'm not here to talk about me or . . . that."

Miss Lottie's eyebrows arched above her thick glasses. "Oh?"

Dani took a second sip and used the moment it bought to find the correct entry point into the sole reason she was there on the woman's porch in the first place. When she was ready, she set the glass on the floor and lifted her gaze back to Miss Lottie's. "Do the Amish ever adopt?"

The woman drew back, clearly caught off guard by Dani's question. "Do they adopt? Why, yes, in certain circumstances."

"Such as?"

"Well, when I was a young child growing up here myself, there was a family who lived a few farms over that perished in a fire. By some miracle one of the children survived. Since no kin claimed him, another family in our district did."

"You were raised *Amish*?" Dani asked.

Miss Lottie nodded. "I was. But like Lydia's brother Caleb, I, too, left before baptism. Only when I left, I left. Spent the next forty years or so traveling the world until I finally realized this place and its people are my true home."

"I see."

"Are you asking about adoption for Lydia?" Miss Lottie asked.

Dani glanced down at her cookie. "I am."

"She could, I suppose. If there was a need for someone to take a child inside her district. But she has four beautiful, healthy children. The Lord has richly blessed Lydia."

"He has also taken much from her."

Miss Lottie's eyes closed behind her glasses. "You are speaking of Rose."

"Yes. And Lydia's ability to bear more."

"Adoption cannot bring Rose back."

Breaking off a piece of cookie, Dani rolled it between her fingers. "You're right; it can't. Nothing can. But Lydia is an amazing mother and she said she wanted more children. Said those very words to me just yesterday."

"It is not God's will."

She lifted her gaze back to Miss Lottie's. "Do you really believe that? Or is it just something you're programmed to say because of your Amish roots?"

"Believe what, dear?"

"That everything is God's will?"

"Of course I believe that. He is all-knowing. It is His plan, not ours."

"Why would God's plan have Him taking a baby from someone like Lydia? It makes no sense."

"I can't answer that any more than I can answer why He took your family the way He did."

Her answering laugh was hollow even to her own ears. "No, that makes some semblance of sense. But Lydia? No . . ."

Miss Lottie set her plate on the table at her elbow and slid forward on her rocking chair until their knees were practically touching. "Dani, dear, I—"

"Please." She held up her hands. "I'm here about Lydia, that's all."

"But—"

"My idea makes all the sense in the world."

"You mean about adoption?"

"About all of it. Adoption, this God's will stuff, all of it."

Scooting back, Miss Lottie began to rock again, her pace slow yet rhythmic, soothing. "Finding a baby is not as easy as you're making it sound, dear. And I don't know of any Amish who have gone the traditional adoption route."

"Meaning?" she prodded.

"Seeking a baby through an agency." Miss Lottie rested her head against the back of her chair. "That doesn't mean it's never happened; it just means I'm not familiar with any who have done it."

"But that's the beauty in all of this. Lydia and Elijah wouldn't have to go through an agency." She brushed the crumbled remains of the morsel back onto her plate and sat up straight. "We'd have to sign legal documents, of course, but that's it. I could even pay the legal fees or court fees or whatever kind of fees it might entail."

Miss Lottie toed her chair to a stop, her ears finally catching up with Dani's words. "Dani, what are you saying?"

"I'm saying that if you truly believe in God's will, there's a reason why I'm here, in the condition that I am. I mean, really, how else can you explain why I left my home and traveled three-plus hours to grieve my family in the home of someone I hadn't seen in twenty-seven years?"

Seconds became minutes as Miss Lottie continued to stare at Dani. "Are you pregnant, dear?"

A heat she hadn't expected pricked at the corners of her eyes, but it didn't last. "I am. I found out last week, even though, in hindsight, the signs had been there for a while. I just thought it was . . ." She stopped, nibbled the tremble from her lips. "I just thought it was everything else."

Again, Miss Lottie sat forward, her hands gathering Dani's inside her own. "Oh, sweet girl, what a beautiful gift your husband left you."

Yanking free, she bolted off her rocking chair and onto a path that took her from the porch steps to the front door and back to the rocking chair before beginning the loop again. "My husband is gone. My mom is gone. My children are gone. I'm the only one left."

"You and that baby," Miss Lottie said, pointing at Dani's abdomen. "Does Lydia know?"

On her third trek toward the stairs she turned back to the elderly woman. "No. But she will. Once I know everything I need to know about doing this."

"Doing what?"

"Giving my baby to Lydia and Elijah to raise. As their own."

Miss Lottie's gasp echoed through the air, cutting short a robin's bath just beyond the side railing. "Dani, you can't be serious. You can't—"

"It's the answer to everything. For Lydia, *and* for me."

"But don't you want to look into that child's face as he or she grows and see your husband? Your children? Because you will, you know. In bits and pieces. It'll be like they're still here, as they are in your memories and—"

She held off the rest of the woman's sentence with a splayed hand. "I know you have Lydia believing that, and if it works for her, great. But the only thing that hurts more than the loss of my family is thinking about them—about their last moments and what they must have been like."

"Things you can't know, because you weren't there, yes?"

Pinching her mouth closed, she nodded.

"The only way you'll be able to pick up the pieces, dear, is to focus on the good, to let the memories you made with them fill you up inside until you're able to keep walking on your own." Miss Lottie retrieved her cane from its resting spot against the table and scooted forward. "And this baby? This child? It will be a living, breathing piece of them that you can hold close. Always."

She didn't mean to laugh, but, in the moment, she couldn't help herself. "There is no *always* when you're talking about death, Miss Lottie. Surely you know that, right?"

"You don't feel them when you think about them?" Miss Lottie asked.

"Oh, I *feel* them, all right. And I hear them, too. Every single night."

"Good . . . Good . . ."

"I feel my children's hands as they're reaching for me, and I hear them crying for me to help them. But I can't stop the accident."

Miss Lottie's answering swallow was audible. "I mean when you think about the good things: the vacations, the holidays, the sleepy kisses, the—"

"Stop. Please. I don't want to talk about me; I want to talk about Lydia."

"About giving your baby to Lydia, you mean . . ."

"Yes." She wandered over to the railing and lifted her chin to the afternoon breeze rustling the leaves of a nearby tree. "I didn't do right by my children. I know that now. But I can do right by this new baby. I can give her a chance to run, and explore, and do all those things kids should be able to do."

The creak of Miss Lottie's chair gave way to the quiet thump of her cane against the porch floor. "So it's a girl then?"

"Not officially, no. But I know it. Inside. I'm feeling many of the same things I felt when I was carrying . . ." Trailing off, she ran her finger along the top of the railing until her breath steadied, her hazy vision cleared. "Anyway, I think a little girl will be perfect for Lydia and Elijah. It'll round things out in their boy-heavy home just a little bit."

Miss Lottie came to stand beside Dani, her gaze slipping across the horizon. "If you don't mind me asking, what makes you think you didn't do right by your children?"

"Seeing Lydia with her kids."

"I don't understand."

"Have you not seen her with them?" she asked, pushing away from the railing. "She's seriously the perfect mom."

The woman's quick laugh gave way to a quiet shake of her head. "I can tell you, with absolute certainty, Lydia would be the first to dispute those words."

Dani took in the porch, the pair of idle rocking chairs, the cookies they'd yet to really eat, and the still-full glass of lemonade beside her own abandoned rocker as Miss Lottie's words rang a distant bell of familiarity. "Just because she practices humility doesn't mean it's not true."

After a beat or two of silence, Miss Lottie turned, her right hand atop her cane, her left braced against the railing at her back. "Tell me what you see when you see Lydia. As a mother, I mean."

"I see someone who lets them be kids. I see someone who lets them play in the rain, dig in the dirt, and chase barn cats. I see someone who teaches her children empathy and compassion in a hands-on way with animals. I see someone who will slow her day down just so she can soak them up in the moment. I see someone who listens to them talk, and who rolls up her sleeves and enjoys the things that make *them* happy."

"And you don't think you did that? With your children?"

"I know I didn't."

"I see." Miss Lottie flexed her hand around her cane, rolled her shoulders forward and backward, and then ventured back over to her rocking chair and her own waiting glass of lemonade. "What were they like?"

"Who?"

"Your children . . . Your husband . . . Your mom . . ."

She closed her eyes against the sudden slide show of faces and expressions flipping past her mind's eye and tried to catch her breath. "They were—they must have been so scared," she said, jamming her fist against her lips. "All of them. And I-I didn't know. I *didn't know*."

The tears she hadn't intended to shed were back. Only this time, instead of being alone in an empty room, there were arms to pull her close and a shoulder in which to bury her head. "There was no way you could have known, dear. You weren't with them."

"But that's just it. If I'd been the kind of mother I should've been all along, I'd have been with them that day instead of taking time for myself that I didn't need and shouldn't"—her voice broke, sob-like—"have *wanted*."

Miss Lottie's aging hands slid back around to Dani's shoulders and gently yet firmly moved her back a step. "Good heavens, child, you not being with your family in that car isn't a reflection on you. It . . ." Stopping, the woman waited for Dani's tear-soaked eyes to find hers. "It just wasn't your time. You were meant to stay here, to be"—her hand lowered to Dani's abdomen—"*this one's* mamma."

"I want to be *Maggie's* mamma! I want to be *Spencer's* mamma! I want to be *Ava's* mamma!"

"You will always be those children's mamma," Miss Lottie said, cupping Dani's cheek. "Death doesn't change that."

"They're not with me like they should be!"

"In their physical form? No, they're not. But that doesn't mean they can't still be with you. You just have to let *them*, Dani. For you *and* for them."

Reaching up, Dani pushed away the woman's hand along with the last of her tears. "I have to go. I just came to make sure there wasn't some Amish rule against adoption I didn't know about."

"No, no rule." Miss Lottie caned behind Dani to the top of the steps and halted her departure with a gentle hand. "Please. Sleep on this for a while, dear. You have time. No decisions need to be made today."

"The decision has already been made, Miss Lottie. The only thing still left to do is tell Lydia."

Chapter 22

She didn't know how long she'd been sitting there, staring out at the distant windmills and silos, the utter peace and tranquility of her surroundings little more than white noise against her internal clutter. There was so much she wanted to say, so much she needed to share, but every time she tried, every time she got close, the shake of her hand made it so anything she managed to actually write was completely illegible even to her own eyes.

Maybe, instead of abandoning the litter-strewn table in tearful frustration, she should have just taken it as a sign. A sign that the baby growing inside her would be better off completely untethered from—

"Danielle?"

Dropping her feet onto the patio, Dani turned toward the voice and the familiar face standing just inside the shade of the main house. "Oh. Lydia. Hi . . . I-I guess I didn't hear you walk up. Is everything okay?"

"I knocked on the door, but you did not answer." Slowly, tentatively, the Amish woman approached the patio, her hands tightening around the handle of a different, larger basket than she normally packed for Dani.

"Is it noon, already?" she asked, glancing back at the sun's position in the sky.

"Yah."

She swallowed. "I didn't realize."

"You have gotten it the way you want it to be?"

"It?"

"What you were trying to write."

Heat rose into her cheeks. "How do you know I was trying to write something?"

"I saw the mistakes on the table."

"You . . ." Grabbing the armrests of her chair, Dani tried to process what she was hearing, her mind's eye rewinding through the same sentence she'd tried to write more than a dozen times before finally calling it quits—each attempt crumpled into a tight ball alongside other tight balls. "You opened them up and read them?"

Lydia's eyes widened in horror. "No! I saw them only through the door. I would not read something that was not mine to read."

Dani sank back against her chair and waited for her heart rate to return to normal. When it did, she looked back up at her friend. "I'm sorry, Lydia. I just thought . . ." Waving off her idiocy, she rose onto her feet, her eyes meeting and holding Lydia's. "Actually, it doesn't matter what I thought. I was wrong to accuse you like that and I'm sorry. I'm just trying to work through a lot right now."

"Yah. Perhaps that is why you should come for a picnic." Lydia lifted the basket between them and gave it a little shake. "With me and Nettie."

She looked past her friend but saw no sign of anyone—big or small. "Where is Nettie?"

"She is telling Wooly of our plans for the day."

"Where are you going?"

"To Miller's Pond."

"Where is that?"

"Down the road, past the second bend." A mischievous and knowing smile played at the corners of Lydia's mouth. "Where it has always been since the last time you saw it."

"I haven't been to a Miller's Pond."

"Yah. You have been next to it *and* you have been *in* it," Lydia teased.

She stared at her friend, the woman's words delivering Dani to a different time and place. "Wait. Is that the pond where we tried to make boats out of leaves and race them across to the other side?"

"Yah. That is Miller's Pond."

"Wow," she murmured. "I'd forgotten about that day."

"I do not know how. You got very wet."

"I did, didn't I?" She wandered over to the edge of the patio and tried to remember the direction they'd walked that day so long ago. The different starting point, though, made it difficult to discern. "When I first fell in, I remember being a little scared and just wanting to get out. But then, when you and Caleb jumped in, too, I didn't ever want to get out."

"Yah."

"I imagine it looks the same?" she asked, turning back to Lydia.

"Come with us. You will see."

"Lydia, I really can't. I have something I need to . . ." She let the words trail away in favor of truly seeing the woman in front of her, a woman she needed to talk to preferably sooner rather than later.

Pulling in a deep breath, Dani nodded. "Actually, on second thought, I think a little time with you at the pond would be nice."

"Yah?" When Dani nodded again, Lydia beamed. "Nettie will be happy to hear you are coming. Even if she will be too busy chasing butterflies and picking wildflowers to pay us any mind."

Perfect . . .

"Would you like me to drive?" she asked, falling into step behind Lydia as they made their way around the house toward the driveway.

"No. It is a lovely day for a walk."

And she was right. Together, they walked along the edge of the road, the crunch of gravel beneath their feet muted only by the sounds of life around them—birds chirping, sheep bleating, cows mooing, and even the whir of a gas-powered weed whacker. A few times, Lydia stopped to point out a neighbor's garden or a particular horse she spied in a field, but most of the talking came via Nettie as the little girl urged them to walk faster or slower depending on whatever animal she spotted at any given moment.

Just beyond the one-room schoolhouse and its empty playground, Lydia motioned them off the road and onto a well-worn path. "It is just beyond that last tree."

"I'm not really remembering this at all, but . . ."

The words fell away as they stepped into a clearing and Miller's Pond stood before them. Suddenly, Dani was eight again, and she was there, standing between Lydia and Caleb, their laughter filling the air. To her left, where picnic tables and park benches now dotted the grass, they'd played tag in the once-wide-open space—Caleb the fastest of all of them. Up ahead, where she'd leaned just a little too far in her attempts to move her leaf boat along faster, a sign now stood warning visitors to swim at their own risk. But the large boulder-sized rock to her left? That was still there, still exactly the same, its wide, flat surface perfect for sharing cookies as they'd done, or daydreaming the hours away as she'd imagined doing at the time.

"Oh, Lydia," she whispered. "I remember this place. It's changed a little, sure, but not so much—not too much."

"It is a favorite spot for many Amish that I know." Lydia glanced down at her daughter. "Do you want to eat at one of the picnic tables or on the rock?"

"I like the rock." Nettie grabbed hold of Dani's hand and swung it happily. "Mamm says I can put my feet in the water today!"

"That sounds exciting . . ."

"Yah!" Glancing to the left and then the right, Nettie hopped once, twice. "Do you want to chase butterflies with me first?"

"I—"

"Look, Mamm! The flowers are here!" Nettie took off in a half hop, half run, around the pond to the picnic area. When she reached her destination, she crouched down in the middle of a ring of wildflowers and began to sniff each and every one, the joy on her tiny face mesmerizing.

Dani watched the little girl for a few moments and then turned back to her friend. "So I guess that offer to chase butterflies is off the table?"

"For now. But that is good. It will give us time to talk." Lydia led the way to the rock, set the basket down on top, and then gestured toward a flat patch of ground closer to the water's edge. "Perhaps, until it is time to eat, we could sit there, where I can see Nettie best."

"Of course."

Together, they made their way down to the pond and carefully spread the blanket across a bed of dried leaves. When they were settled, Lydia lifted her face to the sun and closed her eyes. "What a blessing the Lord has given you."

She looked a question at her friend. "Blessing?"

"Luke spoke of your yes and no machine and how it adds."

Confusion quickly switched places with truth. "Oh. Right."

"But I would have known even without such a *machine*." Lowering her chin back to start, Lydia smiled at Dani. "The way you hold your back. It is something I did with Luke and with Rose."

"I'm sorry I didn't say something sooner," she said, resting her hand atop Lydia's. "I didn't get the official word from the doctor until last week and then, well, I didn't want to hurt you with talk of a baby."

Lydia's gaze wandered across the pond, settled on her

daughter for a moment, and then lifted to the crystal-blue sky. "I wish you could have seen her, Danielle."

She recovered her hand. "You mean Rose?"

"Yah. Her eyes were shaped like Elijah's but were most like Luke's. And her nose? It was like Nettie's and like David's."

"Which means it was like yours," Dani mused.

"Yah."

"Tell me more."

Lydia followed a cloud behind a leafy branch above and then slowly lowered herself onto her back, her arm coming to rest across her eyes. "She liked to watch the other children. Elijah said she was paying close attention so she would be ready when she was old enough to run like the others.

"My favorite time with her was at night, though, when I was putting her in her cradle. She would reach for my chin and try to hold it between her little hands." Lydia exhaled against her arm and then struggled up onto her elbow for yet another visual of the flower patch. "When I say it out loud, I know that it does not sound like much—that it sounds silly, even. But it was something that was just us."

"It doesn't sound silly at all," Dani countered between hard swallows. "It sounds . . . *beautiful*."

"Sometimes, when I'm missing her, it is hard to breathe. It's like someone is covering my mouth and I can't make them stop."

It was a feeling she knew well. One she would liken more to being buried alive . . .

"I wonder if she would still be here if I would have taken her for a walk when she napped instead of putting her in her cradle. I wonder if I had waited for one more burp, or checked on her five minutes sooner, would she have lived? I wonder, if Caleb had been in the house with me instead of in the barn with Elijah, would he have been able to . . ." Lydia's words fell away with a deep and labored sigh. "I know it is not for me to wonder, or for me to question. But still, I do."

"If I had shooed everyone away from the breakfast table a little faster, or let that last batch of pancakes cook just a little longer, Jeff and Mom and the kids wouldn't have been in that exact spot when the other driver crossed the center line," Dani said, her voice husky even to her own ears. "If I'd listened to my gut and gotten in that car with them, I'd have been there, with them, instead of at home, completely oblivious to the world around me. Maybe if I *had* been with them, I'd have noticed something about the other car—something that would have made it so I was able to yell out, to warn Jeff so he could've swerved sooner."

Slumping forward, Lydia nodded, her eyelids half-mast. "Do you ever wish you could go back to that day? So you could do it all different?"

"All the time."

Silence grew between them for a moment—a silence broken first by a bird's chirp, next by the faint clip-clop of a buggy's horse just beyond the trees, and, finally, Lydia herself, the woman's grief so raw it was painful to hear.

"I want my baby back, Danielle."

"I know." Blinking against the tears that blurred Lydia's face from view, Dani shifted her focus to the trees . . . The clouds . . . The shafts of sunlight reaching through the branches . . . A pair of squirrels playing chase through a pile of dried leaves . . . The bird watching from his perch above them . . . The patch of yellow and purple wildflowers swaying in the soft breeze . . . The—

She sat up tall, wiped the last of the wetness from her eyes, and looked again at the flowers, the sea of yellow and purple no longer broken by the top of a gauzy white kapp. "Lydia? Where's Nettie?"

Chapter 23

꧁꧂

She heard Lydia's voice blending with her own as they fanned out around the pond looking for Nettie. Lydia went left toward a trio of butterflies she was certain had attracted her daughter, and Dani went right, a second slightly wider stretch of wildflowers beckoning her close.

"Nettie!" Lydia called.

"Nettie!" Dani echoed.

Midway to the flowers, Dani stopped, the flash of white she sought noticeably absent. "Is there a farm nearby? Maybe she caught a glimpse of an animal and went to say hello?"

"Nettie wouldn't go off like that without me. She loves it here at the pond; she wouldn't leave."

Sweeping her gaze toward the pond, Dani took in the dark, marshy water . . . The smattering of thick logs breaching the surface . . . The handful of turtles sunning themselves atop wet bark . . .

"Maybe she just wandered off to look at something without really thinking," Dani offered. "Like she did the other day when you were at the doctor's and she was done feeding the calf."

Lydia's eyes met and held Dani's for a second before sweeping back toward the butterflies. "Caleb didn't tell me she'd wandered off."

"*Wandered* probably isn't the right word. Nettie had a purpose. It just wasn't a purpose Caleb was told and so he got pretty scared when he couldn't find her at first."

Shaking her head, Lydia moved still farther into the trees while Dani skirted the pond's edge. "She went to see Wooly, didn't she?"

"She did."

A flash of purple leaned Dani to the right, her breath whooshing from her lungs in relief at the realization it was just a flower, floating on the surface next to a white—

Pulling her phone from her back pocket and tossing it to the ground, Dani took off in a run. "Use my phone! Call nine-one-one! Now! Now! *Now!*"

Her eyes locked on Nettie's kapp, she rewound her thoughts twenty-seven years to the moment she'd fallen into the same pond. She remembered the muddy bottom, the plant life that had encircled her legs, and Caleb's pleas for her to stay away from the deep side.

She skirted the outer edge of the pond, her mind's eye working to frame the present with the past. Where had she fallen in? Which side was the deep—

In a flash, she saw herself straining forward, trying desperately to blow her leaf boat across the surface, the afternoon sun warm on her face as she fell—face first—into the pond. Sputtering and flailing, she'd pushed the water from her eyes to find Caleb laughing.

"*Just stand up, Danielle! It's shallow on this side. The deep part is over there.*"

She'd followed his finger, the afternoon sun warm on her face once again.

The afternoon sun . . .

Breaking into a sprint, Dani headed toward the western side of the pond and the safest place to dive in—a spot not all that far from where Nettie's white kapp had . . . *been*? Toeing off her shoes, she dove in, headfirst, her shoulder grazing something hard and unyielding as she rose again to the surface.

"Nettie! Nettie!"

Again she dove down, the murkiness of the water limiting her vision to no more than an inch or two at a time. Leading with her arms, she stroked forward, her fingertips brushing a plant, a log, an old tire, another plant, skin—With one powerful stroke forward, she wrapped her arms around the lifeless form and pulled, her only thought a silent prayer.

Please, God, please. Let her be okay . . .

Please.

At the surface, she turned right toward the shoreline, Lydia's shrieks barely registering against her own shallow breaths and the lack of any from Nettie. When she reached the edge, she used the last of her strength to lift the child and then herself up and onto the ground.

"Nettie! Nettie!" Lydia screamed, swooping down between them. "Nettie!"

"Get back, Lydia!" Pushing past her friend, she felt the little girl's neck and wrist but found no pulse. "Please!"

"Is she breathing?"

"No."

"Nettie!"

She tilted the child's head back and pinched her nose. "Did you call nine-one-one?"

"Yah!"

"Go"—she covered Nettie's mouth with her own, breathed into it, and then followed it up with a series of chest compressions—"out to the road"—she breathed into the child's mouth again and then followed it with more chest compressions—"wait for them at the road"—she repeated the sequence a third time, cycling from breath to compressions again—"so they know where to find us."

"He is working! They will know!"

A siren in the distance confirmed Lydia's words. Louder

and louder it got until its sudden silence was broken by the echo of doors being slammed, metal clicking into place, and, finally, a familiar voice shouting through the trees.

Again, she breathed into the tiny mouth. Again, she compressed the tiny chest. And then, finally, Nettie coughed, a spray of pond water exiting her mouth and hitting Dani on the cheek.

"That's my girl . . . that's my girl . . ." Gently, she slid her arm underneath Nettie's shoulders, tilting her until her cornflower-blue eyes widened on Dani's. "It's okay, sweetie . . . I'm here. And your mamm's here . . ."

"Nettie!"

Caleb?

A quick glance over her shoulder yielded Lydia's brother, dressed in dark navy trousers and a pale blue shirt emblazoned with a paramedic's badge on the sleeve. In his calloused hand was a medical bag, and in his eyes was a mixture of both fear and confidence. Behind him, no more than ten feet away and moving fast across the dirt, was a young woman, clad in dark pants and a white EMS shirt, pushing a stretcher.

"Is she breathing?" he barked as he traversed the subtle pitch of the shoreline and dropped to his knees.

"Yes." Dani slid to the right to give him access to the child and then, while he set about assessing the situation and talking to Nettie, she picked herself up and onto her feet, her heart thudding, her shoulder stinging.

"May I take a look at that, ma'am?"

She looked up, her gaze settling on the young woman wearing a pair of latex gloves and staring at Dani's shoulder. When she followed the woman's eyes, she saw that she was bleeding. "Oh, that's nothing. I think I scraped it against a log or something when I first dove in."

"You're probably right, but we should get it cleaned up, anyway. Make sure it doesn't require stitches."

Shrugging, she stood in place as the young woman

cleaned, treated, and covered the surface wound, Dani's own attention returning, again and again, to the little girl now lying on the gurney, looking up at her beloved mamm while her uncle hovered nearby.

"It's not deep enough to need stitches, but you'll still want to change out the dressing and treat it with an antibacterial ointment once or twice a day for the next few days to prevent possible infection." The EMT gathered the wrapper from the bandage, tossed it into her own medical bag, and then glanced back at Dani before she hustled to catch up with Caleb and the Nettie-topped gurney now making its way back around the pond toward the path and, presumably, the waiting ambulance. "Looks like you were a hero today, ma'am."

Before she could truly process the words, or the fact that every sound around her made her feel as if she were standing in a tunnel, Nettie's tiny hand popped up from the gurney and waved, slumping Dani's shoulders with the powerful weight of relief. For a moment, maybe two, she stayed where she was, rooted to the dirt, her gaze returning, again and again, to the purple flower still floating on the surface of the pond, its tiny would-be rescuer seemingly okay after being close to—

She shook the horror from her thoughts and, anxious to see Nettie's face one more time, took off in a run around the pond, down the path, and out to the road in time to see Caleb push closed the door on the back of the rig and lift his head to the sky in what she knew was surely a prayer of gratitude.

"Caleb?"

Dropping his chin, he turned to Dani, the fear she'd seen in his eyes at the edge of the pond still alive and well. "Danielle . . . I-I can't even begin to thank you for what you did back there. You saved my niece's life."

The words bounced off like gravel on a moving tire. "Will she be okay?" she asked, moving her gaze between Caleb and the ambulance. "I mean, *really* okay?"

"She's going to be fine. Because of you."

"Where is Lydia?"

"In back, with Nettie."

She nodded. "Did you get word to Elijah somehow?"

"No. When the call came in, my only focus was getting here."

"I'll tell him now. As soon as I get back."

"Thanks."

"Should I bring him to the hospital?"

"You can, but I don't think they're going to keep her beyond a few tests. All precautionary stuff that is more about checking boxes." He pointed at the back door. "Do you want to say something to them?"

She stopped herself, mid-nod, and changed it to a quiet yet audible "no." "I'd rather you get her where she needs to go so she can get back home as soon as possible. Her family needs her."

"Roger that." He started toward the passenger side of the white and red rig but stopped before he'd made it more than a step or two. "Thank you, Danielle. Thank you for your cool head, for your quick actions, and for keeping my family from having to endure another tragic loss."

Chapter 24

She was sitting outside the kitchen window when they finally pulled up, Lydia's kapped head in the passenger side window a welcomed sight. Toeing the rocking chair to a stop, Dani stood and made her way down the steps and onto the driveway, her gaze moving from Lydia, to Caleb, and finally, thankfully, to the smaller kapped figure waving out at her from the center of the back seat.

Seconds later, the front door of the main house opened, depositing Elijah and the boys onto their own porch, their destination and their relief equally clear. When the pickup stopped and the engine was turned off, Elijah and the boys swarmed to Lydia's side of the truck, prompting Dani to go toward Caleb's.

Even in the last of the day's light, she could see the strain of the day in everything from the subtle curve of the man's normally iron-straight shoulders to the darkened circles rimming eyes dulled by fatigue. Yet despite all of the indicators it had been a day he never wanted to relive, there was no denying his smile's part in keeping him upright.

"Hey," he said, stepping down beside her. "We're back."

"I see that." Dani drank in the sight of Nettie on the other side of the truck, the child's excitement over the sheet of stickers she'd gotten from the nurses at the hospital bringing a smile to her own lips.

"Nettie?" Caleb said across the hood of his truck. "I think Miss Dani could use a great big hug from you right about now."

"No . . . No . . . It's okay. She's where she should be," Dani said, her voice hushed. "With her family. I'm just so happy to be able to *look* at her."

Lydia popped her head around the long, rectangular side view mirror and covered her answering sob with her hand. "Danielle . . . I . . . I am just so grateful to the Lord for bringing you here to us, and for having you there at the pond with us, today." Slipping Nettie from Elijah's arms, Lydia carried the smiling child around to Dani and Caleb.

When Nettie reached out for Dani, Dani pulled the little girl close and breathed in her sweet scent. "Oh, I am so very happy to see you, little one. How are you feeling?"

"All better!"

"I'm so glad." She snuggled her close for a few more moments and then pulled back just enough to afford some much-needed eye contact. "You tried to get that purple flower, didn't you?"

Nettie shot out her lower lip. "I wanted to bring it to Mamm. But I dropped it in the pond."

"I figured as much. But sweetie?" She tapped the little girl on the nose. "You can't ever go in that pond again without asking your mamm or your uncle or your dat first, okay?"

"Or you?" Nettie asked.

"If I'm there with you, yes. If not, just find a big person, okay?"

Nettie's nod was slow yet intentional. "Yah."

"You can't forget that, okay?"

"Okay."

"Never, ever," Dani added for good measure.

"I won't forget." Reaching for her mamm, Nettie yawned, her eyelids beginning to droop. "I am very sleepy, Mamm."

Caleb leaned in, kissed his niece on her soft cheek, and then extended a second one to Lydia. "It's been a long day for her, and for you, too. Get some sleep and I'll check in on you both tomorrow morning, okay?"

"Yah." Shifting Nettie to her left arm, Lydia hugged first Caleb, and then Dani, with her right. "Thank you—*both* of you."

"Of course." Dani watched her friend cross to the rest of her family and then, as a unit, they headed inside their home, a family once again, a family still.

Sagging against the truck, she tilted up her chin until her only view was the dusky wide-open sky.

"How's that cut doing?" Caleb asked, stealing her focus back to him and then her arm.

"Honestly? I'd actually forgotten all about it until just now."

"That's a good sign, I guess. But you really need to keep it clean and change the bandaging once a day. Don't want to get an infection, you know?"

"I will. Thanks."

"And sleep, you should probably try to get some of that tonight, too," he added. "You had a lot of excitement for one day."

"Trust me, I am *way* too keyed up to think about sleep just yet."

"You sure?"

"I'm sure."

"Could we talk then? Over a cup of coffee or something?" He hooked his thumb toward his truck. "I think the coffee shop in town is open for another hour or so if we head out now."

"Don't you think maybe *you* should get some sleep? You look like you could fall over."

"Hence the suggestion of coffee," he said, laughing. "And heading out now before it gets much later . . ."

She looked from Caleb, to the truck, and, finally, to the darkness beginning to envelop the fields and the barn, the day's events, coupled with the demands of the job she hadn't known he had, leading her to the offer she knew she had to make. "I could make us both a cup if that's okay? That'll get you back on the road to home sooner than if we have to drive into town and back."

He tried to recover his sag of relief before she saw it, but when it was clear she had, he grinned. "Thank you. That sounds perfect."

Nodding, she led the way around the truck and over to her own porch. "You should've seen me a few hours ago, after the boys got home from school. I was doing things I never thought I'd do."

"Like what?" He held the door for her to walk through and then closed it behind himself.

"For starters, I mucked a stall. After that, I took the clothes off the line for Lydia and shuttled them to the right rooms thanks to Mark. And for my crowning achievement, I milked a cow. Or, rather, I tried to milk a cow. Fortunately for me—and the cow, I'm sure—Luke took over after about three pulls."

Caleb's laugh rattled around the room only to stop as his gaze came to rest on the table. "Writing a novel?" he asked, pointing to the pile of balled-up stationery she'd yet to discard.

"Uh, no . . ." She plucked a pair of mugs from the cabinet to the right of the sink and set them beside the stove and the kettle she promptly filled with water. "I've been trying to write a letter and I just can't seem to make it say what I want it to say."

"Keep at it; it'll come."

"I hope so." She held the propane button until the burner lit and then set the kettle on top. While the water heated, she joined him at the table, the battery-operated light he'd flipped on above them drawing her attention to the badge on his sleeve. "I had no idea you were a paramedic. I just thought your job was helping Elijah on occasion."

Setting his elbows atop the table, he rested his chin against his palm. "I do that, sure, but yeah, that's not my job. I work four on/four off out at the ambulance district on Route 322. Started out as an EMT, and worked my way up to being a paramedic."

"Is that why you decided not to get baptized? Because you wanted to be a paramedic?" she asked.

"Not exactly, no. I left because I wanted a little more freedom in my life. I wanted to drive, I wanted to explore new places, and, yeah, I wanted to do something that had me helping people. At first, after I left, I considered being a cop, but it didn't feel right. Then, I thought about being a firefighter, but I could've done that on a volunteer basis and stayed Amish, so that seemed silly. Then, one day, when I was driving around, I saw a sign about becoming trained as an EMT. I gave it a shot and ended up enjoying it enough I decided to go back to school and work toward being a paramedic."

"And you did it."

His grin, while tired, reached clear through to his eyes. "I did."

She traced her finger along the edge of the table and then dropped it into her lap, her thoughts filling with a single question she couldn't help but ask. "Do you ever miss it?"

"Being Amish?"

"Yes."

"Not really, no. But since I left before baptism instead of after, the only thing that's really changed is where I live and how I get around. I still stop out and see Mamm and Dat when I'm not working, I come out here and spend time with Lydia and Elijah and the kids on my days off, and I actually go off and see my older brothers whenever I have some time off and feel like driving myself to Ohio—something I couldn't do quite so easily if I'd stayed."

She considered his words as the kettle began to whistle. "Sugar? Cream?"

"No. Black works for me."

When the coffee was ready, she carried their matching

mugs back to the table, setting one in front of Caleb's spot, the other in front of her own. "Is there anything you *do* miss?"

"Again, not really. I can still participate in just about any-thing I want. Though"—he tugged on his chin, his eyes crackling with mischief—"I think I'll skip the whole beard-growing thing when I get married. I don't think I have the face for it, you know?"

She swallowed back her answering laugh and, instead, stared down into the tannish-colored liquid in her own mug. "Today was terrifying."

"Tell me about it."

"I was afraid she . . ." She pushed her mug forward, shook her head.

"What happened, exactly?"

"Lydia and I were sitting on a blanket near the eastern edge of the pond, talking. Nettie was sniffing her way through a patch of wildflowers on the opposite side. I was just getting ready to tell your sister about the baby when I looked up and realized Nettie wasn't in the flower patch anymore. So I got up, and Lydia got up, and we split off in different directions— Lydia toward some butterflies she suspected as being the catalyst for Nettie's sudden disappearance, and me toward another crop of wildflowers on the northern side of the pond. When I didn't see her there, I started to turn back, and that's when I saw the purple flower floating on the other side of the pond. At first, I was just glad it was a flower and not Nettie. But then, when I looked just beyond it, I saw the white of Nettie's kapp."

Her voice broke, prompting Caleb to reach for her hands and Dani to pull them away. "I wanted to dive in right there, where I was, and swim across to her, but that's when I heard your voice."

"*My* voice?" he echoed.

"Yeah. From twenty-seven years ago. When I fell into the

pond trying to get my leaf boat to go faster than yours and Lydia's."

He stared at her for a moment, his thoughts clearly leaping ahead or, rather, back to the day she, too, had almost forgotten.

"You told me I was fine, that all I had to do was stand up. That the deep side was off the western shore. And so I knew that would be the safest place for me to dive in. By the time I got to the right spot, I couldn't see her kapp anymore. But I could still see the flower and it wasn't really drifting in one direction or the other. So I swam toward the flower and felt my way through the murk around that spot. It didn't take long to find her."

He palmed his face, let his hand slip back down to the table with a quiet thud. "And the rest? How did you know what to do? Because you've gotta know your quick action made all the difference in the world between Nettie being here with us now and . . . *not*."

"When I found out I was pregnant with Maggie, I signed up for a CPR class at the local hospital. I didn't like the idea of standing around helplessly in an emergency."

"You remembered it very well."

She held up her palm. "Actually, I took a refresher when I was pregnant with Spencer, and again with Ava. I hoped that repetition would make it stick in my head better."

"And it clearly did." The bench creaked under his weight as he, too, leaned forward, his gaze fixing on a point somewhere far beyond the confines of the simple kitchen. "Did you ever have to use it? Before today, I mean?"

"I did. Once." She took a sip of her coffee, the liquid warm and comforting inside her throat. "It was at Maggie's sixth birthday party, which meant her entire kindergarten class was in attendance. Jeff and I had taken the kids to a pop-up circus in the next town over and Maggie had been mesmerized by all of it. Needless to say, she wanted her party to have a circus theme."

"You mean like the cake had some circus stuff on it?" Caleb asked, reaching for his own mug. "A couple of clowns? An elephant? That sort of stuff?"

She didn't mean to laugh, but it slipped past her lips, anyway, and sent her scrambling for another sip, another swallow.

"Did I say something wrong?"

"No. It's just clear you don't have kids of your own or"— she paused, thinking how best to rephrase the rest of her answer—"you don't have kids in the area I live."

"Meaning?"

"The cake is but a very minor part of the whole birthday experience. At least in my neighborhood, anyway."

Amusement dulled the fatigue in his eyes. "Oh?"

"Trust me when I tell you, those kids stepped into a veritable circus when they walked through my front door that day."

"How so?"

"Jeff—wearing a top hat and coat—greeted each child when they came inside, announcing their name in true Master of Ceremonies fashion. Spencer, who was not quite four at the time, handed each child six tickets since, of course, it was Maggie's sixth birthday."

"Clever . . ."

"Oh, it gets better." Buoyed by a sudden boost of energy and a desire to move, she pushed her mug into the center of the table and stood. "I set up a bunch of different stations in the backyard that they could visit with their tickets. At one, they could train a lion—"

"A lion?"

"I put Spencer in a lion costume."

He grinned. "Go on . . ."

"At one station, they could get a box of popcorn from the popcorn cart I rented. At another, they could jump through a Hula-Hoop lined with paper flames onto a trampoline. At another, they could pick their favorite circus animal and have the balloon artist I hired for the day make it for them. And on and on it went. And the cake? I made a 3-D one to look like a circus tent with little clowns peeking out."

"*You* made it?"

She wandered over to the window, the door, the refrigerator, and, finally, back to the table, her steps light. "I did. That's another class I took before Maggie was born—a cake-decorating class. I knew that I wanted to be the one who made treats for all the special occasions."

"Wow."

"But no matter what theme they wanted for their birthdays each year, I always made sure there was pin the tail on the donkey. It was a favorite for all three of them and, therefore, a real must-have. I just doctored it up to coincide with whatever the chosen theme was for any given party."

"Let me guess," he said. "For Maggie's circus party, the kids played pin the trunk on the elephant?"

She grinned. "No, but that would have been a good option."

"So what *did* you do?"

"We played pin the nose on the clown. With *me* being the clown."

"Ouch," he said, pulling a face.

"No pins at my parties. Just tape."

"Oh, okay, good. That's a relief." He took another sip of his drink and waved her back to the table. When she acquiesced, he pushed her mug back into reach. "So what happened that you needed to use your CPR training?"

"One of the little boys—Adam . . ." Closing her eyes for just a moment, she conjured up an image of the little boy who'd given his kindergarten teacher more than a few gray hairs that year. "He was . . . How shall I say this? A . . . busy one."

"Busy?"

"As in, he was the kid who lived to do the opposite of whatever he was told. If Maggie's teacher told the children it was time to sit, Adam would not only stand; he'd do so on his desk. If the teacher told the children to keep their hands to themselves, he'd run around touching everyone and everything, often making some of his quieter, more timid classmates cry."

"So why did you invite this kid?"

She pulled her mug close, noted its now-lukewarm sides, and slowly traced her index finger along its nearest rim. "Because Maggie wanted him there. She said she didn't want to make him sad by not inviting him. When I pointed out there was a chance he might dampen her special day with his antics, she said that was okay. That she would have fun no matter what."

"Wow. I'm not too sure how many adults could say that in the same situation."

"I know. But that's the way Maggie was, the way all three of them were. They had an uncanny ability to consider the feelings of others."

He took another sip of his coffee. "Clearly you instilled that in them through your words and your actions."

"I'm not sure you're all that qualified to make a statement like that about me when, truth be told, you really don't know me all that well."

"I know enough," he said, lowering his mug back to the table. "You ever notice how each and every piece is critical in a puzzle? People aren't much different in my opinion. All the pieces come together to form the complete picture."

She pushed her mug away, the lightness she'd felt while walking around the kitchen all but gone; in its place, a sudden wariness. "Anyway," she said, releasing her breath. "I made sure to tell each and every child that the popcorn could only be eaten while watching their friends at the assorted stations. When they were done eating, they could join in again. All of the children heard my instructions and followed them. All but Adam, that is. He stuffed a handful of popcorn into his pocket and pushed his way to the front of the trampoline

line. Next thing we knew, he was jumping and eating and making sure—quite loudly—that I knew what he was doing."

Caleb scrubbed his face with his palm. "I'm guessing he started choking?"

"He did. So there I am, in my clown suit, performing the Heimlich. Fortunately for Adam, me, and the bevy of little ones watching in horror, a few quick pulls of my wrist brought up the offending piece of popcorn."

"Nice job."

"Needless to say, I wasn't all that sad when, the following year, he and his family moved to Florida about a month before Maggie's seventh birthday."

"I'm sure."

"But Maggie? She wished he could've come, anyway." She nudged her chin at the pile of balled-up paper. "That's why I've had to start over so many times. I just can't seem to do her justice in my letter to the baby."

He shifted on the bench, his gaze moving from Dani to the balled-up papers and back again. "You're writing a letter to the baby?"

"I'm trying to. But I'm failing miserably."

"You could just tell her . . . or *him* about his siblings."

She was shaking her head before he'd even finished. "No. I-I can't. It's either write it, or just not say anything about them at all."

"Not say anything about them at all? Why? That baby is going to want to—"

"Please." Dani pushed back on the bench and held up her hands. "Can we actually not do this right now? It's been a long day."

Understanding dawned in his eyes, silencing his mounting protest. "Right. Sure. Yeah. It's been a very long day. Especially for you."

"Especially for both of us," she corrected.

"Oh no, the credit for this is all yours. If you hadn't gotten her breathing when you did, it's quite likely it would've been too late by the time I got there. Story of my life where my nieces are concerned."

She waited for him to explain his last comment, but, instead, he stood, gathered their coffee mugs in his strong hands, and carried them over to the counter.

"Nettie adores you, Caleb. Surely you know that. She's not going to see what happened today as you failing her."

He set the mugs in the sink, squirted a drop of dish soap into each one, and then filled them with water from the tap. While they soaked, he turned back to the table and Dani, the half-moons of fatigue he wore under his eyes seeming to deepen with each passing second. "I went into my line of work so I could help people out of some tight jams and, when the Lord allows, do my part to keep them here on earth. And the funny thing is, I actually thought I was pretty good at it. Even won a few community-based awards because of some of my trickier saves. But when my sister came running out to Elijah's barn with Rose in her arms that afternoon, I was right there and I couldn't do anything to bring her back. She was just . . . gone."

"Caleb, you can't blame yourself for what happened to Rose," she said, standing.

"Why not? Saving people is my job. I do it all the time. Yet when my sister needed me—when *my infant niece* needed me—I was worthless."

"But you said she was gone."

His gaze dropped to the floor. "She was."

"Did you give up right away?"

"No, I worked on her right up until my coworkers got there, and even beyond."

"Then you can't beat yourself up, Caleb. There was nothing you could've done."

His answering laugh was hollow. "And while there's a part of me that knows you're right on some level, the guilt still eats me alive every time I see that haunted look in Lydia's eyes or hear Nettie crying because she misses her baby sister."

"It wasn't your fault, Caleb," she whispered, her voice tight.

"Maybe. But it was my job. As a paramedic."

"And being with my kids and keeping them safe and happy was *my* job. As their mother."

His eyes shot back to hers. "Wait. Those are two very different things."

"How do you figure that?"

"I was here—on the farm—when Rose stopped breathing. I'm a paramedic. I'm trained to get people breathing again." He stepped forward, cutting the space between them to little more than a foot. "You weren't anywhere near your family when that accident happened."

"My point, exactly. I *should've* been with them."

He splayed his hands. "That's not the same thing, Dani. Not even close."

"Isn't it, though?"

"No. It's not. But if you can't hear that, can't believe that, then at least hear the very thing you just told *me*—someone whose *job* it is *to save* people."

"What I just told you?"

His eyes found and held hers. "It wasn't your fault, Dani."

Chapter 25

"Beautiful day we're having, isn't it?"

Dani glanced to her right, her gaze skirting the road in favor of the simple wooden farm stand and the array of plants for sale across its top two shelves. Beside them, on a separate shelf unit entirely, were a half dozen hand-painted birdhouses and milk cans.

Drawing her hand to her forehead as a shield against the sun, she strained to pick out the face she knew was there, somewhere.

"Over here."

Dodging her eyes left, she could just make out the jeans, the flannel shirt, the cowboy hat. But the object in his hands? Not quite yet . . .

"The sun is so bright I couldn't find you for a minute." She ventured off the road and closer to her friend's brother, the watering can in his hand now easier to see. "Do you ever get a day off?"

Caleb set the can on the ground, repositioned the freshly watered plants on their shelf, and then wiped his hands down the sides of his jeans. "I'm off today."

"It doesn't look like that to me."

"You mean this stuff here?" He shrugged off her answering nod. "I don't consider helping Elijah work. I see it more as exercise and getting to be outside without my hands being idle. That's why, on my days off from the station, I'm either here or at my parents' place."

"What makes you decide which farm to go to?" She made her way over to the shelf of painted birdhouses and milk cans and ran her finger along the fine detail work, her ears on alert for Caleb's answer.

"Depends on the day. This morning, after I saw my tenants off, I came out here to check on Nettie. I didn't necessarily think there would be any leftover issues from yesterday, but I guess I needed to be sure."

"Trust me, I get it. I did the same thing this morning when I practically pounced on your sister when she brought over my breakfast basket."

"You eating any better?" he asked.

"I'm trying to." And it was true. She was. It wasn't easy; the instinct was still there to just shove everything into the refrigerator. But she did her best to resist, even if only for a few bites.

"Good. I'm glad to hear it."

She leaned forward for a closer look at a birdhouse painted to resemble an old Victorian home. "A few seconds ago, you mentioned tenants. Do you own an apartment complex or something?"

"Nope. Just a small cottage on my own property. Been renting it out to the same young couple for close to three years now. Or I was until today when they moved out."

"Were they Amish?"

"Nope."

Straightening up, she leaned against the edge of the farm stand. "So why did they move?"

"He got a job out of state."

"Ahhh . . ." She swept her hands toward the birdhouses and plants. "So how does this work, exactly? Don't Elijah and Lydia worry that someone will just pull up and help themselves to any or all of this stuff without paying?"

"Not really. They believe in the honor system." He pointed

to a small metal box sitting atop the left side of the shelf, its Place Money Inside sign faded from the sun. "That's why that box isn't locked, either."

"It's almost hard to imagine being that . . ." She trailed off in search of a better word than *naïve*.

"Trusting?" Caleb supplied.

"Yes. Trusting."

Shrugging, he moved on to a second set of plants— vegetable plants, based on the signs attached to each one. He picked up a second watering can, gave each plant a healthy drink, and then moved on to a third row. "So you told Lydia about the baby this morning? When you were asking about Nettie?"

"No."

"Then how did she know? I thought you said you were *getting ready* to tell her when you noticed Nettie was missing."

She stepped out from the shaded protection of the farm stand and hurried to right a plant his foot had tipped over. "Lydia had actually guessed on her own before the pond."

"I don't understand then," he said, lowering the now-empty can back onto the ground. "If she already knew, then what were you getting ready to tell her when you noticed Nettie wasn't sitting by the flowers anymore?"

"I was getting ready to tell her my intention for the baby."

He stilled his hands against his jeans, mid-wipe. "Your intention?"

"To give her—or him—to Lydia and Elijah to raise."

For a second, maybe two, it was as if Caleb froze in place, his body, his expression, utterly motionless. But then it all changed.

His mouth gaped.

His eyes widened.

He cupped his mouth only to knock off his cowboy hat as he laced his hands atop his head in conjunction with a loud and prolonged exhale. "Dani, you can't do that. You just can't."

"Why not? Miss Lottie said—"

He stared at her. "Wait. You spoke to Miss Lottie? When? Where?"

"At her house. A few days ago."

"And she told you to do this?"

"No. Of course not. She just answered my question as to whether Elijah and Lydia could even take the baby. And she thinks they can."

He was still staring, but she was no longer certain he was seeing. "You're telling me Miss Lottie thinks this is a good idea?"

"I wasn't there to seek her opinion, Caleb," she countered, her voice beginning to rise. "I was simply there to find out if there was any sort of Amish rule against it."

"But why?" he volleyed back. "Why would you even let your mind go there? Especially after what happened to your family?"

"My mind is there *because* of what happened to my family—because I failed them in ways I know Lydia won't."

He held up his hands. "Did you not hear what I said last night? How it was an exact match of what you said *to me*? The accident that killed your family was not your fault, Dani. Please! Giving up your baby because of it is just . . . *wrong*. And-and crazy."

"You think it's crazy for me to want this child to have a mother like Lydia? A mother who lets her kids be kids? Who enjoys the little moments with them?"

"No, of course not. But I think it's crazy you don't see that you did the same things with your own kids."

It was her turn to stare. "You never saw me with my kids, Caleb. You know nothing."

"I didn't see you with them, no. But I've listened, and I've heard."

"What are you talking about?" she hissed.

"I'm talking about a mom who made her children's birthdays beyond special. I'm talking about a mom who clearly modeled the notion of inclusion if her daughter couldn't imagine not inviting the bad seed of the kindergarten class to her birthday party. I'm talking about a mom who clearly instilled such a gentleness in her son that *a stray cat* was able to pick it up. I'm talking about a mom who not only had the foresight to learn CPR before her first child was born, but to make sure she was current every few years, as well. I'm talking about *that mom*, Dani. I'm talking about *you*."

"That's what?" she spat. "Four stories?"

"It's the only four stories you've shared."

"Four stories doesn't make you an expert on what kind of mother—what kind of person—I was."

"Then share more. Tell me about Maggie, about Spencer, about Ava, about your husband, about your mom. It'll do you good. Just like it did for Nettie in the barn the other day."

She raised his step forward with her own three steps back. "I-I can't. It hurts too much. They're *gone*. And *those moments* are gone."

"Not when you share them with someone, they're not. That's why, the four times that you have, you've smiled real smiles every single time, Dani. The kind that go from *here*"— he moved his finger from his lips to his eyes—"straight to *here*."

"Caleb, please. You don't know what you're talking about."

His eyes darkened. "You don't think I've known grief?"

"I'm not saying that; I'm just—"

"You know about Rose. But what you don't know about is my fiancée, Sheila."

"Your fiancée?"

Again, he cupped his mouth, his gaze fixing on a point far beyond Dani. "I met her when I was out on a call as an EMT. Her friend was sick. Saw her again a few weeks later. We began dating and, about a year later, I asked her to marry me." He shook his head at the memory. "One minute we were planning a simple wedding in her parents' backyard. The next she was facing down a stage four cancer diagnosis. She died a month later."

"Oh, Caleb. I'm so sorry. I-I had no idea."

He stepped forward again, his eyes back on Dani. "I'm not sharing this to make you feel bad, Dani. I'm sharing this so you see that I get it. At least a little. And like you, I closed myself up when she passed. I didn't want to talk about her, didn't want to think about her, didn't want to step foot in even so much as one place where we'd been together because it all hurt too much—the reality, the memories, all of it. I was literally misery walking.

"Then, one day, we got a call out to a park I'd been to for picnics with Sheila countless times. Not going wasn't an option. When we got there, we realized it had been a prank, but once I wrapped my head around that and really let myself look at my surroundings, it was like a dozen little visits from Sheila. I saw her on a picnic blanket near our favorite tree . . . I saw her swinging on a rope swing . . . I saw her running ahead of me on a path . . . I heard her laugh . . . And you know what? It made me *happy*, Dani. Really, really happy. Because, for those moments, in that place, she was there. The time we'd spent together and the memories we'd made were still there, still"—he smacked his hand to his chest—"*here*. And that's when I realized she'll always be with me as long as I *let* her be with me. Hearing you say that to Nettie the other day was simply a reminder."

She knew he was waiting for her to say something, anything, but the noise in her head was making it difficult to think, let alone speak.

"So tell me something. Share another story."

"Another story?"

"Yes. Tell me something Ava liked. Something that made her happy."

Ava . . .

Sweet, precious Ava . . .

Wrapping her arms around her body, she stumbled backward. "I can't. I just . . . *can't.*"

"Yes. You can. Just tell me one thing. *One thing*, Dani. One—"

"She liked flowers! My little girl liked flowers!"

"I like flowers, too!"

Together, they turned in the direction of the excited voice and the equally excited face peeking out from a row of large sunflowers denoting the property between the farm stand and the farm itself.

"Nettie! Does Mamm know you're out here?" Caleb motioned to the child and dropped down to her eye level. "Because you're not supposed to be wandering off, remember?"

"Mamm is hanging the clothes. I asked if I could say hello and she said yes!"

A wave from Lydia in the distance confirmed the child's words and softened Caleb's tone. "Okay, good. That's important, remember?"

"Yah!"

Nettie stepped around her uncle and grabbed hold of Dani's hand. "Where is your little girl?"

She closed her eyes.

Breathe in . . .

Breathe out . . .

Breathe in . . .

"Dani's little girl is with the Lord," Caleb said.

"Like Rose?"

"That's right, kiddo. Like Rose."

"What is her name?"

Is, *not* was . . .

Dani opened her eyes to the sky and swallowed. "Ava. Her name was . . . Ava."

"How old is she?"

"She was three."

Nettie tugged Dani's eyes down to her own. "What kind of flowers did Ava like?"

Swallowing, she lifted her gaze to Caleb's. *Please*, she mouthed. *I can't do this.*

Yes. You can, he mouthed back.

"What kind, Miss Dani?"

"Tulips," she said, squeezing her eyes closed. "Ava liked tulips."

"What color?" Nettie asked, swinging their arms.

"All of them—red, yellow, pink, and purple." And just like that, she was standing at her bedroom window again, looking down at her little girl's unexpected gift.

"*There* it is . . ."

She didn't need Caleb to clarify what *it* was. She knew it was there. She could feel it just as surely as she could Nettie's little hand inside her own.

"I don't know, Nettie," Caleb teased. "Something sure is making a pretty smile on Dani's face, don't you think?"

"Yah!"

Then, "Care to let Nettie and me in on what you're smiling about?"

Slowly, she opened her eyes to first Caleb, and then Nettie, the curiosity on the child's face guiding the answer from her lips. "Actually, I can show you, if you'd like. It's at the house."

Chapter 26

They were waiting for her at the kitchen table when she emerged from the bedroom, her phone clutched in her hand and powering up for only the third time in weeks.

"You need your phone to show us?" Caleb lifted his chin from its resting spot atop Nettie's kapped head.

Nodding, she glanced back at the lit screen. "Okay, good. It looks like I still have enough battery left; I'll at least be able to show you real quick."

"I can charge that at my place for you if you'd like."

She waved off his offer. "It's okay. There's no one to call."

When the pass code screen came up, she punched in the six-digit number comprised of the kids' birth dates and then waited for the album icon to appear across the bottom.

"I took this picture before I came here," she said by way of explanation.

"I like pictures!" Nettie declared.

Uh-oh . . .

She looked from Nettie to the phone and, finally, to Caleb. "Is it okay to show her a picture without asking Lydia's permission?"

"It'll be fine. I'll see that it is."

Dani pressed her way into the album, her breath catching at the sight of some twenty thumbnail-sized photographs arranged in lines of four. All but one were moments she'd captured at Ava's birthday party.

Ava's eyes filled with wonder as Jeff took off her blindfold to the ocean of balloons scattered across the sunroom floor . . .

Celia, her neighborhood friend, pretending to swim through the balloon ocean . . .

Dexter, her swim lesson buddy, holding his nose as he jumped onto—and popped—a part of the ocean . . .

Ava and Spencer working together to open the treasure chest . . .

Maggie watching Ava blow out the cake with no less joy and excitement than she'd have for her own birthday . . .

Row by row, Dani skimmed her way through her last full day with her family, the sudden heaviness in her chest pushing her down onto the bench opposite Caleb and Nettie.

"Dani? You okay?"

"I want to see the surprise, Dani!"

"Nettie, shhhh . . ." Caleb whispered.

"But she said she wanted to show us something."

"Nettie—"

Willing her gaze down to the last thumbnail in the last row, she tapped it into full screen view and pulled it to her chest. "Last fall," she said, her voice quiet, raspy, "Ava and I decided to plant a tulip garden in the backyard. I thought it would be something fun to do together, and since she loved flowers so much she was all excited.

"We made a bit of an event out of it by stopping at the hardware store the day before and getting our bulbs, some dirt, a pair of gardening gloves for her and for me, and two shovels—one for me and a kiddy one for her. The next afternoon, when Maggie was off at school and Spencer had gone to a friend's house after half-day kindergarten, we got to work. We dug, and we planted, and we watered. After a while, I had to go inside to check something real quick, and when I came back out all of the bulbs that were left when I went inside not more than two minutes earlier were gone. When I asked Ava what happened to them, she pointed at the patch of dirt she'd been working in and told me she'd planted them all. Seeing as how it was time to pick up the kids so I could get Maggie to her scout meeting in time, I just let it go. I figured, come spring, there'd be a dozen or so tulips in one confined area and a lot of emptiness everywhere else. No big deal."

Caleb grinned. "That's not what you got, is it?"

Glancing down at the phone still clutched to her chest, she shook her head. "Later on, during the car ride to pick up the kids, Ava told me she made a flower surprise for me. Since I was just pulling into the car pool line and there were kids walking everywhere, I didn't pay it much mind. Until one morning . . . after the—"

She stopped, slowed her breathing to a more manageable level, and made herself keep going. "I heard this little bird chirping away outside my bedroom window. I almost ignored it the way I ignored everything else those first few weeks, but I didn't. I walked over to the window, peeked outside, and I saw *this*."

Pulling the phone away from her body, she looked down at the picture, felt the instant smile it brought to her lips, and then turned it so Caleb and Nettie could see.

"That's a smiley face!" Nettie said, clapping her hands together.

Caleb's laughter filled the space between them. "Yes, yes it is. The circle of pink tulips for the face, the two yellow tulips for eyes, the one yellow tulip for the nose, and the four yellow tulips in a curve for the smile . . . Wow. I'd say Ava very definitely made a flower surprise for Mommy."

"She sure did, didn't she?" Dani whispered, smiling at Caleb through tear-dappled lashes.

"Who is Spencer and Maggie?" Nettie asked, peeking around the camera.

She pulled the phone back, exited out of the picture of Ava's tulip surprise, and scrolled through her album until she came to a picture of her children—together—hugging on the front step as the last of Ava's birthday guests pulled out of the driveway. Her hand shaking, she turned the screen back into Caleb and Nettie's view. "Spencer was—*is* my son. And Maggie is my daughter."

"Are they with Ava and Rose, too?"

Caleb tightened his arms around his niece. "Yes, Nettie, they are."

"Rose has a lot of friends in heaven!"

"She does, indeed, Nettie. She does, indeed." He looked from the photo to Dani, his smile tender. "They're beautiful, Dani."

Unable to speak, Dani hurried a nod instead, and pulled the phone back against her chest.

"Did Spencer and Maggie give you a surprise we can see?" Nettie asked, wiggling off her uncle's lap and onto the bench beside him, her eyes wide with hope. "I like to see surprises!"

"You mean like the flowers?" she asked.

"Yah. Something I can see!"

Slowly, with Nettie's words playing in her head, Dani pulled the phone away, looked down at the picture of her children, and then set it down on the table next to the pile of balled-up paper she'd still yet to clear away. "No I don't— Wait!" She sat up tall, swung her legs over the bench, and stood. "I *do* have things I can show you from them."

"*With stories?*" Nettie asked.

She nodded—once, twice—and then disappeared into her room, her heart leading the way for her feet. When she reached the wall to the right of the dresser, she carefully peeled Maggie's picture from the wall and carried it out to the kitchen.

Again, she sat at the table, and again held the memory to her chest as she set the scene. "My Maggie, at heart, was a quiet little thing. It's not that she minded people being around—because she didn't—but she liked to observe, often giggling off in a corner about something funny her brother and his friends were doing on the other side of the room. She was also a girly girl in every sense of the word. She loved dolls, playing house, wearing pretty bows in her hair, that sort of thing. She loved books—and I mean *loved* books. She'd read every chance she could. She loved looking out at the stars and making"—her voice faltered—"wishes."

"What's that say?" Nettie asked, pointing Dani's attention back down to the paper pressed against her chest.

"It doesn't say anything. It's a picture Maggie drew of us baking cookies together. See?" Dani set the paper on the table in front of Caleb and Nettie and gently, reverently, smoothed it flat. "She even drew the radio in the background with music notes coming out of it, see?"

At Caleb's nod, she added, "We kept it turned down really low so we wouldn't wake Ava from her nap."

"I like to make cookies with Mamm!"

She smiled, her lips trembling. "I'm sure you do."

"What do the words say?" Nettie pushed up onto her knees and pointed toward the drawing. "Can you read them to me?"

Dani dropped her eyes to the drawing she really didn't need to see to know. The table, the rolling pin, the mixing bowl, the bag of—

"Oh! It says *flour*," she said, pointing at the rectangular bag Maggie had drawn to include the brand's blue stripe and company logo. "Your mamm uses flour for cookies, too."

"Not *those* words, Dani. The other words."

This time she let her eyes lead her around the drawing, continuing from where her memory had left off. Maggie grinning, the can of—

"Oh. That says *icing*. See?" She moved her finger from the icing can to the pile of decorated cookies on the counter behind Maggie's drawing of Dani. "We decorated the cookies with icing and sprinkles."

Nettie listened closely only to shake her head when Dani finished. "The *other* words. The ones back there."

She followed Nettie's slowly inching finger along its path toward the corner of the paper and flipped it over, her eyes coming to rest on seven lightly penciled words she'd failed to notice until that moment—seven words Caleb read aloud for Nettie.

" 'Mommy makes the best wishes come true.' "

Jamming her fist against her ensuing gasp, Dani sank forward against the table. "I-I had no idea that was there," she whispered. "How . . . how could I not have seen that?"

Caleb set his hand atop Dani's and squeezed. "Because now was when you needed to see it most, that's why."

"I-I . . . don't know what to say."

"You don't have to say anything, Dani. Just feel. Let yourself know the love Maggie felt for you when she drew that picture and wrote those words. Because whether you sat and listened to her wishes as much as you wish you had, it's clear you're the kind of mommy who knew them, anyway."

Nettie planted her elbows on the table and bookended her cheeks with her hands. "Do you have a surprise to show from your boy, too?"

"His name is Spencer," Caleb reminded his niece.

Dani forced her eyes off Maggie's carefully written words and onto the expectant face staring back at her, waiting.

"Do you have a surprise to show from Spencer?" Nettie amended.

"I do, actually. Wait here." Again she headed into her room, and again she made her way toward the simple wooden dresser next to the window, her gaze seeking and finding the wooden pencil box with Spencer's name spelled out across the top.

She carried it back to the kitchen table and sat down, her fingers gravitating toward her son's name as they did every night. Only this time, instead of drawing them back at the last minute as she always did, she allowed herself to trace each and every letter—letters she'd filled in with dozens of pictures she'd painstakingly shrunk, copied, cut, and glued into place.

The *S* she'd filled in with pictures of cats and dogs . . .

The *P* she'd filled in with pictures of his favorite baseball players . . .

The *E* she'd filled in with pictures of soccer balls and goals and whistles . . .

The *N* she'd filled in with pictures from swim lessons . . .

The *C* she'd filled in with pictures of Spencer and his best friend, Bobby . . .

The *E* she'd filled in with pictures of his sisters . . .

The *R* she'd filled in with pictures of him sitting on Jeff's lap and hugging his grandma . . .

When she completed her tracing of the final letter in her son's name, she scooted the box across the table to Caleb and Nettie. "Spencer loved sports, and nature, and animals, and learning things, and playing army men with the little boy across the street, and his sisters, and his dad, and his grandma. When Maggie went off to school at five years old, I threw a little Go-to-School party after dinner for the five of us. I made her favorite treat, gave her a special hair ribbon for her first day of school, and sent her off to bed more excited than nervous. She loved it so much, I did it again the night before first grade, and second grade, and then for the two of them the following year when she was starting third grade and he was starting kindergarten.

"He'd been a part of this special gathering for Maggie for three years at that point and so he was just tickled to finally be an honoree even if he was more than a little worried about actually going off to school. So I let him pick the treat knowing it would be one Maggie would like, too, and, for his gift, I got him this pencil box and decided to spell out his name using pictures of the things that made him most happy. I thought that maybe, if he could see these things during the school day, he might feel less homesick."

Leaning over, Caleb took a moment to study each and every letter. When he reached the end, he looked up at Dani, his brow furrowed. "Why didn't you include a picture of yourself?"

"I don't know. I guess I figured I was represented by having made it."

Nettie dropped her hands next to the box. "Can I see inside?"

"I guess," Dani said, shrugging. "There's just pencils inside."

"I like pencils!"

Inching the box closer, Dani snapped open the hinge and spun it back around for Nettie to see. "See? Pencils."

"Can I take them out?" Nettie asked.

"I guess . . ."

Nettie reached in, pulled out the handful of pencils, examined them closely, and then peeked back in the box at Caleb's audible inhale. "That's you, Dani!"

"Me?" she echoed.

"Yah! Right there!"

She accepted the box Caleb pushed back across the table and looked inside, her eyes coming to rest on a photograph of herself, cut into something resembling a circle, and affixed to the bottom of the box with four pieces of tape. "W-when? How?"

"I don't know, Dani. But it appears I'm not the only one who thought you should've been part of that pencil box."

Chapter 27

She'd always been drawn to sunsets. For her, it didn't really matter if the vivid golds and oranges, mauves and reds were streaking the ocean's sky or peeking out behind a shopping mall in suburbia. Either way, it was worth a moment to stop and look or make a mad dash for her camera in the hopes of framing its beauty on a wall. But there was something about the one in front of her now—slipping behind lush green fields dotted by the occasional grain silo and windmill—that quieted her heart in a way that felt almost peaceful.

Pulling her legs onto the Adirondack chair, Dani pointed toward the farthest field she could see. "Is it bad that sheep is still outside, alone?"

"If a coyote or a fox happens by, yes. But I'm thinking it'll find its way back to the barn before long." Caleb took a sip of his lemonade and then set the glass on the armrest of his own chair. "You doing okay?"

She returned her gaze to the horizon. "I'm not sure how to answer that."

"No worries." Stretching out his legs across the patio, he laced his hands between his head and the chair and chuckled. "Those kids didn't give you much elbow room to eat tonight, did they?"

Her lips twitched at the memory. "I was one more body on a bench that was already pretty full."

"Dani? That had nothing to do with the length of that bench and everything to do with Nettie, Mark, David, and Luke being excited that you were finally joining us for dinner."

Not sure what to say, she said nothing.

"And while I got a kick out of watching you play dodge-a-head with your elbows every time you cut a piece of your chicken, I enjoyed seeing you *eat* even more," he said, his own elbows jutting out from behind his cowboy hat like wings. "You needed that."

"I've been eating."

The scrape of his hat's brim on the chair let her know he'd abandoned his view of the sunset. "I saw inside your refrigerator when you opened it for Nettie this afternoon. You have enough food in there to feed Lydia's entire crew for a week, if not more."

She kept her own eyes on the sky. "I just haven't had much of an appetite, that's all."

"You had one at the ice-cream place," he said. "And again tonight."

It wasn't hard to deduce the dots he was connecting. Nor was it hard to see that maybe, just maybe, he was right . . .

"It felt good to talk about the kids with you and Nettie this afternoon," she said as the last of the day's colors slipped away. "It really did. So thank you for that."

"It was my pleasure." Another scrape of his hat against the chair's wooden slats let her know he, too, was drinking in the part of the night responsible for the orange flashes making their way down the otherwise darkened roads of Amish country. The safety lights, mandated by the state, kept buggies and their occupants visible at night. "So how about Jeff? And your mom? Did you bring something of theirs with you?"

"I did."

When she didn't say anything more, he pulled his legs back toward the chair and stood. "Well, I've taken way more of your time today than I should've, but it was nice getting to know you a little bit better, Dani. Thank you."

"Getting to know *me*?"

"Absolutely. Maggie, Spencer, and Ava were—and will always be—a part of you. Learning a little bit about them meant learning a little more about you, too." Palming the front of his hat, he tugged it down across his forehead and then motioned in the direction they'd been facing for the better part of an hour. "You enjoy the rest of your evening."

Something about his words, juxtaposed against the now-darkened fields, stirred an all too familiar feeling in the pit of her stomach. For the first time since the accident, the crushing weight of loneliness had receded for just a little while, enabling her to eat, to smile, to remember, to feel her children close—

"Please." She reached for Caleb's arm only to pull away at the feel of his flannel shirt against her skin. "Could you stay a little longer? I . . ." She glanced back at the growing darkness and then stood. "I want to talk about my mom and Jeff."

"Good, because I want to listen."

Nodding, she led the way through the back door of the grossdawdy house. When he was seated at the table, she ventured into the bedroom, returning moments later with a small pink book clutched tightly to her chest.

"As you know, I was an only child," she said, lowering herself onto the bench opposite Caleb's. "I was also a latchkey kid, if you're familiar with that expression?"

"Not really, no."

"It means I was the kid of working parents," she explained. "I came home from school to an empty house; I got my own snack, did my homework by myself, and, as I got older, had dinner on the table most nights when they finally got home. Being a latchkey kid meant I didn't get to do a lot of the things my peers did after school—like music lessons and playdates and stuff like that.

"Mom always said she thought that's why I went to the other extreme with my own kids—because I wanted them to have the things I hadn't been able to have, that I wanted to be a better mom than I felt I'd had. She said it was the natural order of things between a mother and a daughter. Her mother had stayed home with her, and while her mom had lots of time to play, there wasn't money for anything beyond the necessities in life, like food and shelter. So my mom vowed to do things differently when *she* had a child. Her way to go about that? To work so we had money to take trips like the one that had me meeting you and Lydia."

The bench creaked as he leaned forward against the edge of the table. "Okay . . ."

"And me? I didn't want my kids to be the ones who couldn't do things because their mom was always working. So I stayed home and got them involved in everything and anything they so much as blinked at. But when Mom said to me—about my wanting to be a better mom to my own children than she'd been to me—I felt awful. Because the truth is, my mom was a great mom. Did I miss out on some things growing up because of her work schedule? Sure. Often, actually. But when I needed her, she was always there for me. *Always.*"

She pulled the book from her chest and set it on the table, title side up. "I wanted her to know that my doing things the way I was doing them wasn't a reflection on the job she'd done. So when I came across this book in a specialty shop one day, I knew I had to get it for her." Spinning it around for Caleb to read, she pushed it toward him, her hand gently holding it closed while she continued. "It's filled with poems and special quotes about motherhood. At the back of the book, there is a page where I was able to include the many things I admired about her as a mom, and why she was the best mom for me."

When he looked down at the book, she filled in the final piece of the story. "For whatever reason, when she came to visit this last time, this was in her bag. I-I guess it meant more to her than I realized." She pulled her hand back. "Go ahead, open it."

"Are you sure?"

"Yes. I-I want you to read what I wrote. My mom was a special woman and I want you—I want *everyone*—to know that."

Slowly, gently, he flipped back the front cover to reveal . . . *her mother's handwriting?*

Confused, she lifted off her bench with her own lean. "Wait. That's not my writing. That's my mother's. What does it say?"

"It says: 'Now it is your turn, my love.'"

"My turn?" she echoed. "My turn for what?" Reaching across the table, she flipped the book closed, confirmed it was the same book she'd given her mom, and then opened it once again. "I don't understand why she'd write that. It was my gift to her . . ."

Silence fell across the room as, page by page, he made his way through the book, stopping on occasion to read a particularly poignant quote or to comment on a poem. Some made them laugh; others had her wiping a tear while Caleb sniffled. But it was as they approached the end that she felt the emotion really beginning to kick in.

"Okay, this next one"—she stilled his page-turning hand—"will be the one I wrote. I want you to read it aloud, too."

She closed her eyes at his answering nod.

"'My Dearest Danielle.'"

Her eyes flew open. "It doesn't say that!"

"Yes it does." He spun the book around so it was readable from her side of the table. "See?"

"'My Dearest Danielle,'" she managed past the sudden tightening in her throat. "'I used to believe a mother's greatest joy was in watching her child grow and learn. I was wrong. A mother's greatest joy is watching her child become a mother. And while you have been one for many years now,

I am awestruck at the job you are doing. You are my life, my light, my joy, Danielle, and I am so incredibly proud to be your mother and to have you be my grandchildren's mother.' "

Pressing against her strangled sob, she made herself continue, her lips and her mouth filling with tears. " 'Forever and always, Mom.'

"Oh, Caleb," she whispered, pulling the book close to her body once again. "She didn't pack the book *I* gave *her*; she found one just like it—one *she* planned to give *me*."

"I'm glad you found it."

Seconds turned to minutes as she stared at the book, at her mother's handwriting, at her mother's final message of love. "I wish I had seen this before . . . Before the accident."

"Maybe you needed it more now."

She ran her fingertips across the words one last time and then stood. "I have something of Jeff's, too."

A quick trek in and out of the bedroom had her back at the table in no time, clutching the final item in her hands. "I met Jeff shortly after college. I was sitting on a bench, looking out over the river, when he walked by—or intended to, as he was fond of saying. I was so intent on whatever I was looking at that all his best efforts to get me to look up failed."

Caleb laughed. "Nothing like killing a guy's ego."

"That's what Jeff said. But I honestly didn't see him. I really didn't."

"So what made you finally notice him?"

"He sat on my lap."

He pulled his hand out from beneath his chin and thumped it down onto the table. "Seriously?"

"Not really. But by the time I snapped out of whatever zone I was in, he'd bought me a rose from a nearby flower cart, a balloon from the same place, a cup of ice cream he ended up eating while he waited, and *this jacket*"—she held it up—"from some kid who wasn't wearing it, anyway."

"A jacket? Why?"

"Because he knew a cold front was coming in and he didn't want me to have any excuses for leaving once I finally noticed him."

He laughed. "Wow. Do you remember what you were thinking about?"

"No. I was just thinking or, maybe, not thinking. I just knew it was a sunny day and I didn't have anywhere I had to be."

"Wow," he repeated.

"I know." She smiled at the memory. "But once I did notice him—empty ice-cream cup and all—we hit it off and we were pretty inseparable after that."

"What drew you to him? Once you noticed him, that is?"

"He was sweet. He was always doing little things to let me know he loved me—a note in my shoe, a favorite piece of chocolate on my pillow, a quick mid-day call just to tell me he loved me before he went into a meeting. He was a doer as much as he was a dreamer. And he wanted the same things I wanted—stability, honesty, and family."

Caleb pointed at the jacket. "You kept it all these years?"

"Of course. It, more than any other possession, sums up who he was."

"How so?"

"He was kind and he was generous. He was always thinking ahead to what I might need, what the kids might need. And he made it all look so effortless, so easy, so natural."

"Sounds like someone I would've liked to know."

She held the jacket to her cheek. "Absolutely."

"How come I haven't seen you wearing it at all since you've been here?" he asked.

"Because it's been a reminder of that day, of the way we started. How he made sure we'd be okay and that we'd be together always. Only we're not now. Or . . ." She looked from the jacket to Caleb and back again, her eyes misting. "Or not in the way I thought we'd be. But he is still with me, isn't he?"

"You bet he is."

Hesitancy traded places with conviction and she slid her arms into the sleeves, the soft, familiar fabric a gentle and welcomed hug against her skin. She drew her shoulders alongside her cheeks, breathed in the lingering scent of his cologne she could almost pick out around the collar, and tucked her hands into the narrow pockets—

Pulling out her right hand, she stared down at the familiar blue sticky note folded closed inside her palm.

"What's that?" Caleb asked.

"It-it's one of Jeff's notes."

"You've kept it in the pocket all this time?"

"I didn't know it was there," she whispered.

"Oh. Wow. Do you want me to leave so you can read it?"

She looked at her name and imagined her husband peeking over his shoulder to make sure she wasn't around as he ripped the page from her notepad.

She could see him plucking the black pen from the holder on her desk . . .

Writing the note while listening for the sound of approaching footsteps . . .

Folding it in half . . .

Writing her name across the front . . .

Opening the hall closet and slipping it into the pocket . . .

And, finally, closing the door in triumph . . .

"Dani?"

She let the image play out and then looked back at Caleb, his question catching up to her brain. "Actually, no. I think I'll save this for another day."

"Are you sure?"

Was she?

Glancing at the table, she breathed in the sight of Maggie's picture, Spencer's pencil box, the book from her mother, and the image in her head of Ava's flowers—each one a gift, an unexpected reminder of their love for her, and their forever place in her heart and in her life.

"I wish you could see yourself right now," Caleb said. "Really see yourself."

"Why?"

"If you could, you'd be able to *see* what good it does you to talk about them, to feel them, to remember them. Because in doing those things they're still here. They're still part of you."

"I don't need to see myself."

"But Dani—"

She dropped her hand back to her side. "I don't need to *see* myself because I can *feel* it. I can *feel them*. Thanks to you."

"You were a great mom—a treasured mom, Dani." Palming the top of his cowboy hat, Caleb stood and made his way over to the door. "The people who would know that better than anyone else wanted you to know that today. I, for one, don't think that's a coincidence."

"What are you saying?"

He paused his hand on the doorknob. "I'm saying that Maggie, Spencer, and Ava's baby sister deserves to have *you* as her mother."

My Day's To-Do List

Epilogue

Fourteen months later

She was just taking the cookies out of the oven when she heard the familiar little voice drifting up her driveway and through her front window screens. Glancing at the clock above the sink, Dani wiped her hands on the nearest dish towel and turned back to the chubby-cheeked baby happily gumming a pale yellow teething ring and watching her every move with wonder and fascination.

"Do you hear that, little one?" she asked, grinning. "I think we're about to get a visit from a friend!"

The tiny mouth, wet with drool, spread wide in the same endearingly crooked grin Dani saw, times four, every morning when she opened her eyes. In those framed smiles, as well as the one in front of her now, she found the courage to tackle a new day. And when grief darkened her path forward, it was their light, their beauty, that got her back on track time and time again.

"C'mon, pumpkin. It's a perfect day to—"

"It's me, Dani! Me and Mamm! Are you home?"

Unbuckling the baby from the swing, Dani pulled the sweet wiggly body against her chest and waved the tiny hand at the heart-shaped face now peering back at them through the living room screen.

"They are home, Mamm! They are home! I see them!"

"Perhaps you should not press your face to Danielle's window."

"But I see them, Mamm! I see them both! *See?*" The screen pushed inward with Nettie's index finger, then retracted at Lydia's command. "They are right there. In the kitchen! And I smell cookies! Yummy ones!"

"Yummy cookies? Did someone say *yummy cookies?*"

Bobbing her head to the right, Dani traveled her gaze out the kitchen window to the black pickup truck stopped in line with her front porch. An added lean yielded the man who'd been a steadfast beacon through some of her stormiest days. With his solid hand and quiet friendship, she'd found a way to put herself back together—piece by piece. Very few of her pieces looked as they once had. Some were battered and worn around the edges. Others had required a few strokes of a marker to restore their missing color. And still others had come so close to breaking in two they'd required a piece of tape here and a piece of tape there just to keep them intact. But when they finally fell into place where they belonged, she was still the same person in all the ways that mattered most.

She was still Jeff's wife . . .

She was still Maggie, Spencer, and Ava's mom . . .

And she was still her mother's daughter.

Nothing, not even death, could ever change those things.

But she was more than that now, too.

She was someone who sat outside and savored sunsets . . .

She was someone who looked at the clock merely as a point of reference rather than a timer . . .

She was someone who took walks to nowhere in particular . . .

She was someone who savored the here and now and tried hard to let her battle-tested faith take care of the rest . . .

All good things, no doubt.

But of all the changes that had come her way—good and bad—the very best one was in her arms at that very moment. For in her baby's face she saw a dash of Spencer, a pinch of Ava, and a sprinkle of Maggie combined with equal parts Jeff and her mom. Yet, even with those little reminders she so cherished, Grace was just Grace, too.

Sweet.

Loving.

And a daily reminder of the importance of faith, and friends.

Breathing in her daughter's sweet scent, Dani gathered four cookies in her hand, bypassed the stack of napkins deemed unnecessary by summer's unwritten rules, and headed toward the front door of her new home—a home she'd fallen in love with the moment she'd laid eyes on it.

It wasn't that it was big and fancy like the home she'd shared with Jeff and the kids. Quite the contrary, in fact. But the small rental cottage on the edge of Caleb's property was the new start she needed. It was just far enough away from Lydia and Elijah that she had to learn to stand on her own two feet a little, yet still close enough to know Caleb's listening ears were less than fifty feet away.

In the beginning, she'd worried that she was robbing Grace of the chance to grow up in the same home in which her brother and sisters had once lived—a home her daddy had worked so hard to buy for all of them. But if there was one thing Dani had learned since that fateful day, it was that love wasn't defined by space or time. It was everywhere. All the time. And it was up to Dani to make sure Grace grew up truly knowing her father, her brother, her sisters, and her grandmother via the photographs and stories that would forever hold a special place in their lives.

Swinging her gaze to the table beside the door, she drank in the sight of the blue sticky note now framed and purposely placed in a spot where she and Grace would see it every time they walked out the door. Because while the words had been written for Dani, she knew they applied to Grace, as well.

"We will love you for all eternity, too," she whispered.

ACKNOWLEDGMENTS

In order for you to have this book in your hand, a lot of things must happen . . .

I need an idea for a story (which, in this case, came while visiting friends in Wyoming—a place that always leaves me feeling renewed).

Then, many, many hours—stretched over months—must go into the writing. Which, as my family can tell you, often has me talking to myself and zoning off at odd times. It also means more leftovers than might otherwise be had.

When I finally type "the end," I turn it over to my team at Kensington Publishing, knowing my wonderful editor, Esi Sogah, will help me spit shine the final product. After her comes the editing team, the marketing folks, and the sales team, who are on the ground doing their best to get this book into your hands.

And, finally, you—as the reader—must make the choice to read it. For that, I thank you. If you like what you've read and are curious about what else I've written, please visit my website at: laurabradford.com.

PIECE BY PIECE

Laura Bradford

ABOUT THIS GUIDE

The suggested questions are included
to enhance your group's reading of
Laura Bradford's *Piece by Piece*.

DISCUSSION QUESTIONS

1. In many ways, Danielle lives life on a schedule, her days shaped by to-do lists and appointments. How does her life resemble yours in that regard? What are some pros and cons to the way Danielle is/the way you are?

2. Danielle's mother recognized a fatigue in Danielle that Danielle, herself, is reluctant to see. Do you think it was right or wrong of her mother to insist Danielle take time to herself?

3. Danielle is surprised by how much of her day has passed while she was reading. Have you ever lost yourself in a book like she did?

4. The life Danielle Parker has been living changes in an instant. In the blink of an eye she's gone from a wife, daughter, and mother to being completely alone. Has there been a single instant when life seemingly changed for you? How so? Has the passage of time changed that perspective?

5. Danielle flees to Amish country in an attempt to put a little distance between herself and her reality. What do you see as the benefits/pitfalls of such a move?

6. Watching Lydia with her children, Danielle begins to question herself as a mother. Do you think this is natural? Do you think Lydia is, in fact, a better mother? Why? Why not?

7. Danielle sees talking about her loved ones as too painful and, thus, tries to steer all conversation away from them. Do you know people who do the same thing?

8. In what ways do Caleb, Lydia, Nettie, and even the setting help Danielle heal?

9. What do you think of Danielle's decision to stay and raise her child in Amish country?

10. Helen Keller is quoted as saying, "What we have once enjoyed we can never lose; all that we love deeply becomes a part of us." Do you feel that Danielle's journey reflects this belief? How so?

Keep reading for excerpts from
Laura Bradford's novels
Portrait of a Sister
and
A Daughter's Truth,
available now from
Kensington Books
wherever books are sold.

Portrait of a Sister

❧

For the second time in her life, Katie Beiler prayed for God to change His mind, to make His will reflect hers. But the click of her parents' bedroom door, followed by her dat's sad eyes and pasty complexion, told her it wasn't to be.

"It is time, Katie."

Gathering the sides of her pale blue dress in her hands, she made herself part company with the wooden chair that had been both her post and her refuge over the past twenty-four hours and rise onto shaky legs. "I will get the children."

"No," he said, firmly.

Her answering gasp echoed against the walls of the hallway as she reached toward him, her fingers brushing against the suspenders she'd mended during the night. "She-she's gone? Already?"

"No, Katie. But God will welcome her soon. It is His will."

"His will is wrong!" she hissed through clenched teeth only to bow her head in shame just as quickly. "I-I'm sorry, Dat. I shouldn't have said that."

Bracing herself, she lifted her watery gaze from the toes of her black lace-up boots to the amber-flecked brown eyes that matched her own. For a moment, Dat said nothing, the shock on his face the only real indication he'd heard her at all. Eventually though, he spoke, grief winning out over anger. "She has asked to speak to you alone. Go now, child, before it is too late."

Before it is too late . . .

Her thoughts followed her father's heavy footfalls down the stairs and then skipped ahead to the five young faces she'd tried desperately to shield from reality the past few months. Two years her junior, Samuel would be devastated, of course, but he would cover his hurt working in the fields with Dat. Jakob, at fourteen, would take his cue from Samuel. Mary and Sadie would—

"Katie?"

The weakened rasp propelled her forward and through the partially open doorway, her heart both dreading and craving what was on the other side. More than anything, she wanted a miracle to happen, but short of that, she'd be a fool to waste away whatever time they had left.

"I'm here, Mamm." She stopped just inside the door and willed her eyes to adjust to the darkened room. "Can I get you something? Another blanket, perhaps? A glass of water?"

"You can open the shade and let the sunlight in."

"Of course." Crossing the room, Katie gave the dark green shade a quick tug and then watched as it rose upward to provide an uninhibited view of the fields her dat and brothers worked each and every day. She allowed herself a moment to breathe in the answering sunlight before turning back to the nearly unrecognizable shell that was her mother. "Is that better?"

"Yah." Her mother patted the edge of the quilt-topped bed, her pale blue eyes studying Katie closely. "Come. Sit. There are things I want to say. Before it is too late."

"Shhh," Katie scolded. "Do not talk like that. Please."

"The dress I am to be buried in is in my chest. It is what I wore when I married your dat."

She stopped a few inches shy of the bed and cast her eyes down at the wood plank floor. "Mamm, please. I—"

"It is God's will, Katie."

It was on the tip of her tongue to lash out at those words the way she had in the hallway with Dat, but she refrained. To see the same shock on Mamm's face would be unimaginable.

"Katie, I need you to be strong for your brothers and sisters. They will need you more than ever in the days and weeks ahead."

Sinking onto the bed, Katie covered her mother's cold hand with her own and gave it a gentle squeeze. She tried to speak, to offer the reassurance her mother needed, but the expanding lump in her throat made it impossible to speak.

"In another year or so, Annie will be three and Mary will be old enough to look after both her and Sadie on her own. When she is, you are to live your life, Katie. With Abram. He is a good man. Like your dat. It is my hope that your life together will make you smile again."

"I smile," Katie protested.

"Not as you once did."

She felt her mother's thumb encircling her hand and choked back a sob. "I have tried my best to keep this from the little ones. If I have failed, I am sorry . . ."

"You have done beautifully these past few months, Katie. Dat has told me so. But your smile dulled long before I got sick."

Slipping her arm back, Katie pushed off the bed and wandered over to the window. "I painted a new milk can last night while you slept. It is of the pond in summer, the way it was before the climbing tree fell down in that storm a few years ago." She rested her forehead against the glass pane and watched as her dat entered the fields to summon Samuel and Jakob for one final goodbye. "I will always remember the way you'd help boost me onto that first branch when I was no bigger than Sadie is now. I was so frightened that first time."

"That is because I boosted *you* first. When *Hannah* went first and reached down for your hand, you were not afraid."

Just like that, the tears she'd managed to keep to herself in her mother's presence began their descent down her cheeks. "I do not want you to go, Mamm. I-I need you . . ."

"You need only the Lord, Katie, you know that."

She bowed her head in shame. "You are right, Mamm. I know I should not be afraid."

But I am, she wanted to add. Horribly, desperately afraid . . .

"Do not forget what the apostle Paul said, Katie. To fulfill the law of Christ, brethren must bear one another's burdens. There will be many hands ready to help you, Dat, and the children."

The children . . .

She lifted her gaze to the window again in time to see Dat heading back toward the house flanked by Samuel on one side and Jakob on the other. Their brimmed hats made it so she couldn't see her brothers' faces, but her mind could fill in the blanks.

Samuel would be stoic like their father—any emotion offset by his steadfast belief that Mamm's passing was God's will. He would mourn her, of course, but there would be work to be done.

Jakob would surely mimic Samuel, but she knew that in moments alone, while feeding the calves or milking the cows, the younger boy would grieve the woman he still looked to for hugs when he thought no one else was looking.

"I will hug Jakob for you," Katie whispered. "Until he does not need it anymore."

"Thank you, Katie."

She heard the faint sound of the screen door downstairs as

it banged closed behind her father and brothers. If Dat had told Mary first, the thirteen-year-old would no doubt have Sadie and the baby ready and waiting for the family's final moments together. If he hadn't, Katie could imagine her sister looking up from the chair in which she was giving Annie her morning bottle, wondering if she was late in preparing a meal. The absence of footsteps on the stairs told her it was the latter.

A noticeable change in her mother's breath made her turn and scurry back to the bed. "Mamm?"

"It is almost time, Katie."

She looked down at her mother, at the gaunt face and the dark shadows that encircled hesitant eyes. "Do not worry, Mamm. *Please*. I will take care of them all—Samuel, Jakob, Mary, Sadie, Annie, and Dat. I promise."

"That is not all that I worry about."

Swooping down to her knees, she gathered her mother's cold hands inside her own and tried to warm them with her breath. "There is nothing for you to worry about, Mamm."

"There is you, Katie."

She drew back. "Me?"

"Yah."

"But—"

"I want you to be . . . happy . . . again. The way you were when—"

A succession of footsteps on the staircase cut her mother's sentence short and brought Katie back to her feet. She'd had her time with Mamm. To take more would be selfish. "The others are coming to say goodbye." Bending over, she held her lips to her mother's forehead while she worked to steady her own voice. "I love you, Mamm."

"I love you, Katie."

The footsteps on the other side of the door grew louder as they crested the top of the stairs and headed in their direction. Suddenly, it was as if she were being hoisted into that old climbing tree all over again. And just as she'd been when she was four, she was terrified—terrified at the notion of leaving her mother's arms behind.

"They're here, Mamm," she whispered. "I'll let them in."

Her mother's answering nod was slow and labored, but the sudden grip on Katie's arm was anything but. "Tell her, Katie. Tell . . . Hannah . . . I . . . love . . . her."

A Daughter's Truth

❧

Not for the first time, Emma Lapp glanced over her shoulder, the utter silence of the sparsely graveled road at her heels deafening. On any other day, the mere thought of leaving her sisters to do her chores would fill her with such shame she'd no doubt add their tasks to her own as a way to seek atonement inside her own heart. Then again, on any other day, she *would* be gathering the eggs and feeding the orphan calf just like always.

But today wasn't just any day. Today was her birthday. Her twenty-second, to be exact. And while she knew better than anyone else what the rest of her day would and wouldn't entail, this part—the part she'd been anticipating since her last birthday—had become her happy little secret.

Lifting her coat-clad shoulders in line with her cheeks, Emma bent her head against the biting winds and hurried her steps, the anticipation for what she'd find waiting atop the sheep-tended grass eliciting a quiet squeal from between her clattering teeth. Unlike her five siblings, Emma's birthday wasn't a day with silly games and laughter. It was, instead, a day of sadness—a day when the air hung heavy across every square inch of the farm from the moment she opened her eyes until her head hit the pillow at night. And while she wanted to believe it would get better one day, twenty-one examples to the contrary told her otherwise.

But this—

She rounded the final bend in the road and stopped, her gaze falling on the weathered gravestones now visible just beyond the fence that ran along the edge of the Fishers' property. There, on the other side of the large oak tree, was the reason for both Mamm's ongoing heartache and the unmistakable smile currently making its way across Emma's face.

When she was four . . . five . . . six, it had been this same sight on this same day that had swirled her stomach with the kind of dread that came from knowing.

Knowing Dat would stop the buggy . . .

Knowing she and her brother Jakob would follow behind Mamm and Dat to the second row, third gravestone from the right . . .

Knowing Mamm would look down, fist her hand against her trembling lips, and squeeze her eyes closed around one lone tear . . .

Knowing Dat would soon mutter in anger as their collective gaze fell on the year's latest offering—an offering that would be tossed into an Englisher's trash can on the way to school . . .

It was why, at the age of seven, when she'd asked to walk to school with her friends, Emma told them to go ahead without her, buying her time to stop at the cemetery alone, before Mamm and Dat.

That day, she'd fully intended to throw the trinket away in the hopes of removing the anger, if not the sadness, from her birthday. But the moment she'd seen the miniature picnic basket nestled inside her palm, she'd known she couldn't. Instead, she'd wrapped it inside a cloth napkin and hid it inside her lunch pail.

Later on, after school, she'd relocated the napkin-wrapped secret to the hollow of a pin oak near Miller's Pond. In time, she'd replaced the napkin with a dark blue drawstring bag capable of holding the now fifteen objects inside—objects her mind's eye began inventorying as she approached the cemetery.

The miniature picnic basket.

The pewter rose.

The snow globe with the tiny skaters inside.

The stuffed horse.

The picture of a dandelion.

The bubble wand.

The narrow slip of torn paper housed in a plastic covering.

The sparkly rock with the heart drawn on it.

The red and black checked napkin.

The plastic covered bridge.

The small red rubber ball.

The yellow spinny thing on a stick.

The signed baseball she couldn't quite read.

The dried flower with the pale blue and pink ribbons tied around the stem.

The whittled bird.

Emma savored the lightness the images afforded against the backdrop of an otherwise dark, lifeless day and quickened her pace. All her life, her birthday had been a day to hurry through in the hope Mamm's pain would somehow be lessened. There was always a cake with a handful of candles, but it was set in front of Emma with little more than a whispered happy birthday. There were presents, but they were always handed to her quietly, without the belly laughs and silly antics that were part of her siblings' birthdays. And when the sun sank low at the end of her day, she, too, was glad it was over.

But this? This stop at the cemetery had become the one part of her birthday she actually looked forward to with anticipation each year. Because even while she knew it was wrong to be drawn to a material object, the very act of guessing what it might be felt more birthday-like than anything she'd ever known.

Sliding her focus to the left, she surveyed the long, winding country road that led farther into Amish country, the lack of buggy traffic in keeping with the hour. Morning was a busy time in the Amish community. It was time to tend to the animals and get about the day's tasks. In the spring, summer, and fall, those tasks entailed work in the fields for those, like Dat, who farmed. In the winter months, as it was now, there were still things that needed tending—fences that needed reworking, manure to be spread in the fields, repairs made to aging structures, and assisting neighbors with the same.

A glance to her right netted the one-room schoolhouse where she'd learned to read and write as a young child, and where three of her younger siblings still went. At the moment, there was no smoke billowing from the school's chimney, but she knew that would change in about an hour when the teacher arrived ahead of her students.

Seeing nothing in either direction to impede her adventure, Emma stepped around the simple wooden fence separating the cemetery from the Grabers' farm to the south and the Fishers' farm to the north, eyed the gravestones in front of her, and, after a single deep breath, made her way over to the second row. She didn't need to read the names on the markers she passed. She'd memorized them during her visits there with her parents, when, as a new reader, she read everything she could.

Isaac Yoder . . .

Ruth Schrock . . .

Ruth's twin brother, Samuel . . .

Abram King . . .

And, finally, Ruby Stoltzfus, Mamm's younger sister and the aunt Emma had never met. Instinctively, she took in the date of death in relation to the date of birth even though she already knew the answer.

When she was little, and she'd come here with her family, the numbers on the markers she passed hadn't really registered. But as she'd developed math skills and a perspective on life over the next few years, she'd begun to truly understand the reason behind Mamm's grief. Eighteen-year-olds weren't supposed to die. They just weren't. And when she, herself, had inched closer to—and eventually surpassed—the age her aunt had been at death, the whole occurrence took on an even more tragic undertone.

Shaking off the sadness she felt lapping at the edges of her day's one joy, Emma dropped her gaze from the simple lettering to the stark winter earth peeking out from the dormant grass below. An initial skim of the usual places where the various objects had been left in the past turned up nothing and, for a brief moment, her heart sank. But a second, more thorough look netted a brief flash of light off to the left.

Sure enough, as she moved in closer, she saw it, her answering intake of air bringing an end to a neighboring bird's desperate hunt for food in between and around the next row's grave markers. There, wrapped around a medium-sized rock, was a—

"Levi said he saw you out here!"

Whirling around, Emma turned in time to see her best friend waving at her from the other side of the fence. "Mary Fisher! It is not polite to sneak up on a person like that!"

"Sneak?" Mary echoed, shivering. "I-I d-did not s-sneak!"

"I didn't *hear* you. . . ."

"You did not hear Levi, either."

At the mention of Mary's brother, Emma looked past her friend to the Fishers' fields, a familiar flutter rising inside her chest. "Levi? He saw me?"

"Yah. That is how I knew you were here." Mary climbed onto the bottom slat of the fence and leaned across the top, her brown eyes almost golden in the early morning rays. "Happy birthday, Emma!"

"You remembered. . . ."

Mary's brows dipped. "Of course I remember. We've been best friends since we were babies, silly."

Slowly, Emma wandered between the graves and joined her friend at the fence. "Sorry. I guess I just thought maybe you'd forgotten."

"I didn't." Mary ducked her chin inside the top edge of her coat, muffling her voice as she did. "So . . . it is not any different?"

"It?"

"Your birthday. You know, with your mamm. . . ."

Emma didn't mean to laugh, she really didn't. But somehow it took more effort to refrain. "Thinking my birthday this year will be any different than it's been for the first twenty-one is like thinking your brother would ever notice me in the way he notices Liddy Mast."

"Please . . . Liddy Mast . . ." Mary grumbled on an exhale. "Do not remind me."

"What? Liddy is . . . *nice.*"

"I suppose. Maybe. But she blinks too much."

"Blinks too much?"

"Yah."

Emma closed her eyes against the image of the dark-haired Amish girl who'd shown up at one of their hymn sings three weeks earlier and set her sights on Mary's brother almost immediately. "Levi does not seem to mind this blinking," she whispered.

"Levi is . . . well, *Levi.* The only things I know for sure about my brother are that he eats as if he has not seen food for days, he likes to put frogs in places I do not expect to see frogs, his constant hammering gives me a headache, and I would really rather speak of your birthday at this moment."

"There is nothing to speak of. It is just another day."

Mary's brown eyes disappeared briefly behind long lashes. "She lost her *sister*, Emma. That has to be hard."

It was the same argument she had with herself all the time. But . . .

"When Grossdawdy died last year, Mamm and Dat said it was God's will. And when Grossmudder passed in the fall that, too, was God's will. Shouldn't—" Emma stopped, shook away the rest of her thought, and forced herself to focus on something, anything else.

Mary, being Mary, didn't give up that easily. "Her sister was younger than you are now, Emma. And it was so sudden."

"But that's just it, Mary. I don't know if it was sudden or not. Mamm won't talk about it. Ever. She is just sad on this day."

"Maybe you should ask to celebrate your birthday on a *different* day," Mary suggested. "Maybe then there could be smiles and laughter on your special day, too."

She opened her mouth to point out the oft-shared fact that Mamm rarely smiled around Emma at all, but even Emma was growing tired of the subject. Some things were just a certainty. Like her brother Jonathan's rooster announcing the arrival of morning as the moon bowed to the sun. Like the answering gurgle of her stomach every time she pulled a freshly baked loaf of bread from the oven. Like the cute dimple her sister, Esther, shared with Mamm. Like the way Jakob's footfalls sounded identical to Dat's on the stairs each night. And like the surprise she knew she'd find beside her aunt Ruby's grave that morning . . .

Stepping off her own perch atop the bottom slat, Emma motioned to Mary's farm. "You should probably go. You do not want to upset your mamm by not doing your chores."

"I have a few minutes before I must be back."

Anxious to get back to the rock and the flash of silver she'd spied just as Mary called her name, Emma patted her friend's cold hand. "I am fine here. Alone."

"But it is your birthday, Emma! You should be doing happy things like talking to me instead of standing at . . ." Mary's words quieted only to drift off completely as she, too, stepped onto the ground. "I will leave you to pray alone. I should not have interrupted the way I did."

She met her friend's sad eyes with a smile. "I am very glad you did, Mary. Truly. I-I just . . ."

"You want to pray alone," Mary finished. "I understand."

Unable to lie to her friend aloud, Emma let her answering silence do the work.

"Well, happy birthday, Emma."

"Thank you."

She remained by the fence, watching, as Mary made her way back across her dat's field and, finally, through her parents' back door. For a moment she let her thoughts wander into the Fisher home, too, Levi's warm smile greeting her in the way it had Liddy Mast at the last hymn sing . . .

"Oh stop it, Emma," she whispered. "Levi does not see you any more than anyone else sees you."

Shaking her head, she picked her way back to Ruby's grave, her gaze quickly seeking and finding the shiny silver chain peeking out from around a nearby rock. Mesmerized, Emma dropped to her knees and slowly fingered the chain from the clasp at the top to the thick, flower-etched—

The air whooshed from her lungs as she lifted the chain from its resting spot and set the heart-shaped pendant inside her palm. She'd seen jewelry before many times—on English shopkeepers in town; on the driver Dat hired when they needed to travel outside normal buggy range; on Miss Lottie, the elderly English woman who lived out near the Beilers; and even on her own wrist for a very short time during her Rumspringa when she was sixteen—but nothing so delicately beautiful as the necklace in her hand at that moment.

"Who would leave something so pretty on the ground?" she whispered. "It does not make any . . ." The words fell away as her eyes lit on a thin line around the outer edge of the heart. A line just wide enough to wedge her nail inside and—

With a quiet snap, the heart split in two and she slowly lifted the top half up and back, her answering gasp echoing around her in the cold morning air.

There, nestled against a pale pink background, was a heart-shaped photograph of an Amish girl not much younger than Emma. . . . An Amish girl with brown hair and eyes so like Mamm's. . . . Yet, with the exception of those two things, everything else about the girl was a mirror image of . . . *Emma?*

Confused, Emma pulled the open locket still closer as, once again, she studied the face inside. The same high cheekbones . . . The same slender nose . . . The same wide, full lips . . . The same tiny freckles . . . In fact, with the exception of the hair and eye color, she'd actually think she was looking at a picture of *herself*.

Closing her fingers around the locket, Emma rose to her feet and began to run, the steady smack of her boots against the cold, dry earth no match for the thud of her heart inside her ears.

Connect with Us

Visit us online at
KensingtonBooks.com
to read more from your favorite authors, see books
by series, view reading group guides, and more.

for sneak peeks, chances to win books and prize packs,
and to share your thoughts with other readers.

facebook.com/kensingtonpublishing
twitter.com/kensingtonbooks

Tell us what you think!

To share your thoughts, submit a review,
or sign up for our eNewsletters, please visit:
KensingtonBooks.com/TellUs.